W9-CNU-694

The Tale
of a
No-Name
Squirrel

The Tale
of a
No-Name
Squirrel

Radhika R. Dhariwal
Illustrated by Audrey Benjaminsen

Simon & Schuster Books for Young Readers
New York London Toronto Sydney New Delhi

SIMON & SCHUSTER BOOKS FOR YOUNG READERS
An imprint of Simon & Schuster Children's Publishing Division
1230 Avenue of the Americas, New York, New York 10020
This book is a work of fiction. Any references to historical events, real people, or real places
are used fictitiously. Other names, characters, places, and events are products of the author's imagination,
and any resemblance to actual events or places or persons, living or dead, is entirely coincidental.
Text copyright © 2014 by Radhika R. Dhariwal
Originally published in India in 2014 by Harper
Illustrations copyright © 2016 by Audrey Benjaminsen
All rights reserved, including the right of reproduction in whole or in part in any form.
SIMON & SCHUSTER BOOKS FOR YOUNG READERS is a trademark of Simon & Schuster, Inc.
For information about special discounts for bulk purchases, please contact
Simon & Schuster Special Sales at 1-866-506-1949 or business@simonandschuster.com.
The Simon & Schuster Speakers Bureau can bring authors to your live event. For more information
or to book an event, contact the Simon & Schuster Speakers Bureau at 1-866-248-3049
or visit our website at www.simonspeakers.com.
Book design by Lizzy Bromley
The text for this book was set in Goudy Oldstyle.
The illustrations for this book were rendered in charcoal.
Manufactured in the United States of America
0316 MTN
First Edition
2 4 6 8 10 9 7 5 3 1
Library of Congress Cataloging-in-Publication Data
Dhariwal, Radhika R.
[PetPost secret]
The tale of a no-name squirrel / Radhika R. Dhariwal ; illustrated by Audrey Benjaminsen.
pages cm
Previous title: The PetPost secret
Summary: "The last slave in Bimmau, Squirrel, embarks on a quest to solve riddles in order
to find his name and freedom, along with his friends, a crow and a dog"—Provided by publisher.
ISBN 978-1-4814-4475-0 (hardcover) — ISBN 978-1-4814-4477-4 (eBook)
[1. Squirrels—Fiction. 2. Animals—Fiction. 3. Fantasy.] I. Benjaminsen, Audrey, illustrator. II. Title.
PZ7.1.D496Tal 2016
[Fic]—dc23
2015008135

For
Rashmi, the realist,
and Ravi, for dreaming,
For Humbir, the believer,
and Rakshay, for screaming,
And a very real squirrel,
two dogs, and a crow,
Without whom this story
would never have been
Told

Contents

The Tale
of a
No-Name
Squirrel

Prologue

A GAME OF HANGMAN

It was his first murder; yet the tall, cloaked cat knew exactly what to do. He circled his victim slowly, watching the old, furry body twitch like a fish out of water. The smell of fresh fear tickled his nose. He smiled. It was time.

The cloaked cat pinned his victim's feeble paws to a branch and hissed four little words.

"I . . . found . . . the . . . map!" As he spoke, he twisted a twine around his victim's neck. One, two, three, four loops. "I found the Map of Brittle."

His victim—an old, withered, white cat—began to

choke. "How d'you know abou—about the Map of Brittle? Wh-what d'you want?"

"Patience, my friend," said the cloaked cat. "Haven't you heard the cat-phrase 'A whisker of patience is better than a fur ball of words'?"

His victim went as still as ice; his cheeks melted into his skull. "Wh-who are you?"

"I was wondering when you'd figure it out, old friend," said the cloaked cat, peeling the bat-skin mask off his face. He looked up, right into his victim's blue eyes, and smiled. "Recognize me now, Mr. Falguny?"

The cloaked cat waited for a long moment as old Mr. Falguny stared at him. Then, without warning, Mr. Falguny began to kick, and choke, and twist, and spit. "Lemme go! You'd never . . . I taught you when you were a kitten!"

"Taught me, yes. But you taught me lies. You said the map was long gone, but you knew better, didn't you, Mr. Falguny? You didn't want anyone to know the truth about your precious map. But now I've found it. I've found the map."

Mr. Falguny stopped moving. His breath smelled bitter. Of shock. Of sweat. Of blood. "Why d'you want the Map of Brittle? Who've you become?"

"What I should have always been. I was so stupid when I was young. I lapped up everything you said like a lost little

2

kitten. All your 'purr-fections' and morality—equality, free-dom, and all that horse-spit. But I've changed. I'm a smarter cat now. I call myself Colonel these days, and I've got a plan. I'm going to use the map to undo all the damage you did. I'll enslave all the weak, filthy creatures you tried to protect, Mr. Falguny." The cloaked Colonel's throat was raw with ten-sion. "I'll take us back to the older way of life, the better way of life. I'm taking back what should have always been mine."

"But . . . how can you? It's wrong. It's against everything fair, everything good," said the old cat, his voice splintering with wet hiccups. "It's evil."

The Colonel leaned so close to Mr. Falguny he could almost taste the streaks of salt on the old cheeks. "Don't you dare tell me what is evil, Mr. Falguny," he whispered. "You still think I don't know? You still think I don't know what you did? *Who* I lost because of you? Just because you were trying to save those . . . those flea-filled vermin! Those disgusting slaves!"

The Colonel stepped back. He watched the weight of his words fall on Mr. Falguny.

Understanding flickered in the old eyes; then they went blank, as though they were dead already. "I had to . . . It was for the good of everybody." Mr. Falguny looked down. "I didn't deliberately kill her. But, sometimes, sacrifices must be made for the greater good. For equality. You'll never understand how hard it was . . . You can't . . ."

"I. Don't. Care! Your decision killed her," the Colonel hissed, his teeth clenched. He took a breath of the cool night air, pushing his dead fiancée's pretty face out of his mind. He would get his revenge. But he needed something first. "I'll make you pay for what you did, Mr. Falguny. But, first, you will tell me something only you know." He paused. "I can't read the map. Tell me how to read the Map of Brittle."

Mr. Falguny's cheeks began to pound. He said nothing.

"Don't waste my time, Falguny!" growled the Colonel, digging his claws into Mr. Falguny and scratching down his side. Warm blood oozed down Mr. Falguny's back and dripped onto the cobblestones. The Colonel's fur tingled. "Tell me what I need to know."

"I . . . will . . . not," said Mr. Falguny, clamping his jaw shut.

"But you *will* tell me how to read the map, old friend. Just like you told me all about the lost Map of Brittle when we were playing hangman a long time ago. How ironic," said the Colonel, watching Mr. Falguny dangle from the tree in the cobblestone courtyard.

Mr. Falguny tugged on the twine around his neck. He wrung his body till he looked like a twisted towel pegged to a clothesline. "You will not make slaves out of innocent creatures. That won't happen again. I won't let you do it." Beads of bloody spit flew from his mouth and splattered the Colonel's face. "You will never read the Map of Brittle."

"You have no choice, Mr. Falguny. You will tell me. You will help me become the next Master of Bimmau," said the Colonel, wiping his face. "And you will die tonight. But if you don't tell me how to read the map, I will destroy you—even in death."

"You cannot destroy those who are clean of heart," said Mr. Falguny.

The Colonel felt a smile twist his face. "Clean of heart? Don't fool yourself, Mr. Falguny. I've found proof of what you did that night. Of everybody you hurt. If this got out, it would destroy your spotless reputation."

As he spoke, the Colonel reached into his cloak and removed a dead dried butterfly with scribbles all over its wings. He fanned the wings under Mr. Falguny's nose. "What will the world say when they see this? What will they say when they find out what you did? What you did to me, what you did to the others . . ."

"You don't understand. It was my job. My responsibility. I had to make a choice . . ."

"What about your family? How will your wife show her

crumpled, pink little face in public?" The Colonel let his voice trail off, letting the dark leaves fill the night with their eerie swish. Mr. Falguny would crack any moment. Three, two, one . . .

The old cat gulped—a loud, painful gulp as though he were swallowing a clump of thorns. "If I help you, you promise to destroy that?"

"My friend, you're in no position to make demands," said the Colonel, filing his claws. "But fine, I promise. For old times' sake. Now quick, how do I read the map?"

"To read the map . . ." Mr. Falguny hiccupped. "You need a key."

"What key? Hurry up, Falguny. Or I'll send this dead butterfly to every feline home. Now tell me. What key?" The Colonel squeezed Mr. Falguny's neck as if it were a tube of toothpaste.

Mr. Falguny groaned; it was a groan stiff with defeat. "The key is hidden. Only . . . only . . . one person can find it." Slowly he drew his white tail into his pocket and removed something. He shivered, and dropped a heavy brass button into the Colonel's paw.

"What is this?" growled the Colonel.

"A clue to . . . find the . . . one . . . with the key," choked Mr. Falguny, his forehead scrunching up like old garbage.

"Oh!"

To the Colonel, the brass button suddenly looked prettier than a thousand gold nuggets. He looked closer. A symbol was sketched on the back of the button.

"Is that . . . is that the PetPost emblem?" he whispered.

Defeat swirled in Mr. Falguny's eyes. His neck sagged. His tail went limp like overcooked spaghetti.

The Colonel grinned. It was the PetPost crest indeed. "Thanks, old friend. As always, it's been fun learning something from you."

As he strode out of the courtyard, clutching his clue, the Colonel heard a final shudder.

"You . . . have . . . let . . . maggots . . . into . . . your . . . heart . . ."

"And it's your fault," said the Colonel, not looking back as his childhood mentor went still, leaving a puddle of crimson life on the cobblestones.

A CATTY SOCIETY

Mrs. Sox should have kept her big mouth shut. But, alas, she had not.

Perhaps this is why the fat Persian cat had her face stuck to the window, her yellow eyes darting from the sky to the steps below. Her tail twitched. He was late.

Mrs. Sox snarled. A Pedipurr cat should never have to wait. Especially not for the PetPost slave.

Yet, Mrs. Sox did wait. The fat gray cat did not budge from the window, even though the room was getting crowded and sweaty. With her sausage of a tail she whacked two kittens—who were trying to claw in on her spot—out of the way.

Her claws itched, and a splinter of worry pulsed on her flat forehead.

"If that lazy lump of a Squirrel has run off with Smitten's wedding invitations, I'll catch him, stick him on a skewer, and eat him for dinner," she muttered to herself.

The problem was that Mrs. Sox was scared. She knew that the PetPost Squirrel was delivering Smitten's wedding invitations today, and she had the teeniest fear that she would not be invited.

Indeed, when Mrs. Sox had first heard that the bachelor Smitten, a wealthy Pedipurr cat, had chosen to marry the female dog Cheska, she had bad-mouthed Smitten's choice of bride to every cat she could find. Now, as she waited for the wedding invitations, Mrs. Sox wondered if she had said too much.

But no. The fat gray cat jiggled her head, knocking the shards of regret straight out of her brain. "How can Smitten marry a dog, let alone that smutty, penniless Cheska?" she said to herself loudly. "And if for some doggone reason, dogs really do tickle his tail, he should have chosen a lady from the Pawshine Club, not a tramp from the Wagamutt! At least the Pawshine pups try to be like us at the Pedipurr. The Wagamutt, though! Those dogs are just plain uncivilized."

Mrs. Sox paused just long enough to snarl. "I, for one,

won't talk to any of those disgusting mutts at the wedding." Her eyes darkened to the color of cheddar cheese. "I can't associate with those raggedy dogs. I'll catch fleas or worse . . ."

Right then, a sudden movement on the steps below grabbed her attention. Through the window she saw a stuffed, lumpy sack stagger up the stone stairs of the Pedipurr mansion. When the sack reached the landing, Mrs. Sox saw a bushy red tail flail under the bag's weight.

Her wait was over. The PetPost Squirrel had finally arrived.

"Just . . . one . . . more . . . step," wheezed Squirrel, the PetPost slave, as he heaved the sack up the last stair. For a moment, he just stood on top of the steps, swaying. He dumped the bag on the ground and crumpled to his knees like a floppy puppet. He could have lain on the cool stone landing forever, but a flicker of cheddar yellow in the window upstairs jerked him to his senses.

Get a grip, Squirrel scolded himself. As it is, he was late today—for the very first time. On top of that, if the hoity-toity Pedipurr cats caught him panting like an old toad on a ventilator after carrying just one bag up a flight of stairs, they would mock him till morning. So Squirrel pulled himself up, breathed deeply, swung his sack onto his narrow shoulders, and scurried toward the Pedipurr Society.

The Pedipurr was unlike any country club young Squirrel had ever seen. It stood on the only finger of coastline that strayed into the ocean, so that the gray rock building seemed to swell up from the middle of the sea. The mansion stretched sideways and arched upward; and, as beams of twilight filtered into the belly of the building, the gray rock glistened like quicksilver.

Squirrel had always thought the building looked smooth and graceful and alive—almost like a giant, jumping dolphin. But today he had barely any time to admire the Pedipurr, or its tall, ribbed towers, or the bone filigree on its "Members Only" door. He ran straight toward his destination—a half-hidden doorway tucked into the corner of the building.

He was so worried about being late that he did not notice a big black bird crouched in the shadows of the east tower, watching his every step.

The "Outsiders' Entrance" of the Pedipurr was always manned by Olfisse, a grumpy old security cat. Today, however, Olfisse was nowhere in sight.

Squirrel was surprised. Since he was five, he had delivered the mail in Bimmau. And, in those eight seasons, he had never found the Pedipurr unguarded. Not sure what to do, he signed his name on the leaf register, glanced at the sky, and read the time from the streaks of pink in the clouds. Squirrel bit his lip. He was really late.

He was just about to rush into the Pedipurr's Grand Hall when he caught sight of the mica mirror. "I'm late. At least I better make sure I look all right," Squirrel mumbled, giving himself a quick once-over.

He frowned. He was a head shorter than he would have liked to have been at the age of thirteen. His red fur was groomed neatly enough, but it was not glossy like the fur of the Pedipurr cats. He hated his shoulders, which curled slightly inward, and he thought his head was shaped a bit too much like a squashed acorn.

Squirrel knew that he could not really complain about his features. He had nice eyebrows, dimples, and a pleasant but-tonlike nose. He had a strong jaw that had luckily escaped the Curse of Buckteeth, and his eyes were a clear, crystal turquoise—a playful blue that twinkled in any light.

As he looked at himself, Squirrel rearranged his burnt-red hair to cover the shape of his head and adjusted his faded PetPost uniform to hide the awful S branded into his forearm. The S was not for "Squirrel." The S was for "Slave."

"Well, this is as good as I'm going to look," he said, and

with a sigh the slave Squirrel let himself into the Grand Hall of the Pedipurr Society.

Shock was the first thing that hit Squirrel's pupils.

The Grand Hall was destroyed. Slaughtered cushions and torn yarn were stuck to the checkered marble floor, the busts of the Founding Cats were splattered with brown gunk, teak chairs balanced on hinges like seesaws, and the grandfather clock hung sideways, refusing to tick. Instead time was kept by droplets of milk dripping onto the keys of the piano from a shelf of toppled milk bottles.

"What's going on?" whispered Squirrel, turning right, then left, then right again, spinning on his heel like a malfunctioning robot. "What's happen—OUCH!"

Pain shot from his foot to his brain. A whopping crack echoed through the hall. Squirrel looked down. He had just stepped on, and shattered, a fish-bone saucer.

Not sure what to do, Squirrel dashed toward the door. But he was too late.

The door at the end of the hall swung open; something came pelting toward him—and before Squirrel could make out face or form, he was pinned to the floor by something really heavy, something really orange, something really tickly.

13

Squirrel looked up. The orange face of a cat called Brosher hung above him like a burned, furry sun.

"Sorry about that, Squirrel—I got a little carried away," said the orange cat, pulling Squirrel up.

"Sir, what's going on?" asked Squirrel, rubbing his shoulder. "What happened to this place?"

"Don't worry about this. We were so antsy waiting for you to bring the invitations that a few cat-fights broke out—that's all. All sorted now. But tell me, you have the invitations, don't ya?"

"What invitations?" asked Squirrel, who was as confused as a bumper car.

"The invitations to Smitten's wedding, of course, Squirrel. They're supposed to arrive today! We've been pulling the fur out of our hides waiting for you. But enough yakking. Everyone's waiting in the Tiger's Tooth. Let's go," said Brosher, grabbing Squirrel and jostling him and his sack toward the bar on the far end of the hall.

No place had been more aptly named than the Tiger's Tooth. The walls rumbled with purrs and meows. Darkness and dampness filled the room, with sweaty cats crushed against every inch of the window. A single sliver of light cracked the blackness.

Groping his way toward the bar counter in the center of

the room, Squirrel felt hundreds of eyes on him. The beat of the ocean against the Pedipurr's walls made his pulse quicken. Everyone was watching *him*. Waiting for *him*.

Shaking, Squirrel scrambled onto the bar platform and untied his sack. His paws fumbled. He had never gotten so much attention, and the little red PetPost slave could not help feeling very nervous. He half choked, half coughed, and said, "Sirs, madams, sh-should I begin?"

The room roared yes so loudly that Squirrel almost fell off the counter. Hurriedly he emptied the sack on the platform. Instead of a stack of leaf-envelopes, out came big, rectangular parcels. Each was wrapped in lilac wax paper emblazoned with the letter M. Squirrel recognized the M with awe: the paper itself had come all the way from Mellifera, the walled city of bees.

Reverently Squirrel picked up a package. It had a tiny card on it. Scribbled on the card was the name of each invitee to Smitten's wedding.

Squirrel cleared his throat and called out, "Mrs. . . . Mrs. Falguny."

The room shook as cats started elbowing one another out of the way to catch a glimpse of the recently widowed Mrs. Falguny. Squirrel saw Olfisse, the Pedipurr's security cat, amongst the crowd, craning her neck.

From the pit of fur, a frail little cat with salt-and-pepper hair came shyly forward. The other cats moved aside; the first invitee had been announced.

"For you, ma'am," said Squirrel, handing the package to Mrs. Falguny.

"Thank you, Squirrel. I just wish my husband could've been here," she said quietly before dragging her parcel away. Squirrel waited until she had hobbled back to her spot before announcing the next invitee.

"The next package is for . . . Lady Blouse," said Squirrel. He heard a purr, and then saw a sleek, black Bombay cat with twinkling hazel eyes shimmy up to him.

"Ah buhlieve that's me, dahling," she drawled, and winked at Squirrel. As Squirrel handed her the parcel, his heart hammered in his eardrums. He blushed. He had always been very fond of pretty Lady Blouse.

Squirrel pulled out another parcel. He smiled. "Mr. Brosher."

Brosher ran up to Squirrel, bowed, and said, "Good Squirrel and friend of mine, rip open my gift and let it shine, let us all see if it's fine, and I shall stop this rhyme, 'cos I can think of no other line . . ."

And, with that poetic attempt, Brosher signaled Squirrel to open his package onstage. Every curious cat in the room began to clap.

16

Squirrel was so nervous he could barely remove the soft, lilac wrapper. With clammy paws he opened the box. Inside, on a bed of pink satin, lay an ivory collar. The name "Brosher" was embossed on it.

Squirrel picked up the milky collar. His arms trembled as he held it up in the air.

The effect was perfect. The cats oohed and aaahed and purred and panted. Then, just when Squirrel thought he should read out the name of the next invitee, Brosher pointed to a note that came with the collar. "Read it aloud, Squirrel."

Squirrel's knees turned to putty. He could not imagine reading aloud, especially in front of this crowd. Then again, he could not disobey a Pedipurr cat.

So, trying to keep his vocal cords from splitting like hairs, Squirrel gulped and began to read.

Dear Brosher,

We would be honored if you would join us as we celebrate our wedding. The event will be held on the first full moon after the spring equinox. The venue is a surprise. Please come to the rosewood jetty beside the Pedipurr, and we will have ferries to transport you. We also ask that you

wear this collar, so that if you get lost, our ushers can
help you find your way to the wedding. We look forward
to seeing you there.

Warm wishes,
Cheska and Smitten

When Squirrel finished reading the letter, he realized that the mood in the dark Tiger's Tooth had lightened considerably. The cats seemed to have realized that there were enough parcels for everybody, and they began to relax and wait for their names to be called out. One by one, they whisked up to the stage to get their invitations from Squirrel. Soon all the cats had collars fastened around their necks. All except one. Only Mrs. Sox had not received her invite. Luckily for her, there were still two parcels left in the sack.

With her belly sagging on the floor and a scowl sagging on her face, Mrs. Sox lugged herself over to the bar where Squirrel stood.

As Squirrel reached for the parcel with her name on it, she snatched it out of his paw. "You could not have been any slower, could you? I bet you thought it'd be funny to leave my parcel till the very end? Enjoyed making me squirm, you shriveled squirt?"

Squirrel, who was used to Mrs. Sox's sharp words, said, "I'm so sorry, Mrs. Sox; I didn't mean anything by it. Please don't mind me, I'm nobody . . ."

Mrs. Sox did not listen. She simply turned around and stalked off, her parcel tucked safely between the folds of her fat.

But Mrs. Sox's jibe was enough to bring Squirrel out of his pretend play. For the last few moments he had felt important, like he was someone worth knowing. A room full of cats had focused only on him, and they were the cats of the Pedipurr, no less. He knew he was only getting such attention because he was delivering Smitten's wedding invitations, but he had enjoyed it all the same.

Flushing with embarrassment, Squirrel stuffed the last parcel into his sack as quickly as he could. How could he have been naive enough to pretend that he could fit in with the Pedipurr cats? How could he have been so stupid . . .

"Meeeeaaaaaoooooooowwwwww!"

A sickening peal rattled the room. Squirrel dropped his sack on the floor. He turned around.

A note shook in Mrs. Sox's paw; an angry vein throbbed on her flat forehead. Her empty parcel lay on the floor, torn open. There was not an inch of ivory in sight.

"What's goin' on?" said Squirrel. No one heard him. All eyes in the room were fixed on the snarling Mrs. Sox.

The fat Persian cat meowed again and pounced on the sack that Squirrel had just dropped. She dragged out the only remaining package and ripped it open. Slowly she picked up the ivory collar, her eyes fixed on the name embossed on it.

Suddenly she chucked the collar at Squirrel, almost knocking him off the counter. She dropped the note from her hand and marched out of the room.

Brosher got to the note first. "I wonder what made Sox the Ox so mad," he said, and began to read it aloud.

Mrs. Sox,

We heard that you strongly object to our commitment to each other. We would not want you to betray your beliefs by attending our wedding, and hence, we will not burden you with an invitation. Instead we are thrilled to give your place to Squirrel, the friendly PetPost slave, who has faithfully delivered this and many other messages to both you and us for many seasons. We trust this message will be welcome to him. We hope that we have spared you the hassle of declining our invitation.

Cheska and Smitten

As he finished reading the note, Brosher burst into a flurry of giggles. The rest of the cats were shaking too. Some with laughter. Others with shock.

Squirrel, who was tracing the words "PetPost Squirrel" on the ivory collar that Mrs. Sox had hurled at him, spoke first. "This collar is mine? I don't understand. I'm a slave . . . I've never . . . How's this possible? What do I do?"

Lady Blouse came up to him, a pretty, lopsided smile on her lips. She purred, "Dahling, all you need to do is find sumthin' to wear."

THE OLD AND THE NEW

Squirrel opened his wardrobe. He knew what he would find. Three outfits hung in a row—they were all his PetPost slave uniforms.

Squirrel frowned. The uniform jackets had faded and looked bald—like they had been washed too many times. The pants had shrunk and looked like cuffed shorts. The buttons down the jacket fronts drooped on thin thread. Indeed, one jacket was missing a brass button already. Lady Blouse had been spot-on—Squirrel had to get some new clothes for Smitten's wedding.

The problem was, however, that Squirrel had never

shopped before. After all, he was a slave. The only thing he ever did was run errands for his boss—and for that he would always wear his uniform. Up until this very moment, Squirrel had never needed any other outfits. Hence, he had absolutely no clue where to find clothes for this wedding.

"I'm caught in a bit of a soggy sandwich . . . ," Squirrel was muttering to himself, when an idea struck him. Although he himself was a fashion fool, Squirrel knew the most fashion-conscious creature in Bimmau County very well. In fact, Squirrel was his slave.

Squirrel's boss was Bacchu Banoose, a spectacularly lazy mongoose who happened to own the famous PetPost Mail. Although he owned the business, he himself was not inclined to work. Instead he had his slave Squirrel run around delivering the letters, parcels, and packages in Bimmau, while he himself spent his days shopping, crimping, and primping so he always looked as perfect as a poodle. But now the PetPost Squirrel was going to try to use his boss's one expertise to help him find something to wear to Smitten's wedding.

So, the next morning after his chores, Squirrel went to speak to his boss.

"Don't bother me with work stuff now," Bacchu said with a backward wave when he saw Squirrel. A beret crowned the mongoose's block-of-a-head, and his feet were soaked in an oyster-shell Jacuzzi.

"Actually, boss, I was hoping to speak to you about . . . about . . ."

"Get on with it, Squirrel. My groomer will be here soon. Wait . . . is that homemade Mud Milkshake in your paw? Can I have it?"

"Of course," said Squirrel, gulping down the dryness in his throat as he handed his boss the drink. He had made the thick, muddy slush for himself, but he knew better than to deny his boss anything. Instead he said, "Boss, I don't know if you heard. I've been invited . . . to . . . to Smitten and Cheska's wedding."

"Hmmmm," said Bacchu Banoose, taking a deep, loud sniff of Squirrel's milkshake.

"Sir, I was hoping you'd help me get an outfit for the wedding." He swallowed. "I don't own any clothes except my PetPost slave uniforms."

Bacchu forgot all about the homemade Mud Milkshake. He looked at Squirrel, his thick jaw dropping as though it were weighed down by a sack of potatoes.

"Squirrel, how could you possibly not own anything except *those*?" asked Bacchu, wrinkling his nose at Squirrel's uniform.

"I don't know, boss . . . I've never needed clothes before."

Bacchu shook his head. "I've never worn that hideous uniform. Not when I was young. Not now. In fact, I don't even own it. When I was thirteen, I already owned twenty tunics. And you . . ." Bacchu stuck his bulb-of-a-thumb into his waistcoat. He looked Squirrel up and down. "But, then again, we're . . . very different."

Squirrel nodded. Bacchu was right. When Bacchulius was just a baby, his mother and father had started the PetPost Mail—a business that kept them very, very busy and made them very, very wealthy. Baby Bacchu grew up with tree trunks full of money that he spent on whatever he wanted: spun-silk clothes, a house with snakeskin wallpaper, and even three red slaves—a mother, a father, and their infant son—to do his bidding. Now that very same slave son, Squirrel, decided to play on his boss's love for shopping to find the perfect ensemble for Smitten's wedding.

Squirrel pasted a sugary smile on his face. "You're so right, boss. You're important, fashionable, and wealthy. And me? I'm a slave. I'm a nobody! I've never even been invited to a party before."

"Hmmmm," said Bacchu, scratching his jaw and staring at Squirrel with his big, glassy eyeballs.

"You have such an eye for style, boss. You'll know exactly

what kind of outfit I need," continued Squirrel. "Maybe you could give me some pointers . . ."

"What's the use of pointers? You won't understand them anyway. I'll have to take you myself. My groomer can wait for me till I'm back," said Bacchu, lugging his loglike legs out of the Jacuzzi and letting them drip everywhere. "There's only one place to get clothes for Smitten's wedding—Malmali's Silk Studio. But Malmali is very picky about who he designs for. Luckily for you, I'll be with you—that'll help. But I need to know: How much can you spend?" asked Bacchu, slurping Squirrel's Mud Milkshake noisily.

Squirrel hesitated. "Sir, I'm not sure. I've never been to Priggle's to check how much I have in my bank account. I make do with what I get in tips from the clients. My wages are sent straight to the bank, so that I can pay my rent."

"*Rent? What rent?*" asked Bacchu, spitting the word out as though it were an itchy hairball.

"Sir, because I am a slave, I'm not allowed to own my own home. Priggle's Bank owns the tree cottage I live in. So, my wages go directly to the bank, and Mr. Priggle deducts what I owe him in rent. I guess he deposits whatever is left in my bank account, but I have no idea how much that is." He looked down. "I know I should've figured this out since I'm getting older, but I've never needed to till now."

"That's ridiculous, Squirrel. Come, I'm taking you to Priggle's. We must get you some money." And, with wholly uncharacteristic enthusiasm, Bacchu Banoose took Squirrel to the bank for the first time.

Priggle's Bank stood on a pretty slice of beach. The building was made up of four circular apartments scooped together, sprinkled with sugar-white windows. A brown roof melted gently over the entire building.

Squirrel licked his lips as he and Bacchu picked their way through patches of candy-red flowers spilling onto the sand.

They entered the bank, and Squirrel found himself in an airy room. In the middle of the room, a bespectacled pig sat behind a desk.

"Mr. Banoose! What a surprise! Why, weren't you here just yesterday?" said the pig Priggle as he wriggled himself out of his seat.

"Don't worry. I haven't spent the entire pot I took out yet, Priggle," chortled the mongoose. "Today I'm here with my slave, Squirrel," he said, shoving Squirrel forward.

"Oh my!" said Priggle, shoving a scrubbed, pink hand in Squirrel's face. "So you're the PetPost Squirrel! Yes! The tree cottage you live in is owned by the bank. I've been so impressed with you—you always send your rent on time. Just

27

like your parents used to. Yes, yes. Very impressed. Well, I've been putting your wages aside every full moon. Glad you've finally come to visit," said Mr. Priggle, wiggling his nose so that it hoisted his spectacles up his snout. "Tell me, Squirrel, how may I help you?"

"Hello, Mr. Priggle. Uhmm . . . I . . . I want to know how much money I have in the bank."

"Of course you do! It'll take just a moment," said Priggle, jiggling a chiseled pebble key strapped to his wrist. He ducked and began to fidget with the underbelly of the desk till it shook.

"Hurry it along, Priggle ol' boy," said Bacchu, tapping his foot.

"'Course, sir," said Priggle from under the desk. When he bobbed back up, the pig said, "Squirrel, your balance is seven, three, thirty-four."

"Excuse me?" said Squirrel, not understanding the pudgy pig at all.

"That means you have seven gromms, three bizkits, and thirty-four gufflings in your account," said Priggle with a smile.

Squirrel was shocked. He could not believe he had earned so much. He had thirty-four full gufflings at the age of thirteen? Not bad for a slave! Why, he had never spent a guffling. He had never even held a guffling in his paw!

"How do I take some money out, sir?" he asked, his head feeling as light as a balloon.

"I can give you up to five gufflings now. But, if you want more, you'll have to come to the Wet Vault with me and answer your security questions."

"Security questions?" asked Squirrel, puzzled.

"It's a security measure. The questions were created when your account was opened. Just one way we keep our clients' wealth nice and safe."

"I guess I'll take five gufflings now," said Squirrel. He had been a baby when his account was opened. How could he possibly remember what security questions he had chosen?

"No problem, I'll be right back," said Mr. Priggle, trotting out of the room. When he came back, he was carrying a plate piled with currency. Licking the tips of his porky fingers, Priggle quickly separated the pile into a mound of mud patties, a few wooden squares, and four bronze cubes. He handed the plate to Squirrel. "There you go, Squirrel—four gufflings, seven bizkits, and thirty gromms . . . which makes a grand total of five gufflings."

"Thank you," said Squirrel, scooping the thirty mud gromms and seven wooden bizkits into his pouch. He picked up his four gufflings, twirled them in his paw, and dropped them into his pouch—one at a time.

As his pouch tinkled, Squirrel grinned. "I've never had so much money!"

"Make sure you keep it safe. That's a fair bit you're withdrawing, Squirrel," said Mr. Priggle.

"Don't worry, Priggle. I'm making sure Squirrel spends that bag before he gets home tonight. Toodleoo," said Bacchu Banoose as he grabbed and yanked a suddenly concerned Squirrel straight out of Priggle's Bank.

"Oh, I almost forgot! Malmali, can you make my slave Squirrel something?" Bacchu said, trying on his fourth outfit. "He needs a tunic for a wedding . . . for about five gufflings."

Squirrel, who had been hiding behind a spool of red cloth, felt the air freeze in his lungs. He could not spend his entire five gufflings on one outfit!

He looked at Bacchu desperately. He coughed; he hiccupped; he grunted; he almost oinked; but Bacchu did not glance his way.

To his horror, Squirrel realized that if he did not speak up, he would end up spending five gufflings—more than his rent for three seasons—on one tunic!

31

"Excuse me," Squirrel said softly as he shuffled out of his corner. "Sir, I don't think I can spend more than three gufflings on the outfit."

"Three? You'll get nothing for three! What's the point, Squirrel? I should've just taken you to Animart!" shrieked Bacchu. "You have five gufflings with you. What're you saving them for?"

Squirrel looked at Bacchu, all puffed up and indignant, with yellow and peach and pink cloth draped around him, looking like a swollen meringue candy. Suddenly a tightly stretched cord snapped somewhere between Squirrel's neck and his brain. Bacchu would not bully him this time.

Ignoring his boss's mutterings and gutterings, Squirrel turned to the worm Malmali. "Sir, I can't spend more than three gufflings. That's all I can afford. I just want something simple that'll still fit in at Smitten's wed . . ." He could not finish his sentence because he was too busy ducking to avoid the beret Bacchu had just chucked at him.

When he stood up again, Squirrel felt the worm's X-ray-like eyes measure every part of him—from his acorn-shaped head to the S branded into his forearm to his bushy red tail. Squirrel's legs began to sweat. Then, abruptly, Malmali nodded and swept out of the room, his cape trailing on the floor behind him. The meeting was over.

32

"What happened?" Squirrel asked, looking back at a scowling Bacchu. "He didn't say a word."

"Malmali never speaks, you bumpkin!" said Bacchu, his voice as sour as old cream. "That lunatic of a worm actually agreed to outfit you for a measly three gufflings. But why he decided to help such a cheap, uncivilized rodent, I will never understand!"

Bacchu was so annoyed with Squirrel for not spending five gufflings on a Malmali tunic that he refused to tell Squirrel how to complete his outfit and what gift to give Smitten and Cheska. All Bacchu said was, "Since you have such a mind in that egg-head of yours, figure it out yourself."

Well, this was exactly what Squirrel did—which is why, on the evening of Smitten and Cheska's wedding, Squirrel was skipping toward the rosewood jetty, carrying a big wooden crate, and wearing an umbrella-like straw hat on top of his new tunic and his ivory collar.

Squirrel recognized the jetty for Smitten and Cheska's wedding by the puffs of pink smoke bursting from the planks. He scurried over and saw the famous comedians, the Funny Frogs, entertaining the crowd. Excited, Squirrel hopped onto the jetty. Immediately many guests turned and stared at him.

"Hey, catch a load of Cowboy Red! He's stealing our

laughs," croaked one Funny Frog, pointing a webbed finger at Squirrel.

The frog had a point. Since Squirrel had gotten onto the jetty, the comedy troupe was only getting half a laugh from the crowd.

Squirrel felt his cheeks crisp to a deep maroon, when somebody purred, "Dahling, you look sennnsational!"

He turned to find Lady Blouse shimmering in a silver fish-scale dress, which made her look like a slinky mermaid. She was smiling her delightful lopsided smile.

Touching his tunic, she said, "It's the new Malmali blue, his latest work. I like! And the hat—inspired! Though, perhaps, not everyone is ready for Malmali topped with straw quite yet," she said, glancing at a little kitten who was pointing at Squirrel's straw hat and giggling.

"Should I take the hat off, Lady Blouse?" whispered Squirrel, lifting the hat off his head, and putting it back on. "Off. On. Which looks better, m'lady?"

"Take it off for now. You can put it back on when we're at the wedding. But, dahling, that wooden crate is a bit of a pimple on your outfit. Do hide it when we get there."

"I will. I'll put it in the gift pile. It's my present for Smitten and Cheska. I'm giving them a case of Pretty Piths," said Squirrel, taking off his hat and tucking it into his tunic.

At that moment, a canoe glided up to them and a crow with a dented beak hopped out.

"Ladies and gen'men, I'm your usher this evenin'. I'll be ferryin' you through this 'ere mangrove till we get to the weddin' site. All 'board," announced the crow, helping the guests onto the raft one at a time. When he turned to help Squirrel, he stopped.

"Careful. It's 'ard for small animals to get on. If I ain't mistaken, you're a squirrel, aye?" As the crow helped Squirrel on, a hungry glint flitted into the bird's eyes.

"Yes, I am. Thank you," said Squirrel, scrambling onto the boat. He turned away from the creepy crow, back to the so-much-nicer Lady Blouse. She was wearing a puzzled expression on her pretty face.

"Pretty Piths? What in the world are Pretty Piths, dahling?"

"Magical mangoes. When you eat the flesh of the fruit, you become more beautiful: Your fur glows, your eyes twinkle, your smell sweetens. And that's just the half of it. If you crack open the pith of the mango, a drop of juice oozes out. Drinking this juice makes everything around you lovely. Like you're living your favorite dream."

"How wonderful! What a splendid present for a newly married couple," said Lady Blouse. "Where in Cats' Kingdom did

35

you find these Pretty Piths, Squirrel? I've never even heard of them."

"I have the recipe for them in an old book in my tree cottage in Wickory Wood . . . I've made them once before . . . ," Squirrel was saying, till he got utterly distracted by his surroundings.

The canoe was slicing through a floating forest that seemed to have been sprinkled with apple-green fairy dust. Gummy bubbles slid from leaf to leaf, popping with silly smacks; roots swayed in the water like long, hairy jellyfish; a woody lullaby hummed in the thick, warm air.

Just as Squirrel was slipping into this fairy-tale-like dream, the tangle of trees parted. A bright clearing was bobbing on the mangrove.

"Dahling, are you listening? Or has all my purring bored you already?" teased Lady Blouse as the boat pulled up beside a platform and the usher jumped out.

"Sorry, Lady Blouse. I just got, uhm, sidetracked."

"This mangrove is enchanting, isn't it? But back to what I was saying: You think you could make me some Pretty Piths sometime? I should quite enjoy them, I think," she said as the dented-beaked crow helped her slink onto the platform.

"Anything for you, m'lady," said Squirrel, letting the crow help him ashore. Clambering out of the raft, Squirrel wondered if it was possible for even a Pretty Pith to make

Lady Blouse prettier than she already was. The image was so striking that even after he was off the boat, Squirrel did not notice that the crow was still holding his paw in a knuckle-crushing grip.

"Usher, what're you doing?" asked Lady Blouse, pulling Squirrel free.

"Sorry ma'am, I jus' wanted to make sure 'e got off the raft safe. It can be hard for 'em smaller animals," said the crow as Lady Blouse laced her arm through Squirrel's and led him toward the celebration.

3

A Sip of Mischief

Lady Blouse and Squirrel strolled down a walkway covered with butter-colored magnolias. The fleecy blossoms tickled Squirrel's heels, and a chuckle bubbled out of his mouth.

"Dahling, what's so funny?"

"The petals on the floor . . . they're tickling me," said Squirrel.

"Wait!" called Lady Blouse, staring at Squirrel's feet. "Squirrel, where're your shoes?"

"Shoes?" The smile slipped right off Squirrel's face. "I didn't think of shoes . . ."

He felt like jumping straight into the water and paddling back to Bimmau. He was just about to turn around when Lady Blouse said, "Never mind, dahling. Don't go worrying your little red head about shoes. I didn't even notice you weren't wearing any until you actually said so. Trust me—no one will be able to tell!"

"But . . . I look foolish," said Squirrel, staring at his naked, calloused feet, furious with himself for not thinking of shoes.

"Dahling, no one looks foolish in Malmali," purred Lady Blouse, stroking his tunic. "Now let us not speak of silly things like shoes. Go put your crate down there. Excellent. And now escort me to a seat, won't you? Lord Blouse is traveling again and I don't fancy being seen alone."

"Of course, m'lady," said Squirrel, dumping his crate and rushing back to Lady Blouse.

As he tucked his arm in hers, he forgot all about shoes. His eardrums hummed with a soft bum-di-bum-bum; he saw a row of goldfish in bowler hats popping water-jazz beats with their lips. Baboons in suits sprayed him with jasmine mist, and a troupe of golden-purple butterflies swished above, looking like a banner of double-paneled silk. Squirrel glanced at Lady Blouse and sighed; he felt like the hero of a romantic midsummer musical.

They saw the tables, and Lady Blouse picked one topped

with a bright pond-apple lantern. Two tall fountains babbled next to it. Squirrel watched as Lady Blouse shimmied up to the fountains, swept her arms out, and spun. Her paws grazed the tops of the gushing liquid.

"What are those? Why are the fountains gold and fizzy?" asked Squirrel.

Lady Blouse brought a soaked finger to her mouth, licked it, and smacked her pink lips. "As I thought . . . Shell Champagne."

Squirrel began to choke, as though a big, bronze guffling were stuck in his throat. A bottle of Shell Champagne cost more than he made in a moon cycle; these two tall, frothy fountains were probably worth more than everything in his tree cottage.

"You okay, Squirrel?" asked Lady Blouse. He managed to nod.

"Good. I think I shall sit here." She pointed to a seat and Squirrel hurried over and pulled a chair out for her. He was just settling down beside her when his nostrils caught a whiff of something. His stomach gurgled.

"Excellent! They've put out some food already," he said. Sure enough, pitchers of churning cream and sculptures of sugarcane and cheese dotted the room. He watched as guests broke off bits of the statues for a quick nibble. He was about to get up and do the same when two doves carrying a tray floated up to him.

"What are these?" Squirrel asked, looking at the macaroni-like brown swirls.

"Brittle butter snails, sir," cooed one of the doves. "Would you like one?"

"Sure would," piped Squirrel, popping one of the slippery shells in his mouth. His jaw splintered the shell into billions of sharp, salty crumbs that crackled on his tongue. As he chewed, he felt something squishy and chewy, which tasted of butter and mint.

"Hmmm . . . That just made me feel hungrier," said Squirrel, gulping the snail down.

"Dahling, that's what it's supposed to do," said Lady Blouse with a wink.

"Right, of course!" mumbled Squirrel, looking away before he said anything even stupider in front of Lady Blouse.

To his left, he saw a dance floor carpeted with skins of velvety peaches. Millions of fireflies twinkled above the waltzing guests, like a chandelier strung straight from the night sky. To his right, a giant lily with five ribbonlike petals formed a tent that quivered in the breeze.

Squirrel had just decided that this wedding was the most spectacular event he would ever attend when something caught his attention. In the corner, next to a golden spring, was a crumpled ball of orange fur and black silk. A broken ice-crystal cup and a few daisies lay next to it.

Excusing himself from Lady Blouse, Squirrel dashed over to the orange-black mess and prodded the mass of fur with his foot. It let out a long groan.

"A sslower ssor you, misss," slurred the orange heap, rolling over.

Squirrel knew he should not laugh. He hugged himself to control his chuckles. Finally he managed to say, "Brosher, sir, let me help you up."

"You don't want a sslower?" said Brosher as Squirrel tried to uncurl the cat and straighten out his black silk jacket. But Brosher was too heavy for Squirrel's narrow shoulders. Squirrel was trying to sling Brosher on his back when the cat suddenly became lighter. Someone else had grabbed Brosher from under the arms.

Within moments Brosher was standing, with one floppy arm around Squirrel, and his other arm around a young dog wearing a white tuxedo with a red butterfly bow tie.

"Thanks," said Squirrel to the dog.

"No worries! Last I saw, Brosher was standing on the dance floor giving daisies to every pretty girl, saying, 'A flower for you, miss?' He must've got bored 'cos he seems to have guzzled a pig's weight of Shell Champagne from the spring. Poor fella," said the dog as they lowered Brosher into a chair. "I'm Des, by the way," he added, extending a paw to Squirrel.

"Nice to meet you, Des. I'm Squirrel."

"Squirrel? Well, that's an original name, isn't it?" said Des with a grin.

"Tell me about it," said Squirrel, who had always wished he could have had a proper name. "So, is Des short for something?"

"'Tis my nickname. My sister named me. You see these patches?" Des pointed to a dark brown ring on his left eye and to another oval on his right ear. "When I was born, she screamed, 'There's patches on him.' 'Course she could barely speak, so it came out as 'Despatches.' And my mean parents thought it'd be funny to name me that—Despatches," he said, shaking his head.

"You don't like your name either?" asked Squirrel, glad to have something in common with this dog.

"I hate it. Despatches? It makes me sound like a two-hundred-season-old sailor with sardine breath, doesn't it? Sometimes I could just kill Cheska for coming up with it."

"Cheska?" asked Squirrel, confused. Then it clicked. "You're Cheska's brother?"

"Yup, that's me. And who're you? You look familiar . . ."

"I'm Bacchu Banoose's slave—the PetPost Squirrel. I deliver the mail in Bimmau."

"Oh! Of course! I didn't recognize you without the uniform. You wear that a lot, huh?"

Squirrel nodded. "Every day since I can remember. That's who I am. I'm the PetPost slave."

"But, how'd you end up a slave, Squirrel? There are barely any slaves left."

"I'm the last slave in Bimmau," said Squirrel, trying to ignore the itching of the S branded into his arm. "My parents . . . ," he started, when he heard a soft humming.

"Wait . . . are those the nightingales?" asked Des.

Squirrel nodded, glad to be interrupted.

"That's the wedding march. Which means I'm supposed to be up there. How do I look?" Des asked, tweaking his bow tie.

"Like a bride's brother," said Squirrel, grinning at his new friend.

"Excellent! I'll come find you when I'm done. Go get a seat and watch me strut down the aisle. I'm escorting Lexy. At the Wagamutt we call her Leggy Lex," said Des, his brown eyes twinkling before he bounded to the tent.

As he watched Des's tail wag happily, Squirrel decided to head to the tent himself. He scanned the room for Lady

Blouse, but when he could not see her anywhere, he strapped his straw hat onto his head and followed Des into the massive Lily Tent.

Candles, candles, and more candles lit the space. Vines crept up the sides of the tent, with bunches of grapes hanging within easy reach of the guests. Olfisse, the Pedipurr's security cat, had an entire bunch of grapes on her lap and was munching them noisily. Today she did not look grumpy at all. Squirrel chose the seat next to her and settled down just as the nightingales' song became quick and loud.

On cue in walked Smitten, wearing a tuxedo and looking as dapper as ever. He got onto the stage, bowed to his guests, and stood tall, waiting for Cheska.

He had to wait for a bit. A kitten crawled down the aisle first, throwing fistfuls of fluttering ladybugs into the air. Then came the groomsmen, with pretty bridesmaids on their arms. Des was the last. When he swaggered down the aisle with a very leggy she-dog, a couple of young dogs in the audience actually whistled—winning many dirty looks from the Pedipurr cats.

But when the nightingales' song became as soft as a cloud, everyone grew quiet. It was Cheska's turn.

Wearing a flowy orange petal dress that made her fur look

like honey, Cheska drifted down the aisle. Her curls bounced in tune with the music. Smiling, she walked toward Smitten. She stepped onto the stage and the ceremony began.

Hand in hand, Smitten and Cheska sang the Wedded Vow together.

My hand in yours, my love pure
I wish to wed, I am sure
To you I pledge, to share life true
I wish for joy, for me and you
With this crown, I take and give
My heart, my soul, as I live

Smitten and Cheska each held up a wreath of baby's breath flowerbuds and placed it on each other's heads. They smiled at each other—they were married.

Squirrel watched mesmerized as Smitten and Cheska finished the wedding ritual by feeding each other caramel rocks and sharing a goblet of the sacred Walnut Wedded Wine. Then they turned to their guests and said, "Friends, thank you for coming. Dinner is now served."

Instantly the sound of wings filled the air. Pigeons carrying trays, bowls, logs, and ladles flew in and laid the feast around the dance floor.

Squirrel grinned. He had been so excited about this dinner that he had starved himself since dawn. Tonight he would taste everything, go for seconds, and maybe even go back for thirds. He hurried over, grabbed a shell plate, and started heaping dollops of every dish on it. When his plate was the heaviest it could possibly be, he sat down at the nearest table and tucked into his meal.

In moments he had picked the dishes he liked best: fried chilly cocoons and caramelized lizard's gizzard. But his favorite was the creamy bark-nut soufflé, which melted on his tongue like a cotton ball of flavor. Squirrel was on his way to help himself to one—who was he kidding—two more soufflés, when Des grabbed his shoulder.

"Squirrel, I almost didn't recognize you with that hat on! Anyway, come with me. I have a surprise."

Squirrel followed Des to a corner. Des whispered, "Check it out. I stole some of the Walnut Wedded Wine. It's both spiced and spiked. You want some?"

Squirrel paused. "We can't drink this, can we? I thought you could only drink it at your own wedding! It's not allowed . . ." But as he looked from the glowing amber liquid to the glowing golden excitement in Des's eyes, he felt something he had never felt before—the thrill of doing something forbidden. "I've never had Wedded Wine before."

"It's fantastic. And this bottle's the best there is—Smitten's doin', of course. Just try some. I'll get you a glass 'fore we get caught," said Des. "I can't wait to see your face when you taste this stuff."

"This is the best wedding I'll ever go to. And it's my first one," said Squirrel, his mind a tangle of nerves.

"Makes sense. I'm thirteen and the only weddings I've been to are my sisters'. But I managed to sneak some Wedded Wine at each one of them," said Des.

"I'm thirteen too," Squirrel said. "How many sisters do you have?"

"Three: Aubry, Brioche, and Cheska. That's them over there, all gabbing in the corner. They're always whispering to each other—very annoying," said Des, pointing to three she-dogs talking to one another. Cheska was radiant, but anyone could see that the other two sisters were equally pretty.

"I've never seen dogs who look like you guys," said Squirrel. Des and his three sisters looked very similar. They all had fur the color of liquid toffee and gentle features. The only difference was that Des's nose was upturned and his face was flatter and patchy.

"That's 'cos we're Puggles," piped Des, picking two wine glasses off the counter. "Dad's a Pug and Mom's a Beagle. They met at the Wagamutt and 'twas love at first sight. They love telling that story," he said, rolling his eyes. "I guess whose family ain't weird, huh? What're your folks like?" asked Des, pouring the Wedded Wine into the glasses and handing one to Squirrel.

As he took the glass, Squirrel tipped the brim of his hat down so that Des could not see the dampness in his eyes. "My parents aren't around anymore. They died when I was three."

"I'm so sorry, Squirrel," said Des, putting his paw on Squirrel's shoulder. After a long pause, the dog asked, "Do you remember them?"

Squirrel blinked hard so his eyes would stop stinging. "Not their faces—just their smells. And their voices, I guess. I wish it wasn't all so . . . foggy." With a gulp he continued, "They were PetPost slaves too. We lived in the tree cottage we rent from Priggle's Bank. I still live there. One night my mom was cooking and the oil lamp in the kitchen fell. The floor caught fire. My dad jumped into the kitchen to save her, but . . ."

Squirrel stopped, choking.

"Where were you?" breathed Des, his brown eyes warm with sympathy.

"In the kitchen with them. They threw me out the window just before the roof fell," Squirrel whispered.

After a long moment, Des said, "Squirrel, I'm so sorry . . ."

Squirrel shrugged. "I try not to think about it."

"That's the best thing to do. So here's to not thinking," said Des solemnly, clinking his glass against Squirrel's.

Squirrel looked at the Wedded Wine and then chugged the whole glass down, trying to drown his thoughts in the forbidden sweetness of the liquid.

He waited for the sinful wine to warm his belly. But something went horribly wrong. Pain cleaved Squirrel's brain. A scorching current surged through his skull—his eardrums ripped, his eyes went blank. His muscles stiffened and he crashed to the floor like a bowling pin.

Then, out of nowhere, a woman's voice rang clearly in Squirrel's head. The voice sang slowly, carving every word into his mind.

> *You're wed, my son, now you'll see*
> *All you were and what you could be:*
> *Under soil, above a tree*
> *You're tightly bound, yet wholly free*
> *Find, my son, a gift from me*
> *A puzzle as a recipe*
> *Solve it, and start your journey*
> *That leads to long-lost Brittle's Key*
> *But you must prove you're worthy*
> *To use this weapon most mighty*

So find and sip liquids three
The first one lies with the Queen Bee
It is called Marbled Honey
Go find, my son, your destiny

The song ended, but Squirrel kept gripping the hat strapped to his searing-hot skull. Slowly he forced his eyes open and looked up. Des was standing over him, gaping at him like a dumbstruck donkey.

"Squirrel, wh-what happened?" asked Des, pulling Squirrel up. "You okay?"

But before Squirrel could answer, a sudden chill pressed against him. The words became icicles in his mouth. He looked at Des, and saw the sky around the dog go dark, as though a bulb had blown. Squirrel saw the dance floor go black. Then, the tent. Then, the tables—until the whole wedding swilled in darkness.

A stream of smoke punched Squirrel in the face. And everything was drowned by a terrifying, thumping beat.

FOES AND FRIENDS

It was as though the earth had cracked open and was spitting up its insides.

Flecks of soot stung Squirrel's eyes, and his nostrils were punched by the stench of rot. He staggered over to the outline of what he thought was Des and choked, "Wh-what's goin' on?"

Des did not speak; he just pointed to the smoky sky.

Through the haze Squirrel saw crows—at least a dozen of them, cloaked in black, circling the wedding. One at a time, they swooped down, filling the night with their demented cackles.

With growing dread, Squirrel watched as the crows began to smash everything they could with their bladelike wings. He watched them lob rock grenades at guests. He watched as they fired slingshot pellets blindly into the crowd, the whole while laughing their glass-shattering laughter. Their cold, crazy cackles stung fear into his veins.

Squirrel felt Des grab his shoulder. Through a row of glasses he saw guests shriek and scatter like marbles. Some ducked under chairs. Others flung themselves into the water. Escape was the only thing on everyone's mind.

Squirrel realized he had to hide. But before he could do anything, he heard a sharp yelp. He turned and saw Des wincing in pain. The dog was clutching a blot of red on his sleeve.

Squirrel rushed over to his new friend, and almost tripped on the stray pellet that had punctured Des's shoulder.

"Des, you're hurt!"

Though his lips were pale and pursed, Des shook his head. "I think it looks worse than it is," he said as the dyelike blood soaked through his white tux.

"You're losing too much blood," said Squirrel. "We need a bandage." On pure instinct he grabbed Des and pushed him to the closest counter. As a dense cloud of smoke passed over them, he pulled Des under the counter so they were both hidden under the tablecloth.

Squirrel blinked in the darkness. His chest grew tight and his head spun. But, somehow, he managed to swallow his fear of small, narrow spaces.

Ripping a long swab from his new Malmali tunic, he wrapped it tightly around Des's wound. The lush fabric soaked up the blood. In moments Des stopped bleeding.

As the cacophony grew louder, Des said, "My family! It's my sister's wedding. What if they're after her?" His voice was pulled with tension.

Squirrel was about to say something, but then he heard an odd, low rustle. From somewhere—somewhere very close—a strange voice said, "They're not after your sister."

"Who's there?" said Des, trembling. He whispered to Squirrel, "Mate, d'you hear that?"

As a grenade exploded, a deep voice said again, "They're *not* after your sister."

Squirrel felt the words prick his ears. Alarm chilled his cheeks—the voice was definitely speaking to them. He reached for Des and steadied himself. "Wh-who are you?" he said, as bravely as he could.

"A friend. I can help you get out of here."

"Let's make a run for it," said Des hoarsely, pulling Squirrel toward the tablecloth.

"You're surrounded. Don't go anywhere. I'll be right

back," whispered the voice, before dissolving into a soft swoosh.

Three heartbeats later, two more voices pierced the table-cloth.

"We ain't on a hit tonight. No killings," said one loud, metallic voice.

"I don't undershtand. We jusht bring 'im in? No torshture, no blood?" asked a second scratchy voice.

"We bring 'im in as he is. Alive. That's the order. Got it?" said the metal voice.

A few scratchy grunts followed. "Yesh, bosh."

"Good. Now stop mumblin', fool. Just find 'im!"

Squirrel heard heavy footsteps followed by the flapping of wings. When he was sure that the scratchy voice had flown off, he whispered, "Whad'ya think's going on? Who're they looking for?"

"You, Squirrel." It was the deep voice from before.

"Me? What're you talkin' about?" mumbled Squirrel.

"Shhhh!" whispered the voice—a voice Squirrel could tell was definitely female. "I'll get you out. Follow me. But be completely quiet." Her words were so soft they could have been crafted from a gentle breeze. "I'm coming in."

There was a swish of fabric, a flash of light, and a crisp crackle. A blue flame flickered into life on the tip of a long, black feather. Holding this feather was a crow—a big crow, with a face full of angles and beads for eyes.

Squirrel grabbed Des and was about to dash out when he heard the scratchy voice again. "I tell ya, I've searched everywhere. There ain't no red Squirrel here."

Squirrel's flesh squirmed and his toes went dead. Black panic filled his lungs.

"Checked under the tables?" said a new voice, so high-pitched that Squirrel heard the glasses on the tabletop shake a little.

"No, Misshy. You do it."

"Me? You're the one that's searchin' this part. You do it!"

"Not gonna. Where'sh Zulf? Make her do it," said Scratchy.

A frog's leap away, under the tablecloth, Squirrel went so pale he could have passed off as a wax candle. Luckily, Screechy and Scratchy were too busy cursing each other to look under the table, and eventually their arguing voices drifted away.

Under the table, the crow with the blue flame tightened Squirrel's straw hat on his head and motioned to him and Des to follow her.

Squirrel watched the crow pierce the tablecloth with her beak, press an eye to the hole, and wait. She waited till an earsplitting crack shook the floor. At that very moment, the crow sliced the tablecloth and slipped out, pulling Squirrel and Des with her.

The area around them was deserted. The firing was coming from the entrance of the wedding, where the cloaked birds were snatching guests, searching them, and chucking them aside. They were looking for someone. Squirrel gulped. They were looking for *him*.

To the tent, mouthed the crow, pointing to the giant white lily in which Smitten and Cheska had gotten married.

The tent itself could not have looked more different than it had earlier. It was empty. Candles had scorched the white ribbon petals. Smashed grapes littered the floor. Seats were smattered with dark red streaks that could have been either grape juice or blood.

Jumping over a mess of wood, Squirrel followed the crow to the farthest corner of the tent, along with Des. They ducked behind the last petal so they were completely hidden. Around them the green sea splashed and sprayed angrily.

Looking at Des, the crow said, "Dog, you can swim from here to that bush. They won't find you there."

"What d'ya mean? Where're you going?" said Des.

"Shhh! Keep your voice down," whispered the crow. "I'm getting Squirrel out of here."

"Huh? Where?" said Squirrel, desperately looking for any other way off the platform.

"You think we're as dumb as ding-dongs? You're not taking Squirrel without me!" said Des, squaring himself.

"Suit yourself. Though, I warn you, it'll get dangerous," said the crow, narrowing her small, beady eyes.

"I'm not leaving Squirrel," repeated Des.

The crow's jaw tightened, but she nodded. Slicing a long strip from the petal tent, she tied the middle portion of the strip to her talons, and threw one end to Squirrel and the other to Des. Squirrel tugged on the petal. It was surprisingly strong.

"Tie these around your waists tightly. They must hold your weight as we fly. Quickly."

"We're flying?" gasped Des.

"Of course we're flying," said the crow, looking around shiftily. "But don't let the blood from your wound drip. They can spot blood from miles in the air." And having imparted that worrying information, the crow took flight with Des and Squirrel trailing behind her.

The crow glided into a thicket of trees. She did not slow down; she did not look back. Six times Squirrel had to clamp his eyelids shut for fear of smacking into a tree or getting tangled in a hanging branch, but each time the crow plunged or swerved at the very last moment. Just as Squirrel was beginning to trust the crow's flying skills, he found himself heading straight for a painfully solid wall made of tree trunks. He was about to yell when the crow stopped midair and pointed to a small opening at the base of the wall.

"It's clear," said the crow. "Jump in. Through that hole. Quickly."

Jumping was the last thing Squirrel wanted to do, but he had no choice. With shaking paws he untied himself, took a deep breath, and let go of his petal harness. He tumbled through the mess of leaves, through the hole, and landed, with a thump, on his bony bottom.

"Ouch," moaned Squirrel as he picked himself up and looked around. He was standing in a square room, bare except for a bed, a desk, and a stove. One small window let in the swampy, green light.

Squirrel jumped as Des landed next to him. A moment later, the crow flew into the room, went to the wooden stove, filled a coconut shell with water, and put it to boil. She was mumbling something that sounded like, "Would have realized I'm not there."

"Who are you?" said Des, looking squarely at the crow.

The crow looked from Des to Squirrel. "I'll explain everything to you in time. But first we need to bandage that up." She removed a cotton pod from the desk, burst it open, and tossed it into the boiling water.

"I'll bandage it up at home. We have to leave. I've got to tell my family I'm all right . . ."

"If you leave here now, you won't make it out of this mangrove alive. I tried to tell you to leave when you could. Now you must trust me," said the crow matter-of-factly. Then, softening a little, she said, "But I may have a way for you to contact your family. You're a Verza, aren't you? You live on the Prowl Promenade?"

"How d'ya know that?" asked Des, his coffee-colored eyes brewing with suspicion.

"I'm a crow. I watch everything and everyone I have to," she said as she brought over the sterilized cotton pad.

"What? You've been spying on . . . OOOOUUUUCHH!" The crow had just taped the cotton on Des's bleeding arm. "Watch it!" Des yelled, but the crow ignored him. Instead she threw open the window and whistled a melody that sounded like rustling leaves. A muddy, thick-lipped fish with two tusklike teeth swam up to the window.

"Whaddup, Zulf?"

"I need a favor. Tell the Verzas their son is fine and that

he'll be in touch with them soon. Tell only them. No one else."

"Sure, Zulf," grunted the fish before diving into the green water and swimming off.

"Who's that?" asked Des.

"An associate of mine," said the crow, turning around.

Squirrel, who was sitting on the tiniest corner of the bed, felt the crow fix her eyes on him. Though he was shivering, he looked straight at the crow and asked, "Who were they?"

The crow sighed. "Kowas."

"Kowas? Who are Kowas?" asked Squirrel.

"I know Kowas! They're crows who kidnap, sometimes even kill. All for cash. They're real cruel. Apparently they've got more guns than the Gander Cops," said Des, the words tumbling from his lips.

"But . . . why're they after me?" asked Squirrel.

The crow's eyebrows furrowed tightly. When she spoke, her voice was tense. "The Kowas have been hired to bring you in. The client wants something you own."

"What could they possibly want of mine? I am nobody. I have nothing."

"D'ya own anything valuable, mate? Something others may want?" Des asked.

Squirrel pictured his most expensive belonging—his now-ripped Malmali tunic. The Kowas could not possibly want a piece of cloth. "Nothing. There has to be some mistake," he insisted. "They've got it wrong."

Azulfa shook her head. "It's definitely you. They are looking for someone from the PetPost. Someone who wears a button with the PetPost emblem on it. Now tell me, is there anyone else like that?"

Squirrel scratched his head. Bacchu came to mind, but Squirrel knew that the fancy mongoose would never wear anything that associated him with the PetPost Mail.

The truth was that the only creatures who had ever worn the PetPost uniforms were his mother, his father, and he himself. Bacchu did not have any other slaves. He did not even have any other employees, as most free creatures found him too difficult to work with. And, since his mother and father had died ten seasons ago, the only creature who wore the PetPost emblem was Squirrel himself.

"Maybe you are right," said Squirrel, still not believing the words coming out of his mouth. "But why'd they attack me at a wedding? I don't get it!"

"They were told to attack just before the guests began to leave. And Kowas always do as they are told. The boss makes sure of that. The motto is 'Kill by Law.'"

As the crow spoke, Des stepped away from her. "How do you know all this? No one knows details about the Kowas."

The crow crossed the room. "Because I'm a Kowa too."

"Mate, we're outta here," said Des, shoving Squirrel toward the only exit and darting after him. But the crow was too quick. Slipping in front of them, she unfurled her wings—much like a dark magician unfurls his cloak—and blocked all possible escape for Squirrel and Des.

"You cannot leave," she thundered. The room quivered with the treble in her voice.

"It's me you want," said Squirrel, pushing Des behind him. "Let Des go."

"I would let both of you go if I could. But I can't," she said, folding her wings back to her sides. "It's not safe for you out there. You must trust me."

"You're insane! You're a murderer!" yelled Des, pulling a tuft of fur on his head.

"I'll explain everything in time. But, for now, know that I'm here to help. Trust me."

"Trust a Kowa? Bah!" growled Des.

"What other choice do you have?" asked the crow, pausing just long enough for her words to seep into both Des's and Squirrel's brains. "I realize I haven't introduced myself—I'm Azulfa."

Squirrel raised his arm to take hers; it had never felt heavier. "I'm Squirrel." As he shook her hand, he realized he had no way out. He just stood there—paw-in-claw with the Kowa, rooted in her wooden lair.

Azulfa turned to Des. "And . . . you are?"

"Des," came the grudging reply.

"Nice to meet you, Des. You too, Squirrel. Now rest—I'll brew you two some Algae Ale. It'll calm you down," said Azulfa, moving toward the stove.

"So we're giving this murderess a chance?" whispered Des to Squirrel.

Squirrel tried to swallow the tightness in his throat. He leaned toward Des and said in his ear, "We don't have a choice. We're in the middle of nowhere, and we can't escape . . ."

"And, don't forget, I saved you at the wedding. That should count for something," said the crow. She ignored Des's and Squirrel's shocked expressions. "Surprised that I could hear you? I have ultrasonic hearing; I can hear everything near me."

When neither Des nor Squirrel spoke, Azulfa continued, "I'll prove myself in time. But, for now, let's start with what happened to you at the wedding, Squirrel. You seemed to be having a convulsion just before the attack."

The words that had rung in his head before the attack swept every other thought to the corner of Squirrel's skull. He wanted to talk about what he had heard; he needed to understand what it meant. So Squirrel made a snap decision: He would trust Azulfa. At least for now.

A STARTING POINT

Squirrel stared at Des and Azulfa. They stared back. He had just told them about the song he had heard at the wedding, and both the crow and the dog looked as confused as he felt.

Finally Azulfa asked, "What kind of voice was it?"

"A woman's." He gulped. "I think it was my mom."

Azulfa nodded. "I guessed as much. The voice called you 'my son' three times."

Des looked hopeful. "If it's your mom, the message must be a good thing! She wants you to find something . . ."

Azulfa frowned. Pacing the room, she repeated the words

Squirrel had told her. *"You're wed, my son, now you'll see; All you were and what you could be: Under soil, above a tree; You're tightly bound, yet wholly free."*

Azulfa cocked an eyebrow at Squirrel. "Does this mean anything to you?"

Squirrel felt his cheeks flush. "No."

Azulfa's frown deepened. "But why would she say, *You're wed?* You're just about thirteen seasons old. You're still a kid!"

Squirrel stole a glance at Des, wondering if his new friend had the same smidgen of doubt that he had. But Des's face was as blank as before. So Squirrel decided not to say anything. "No idea," he mumbled.

"How about the rest?" said Azulfa. "You remember the next few lines, right?" Her words were quick, almost urgent.

"'Course I remember," said Squirrel, a bit more defensively than he had meant to. The truth was, even he was surprised by how well he remembered the verse. Though he had heard it just once, each line, each word, burned clearly in his mind—as clearly as the S branded into his arm. "The next lines were: *Find, my son, a gift from me; A puzzle as a recipe; Solve it, and start your journey; That leads to long-lost Brittle's Key."*

"So this whole thing is about some Brittle's Key? Any clue what that could be, mate?" asked Des.

Battling the hurricane swirling in his mind, Squirrel said, "No idea." He knew he sounded like a brainless parakeet, but he did not know what else to say.

"No matter, mate. We'll figure it out soon 'nuf," said Des.

"But how about the part that says, *A gift from me; A puzzle as a recipe*—any of that? This part seems to have some direction," said Azulfa, her voice drumming against Squirrel's skull like a hungry woodpecker knocking against a tree.

Squirrel stared at the floor, holding his head. His brain felt raw—as though little bits of it were ripping open.

Then—deep inside—he felt the click.

"I know! I know where I'm supposed to start!" The words came out before he realized what he was saying. "We need to go to my tree cottage. Can we?"

"If we must. We could fly like we flew here. But we must go now. The Kowas don't know where you live yet. When we were told to kidnap you, we were just given a sketch of you. But they'll find your address soon." She looked out the window into the night sky. "They'll be camped around your cottage by the time the wind changes."

"Who first spotted Squirrel at the wedding? Was it you?" Des asked, jabbing Azulfa as though she were a stuffed toy.

For a blink of a moment, Squirrel saw Azulfa's jaw tense

and he was sure that she was about to swat Des's paw with her wing. But, instead, she shook her head and said, "It was the usher who rowed Squirrel to the wedding. He's the Kowa boss. He recognized Squirrel and told the rest of us who to watch out for." Turning to Squirrel, she said, "You're lucky you had that hat. It was a great disguise . . ."

But Squirrel was not listening. Fear gripped his brain as he realized what he had done. "We must leave. Now!" With one arm he grabbed Des, and with the other Azulfa, trying to drag them out of the room. They did not budge.

"What happened?" asked Des.

"I think . . . I think I mentioned that I live in Wickory Wood in front of the usher," Squirrel mumbled, wishing he had not been such a blabbermouth.

Azulfa went still. "Did you mention your exact address?"

Squirrel thought back to his conversation with Lady Blouse. "No."

"So we still have an advantage," she said. "If we go now, we can still get there first."

"Then what're we waiting for? Don't know 'bout you, but I don't fancy bumping into any more Kowas," said Des, rubbing his wounded shoulder. "With my luck I'll end up as their pre-supper snack."

Azulfa stared at Des, her face serious. "Kowas don't eat

dogs, Des. Squirrels, yes. Dogs, no. But you're right. We should leave." She stretched her wings. "Squirrel, keep that hat on your head. We need to keep you as much disguised as possible. Good. Now tie the petals around your waists tightly. You're in for a bumpy ride."

Azulfa stuck to the shadows. Whenever she heard a sound, she darted into the thickest shrubbery she could find. Much to Squirrel's dismay, many of these were full of thorns.

"Those bushes were downright brutal, huh?" said Squirrel after they had landed in Wickory Wood. He plucked a thorn from his thigh. "Ouch! These really hurt."

Des grumbled in agreement as he tweezed a spike out of his own tail. But Azulfa was too distracted to care.

"Hurry up! We have no time for thorns now," she whispered. "I think I can hear wings. It may be the Kowas." Sure enough, two black birds flitted into view, and began circling the clump of trees.

Forgetting the thorns, Squirrel darted to the entrance of a wide ash tree with the number 24 carved into it, his heart beating like a wildebeest's. He felt Des and Azulfa right behind him. Shaking, he slid his left claw into the keyhole. It clicked open.

Squirrel opened the old wooden door, and the three of

them slipped into his cottage as quickly and as quietly as the moonlight slipped through the windows.

Once inside, Squirrel locked the door and bolted the windows. He tried to light the sunflower oil lamp, but he was shaking too much.

"Mate, you look like you're caught in an earthquake. Here, give those to me," said Des, taking the small flints from Squirrel and lighting the lamp.

As the warm, orange glow filled the room, Squirrel felt his heart slow down and his breath begin to steady. He had had more excitement since sundown than he had had in his whole life. He looked around his cozy living room, breathing in its familiar, lived-in scent. The sheepskin rugs, the reed armchairs, the nutshell coffee table, the crooked pollen paintings—they all looked wonderfully normal. Even the dizzying spiral staircase, which led both upstairs and downstairs, was a welcome sight today. He was home.

"Don't relax yet, Squirrel. We should check the rest of the cottage," said Azulfa, giving Squirrel a stern look. "I'll check upstairs."

Before Squirrel could say anything, Azulfa flew up the stairs.

"All clear," she said as she stalked back down. "We just need to check downstairs."

"Let's all go," said Squirrel. "The thing I want you to see is downstairs."

"All right, but shhhh!" said Azulfa, blowing out the lantern. "Remember, all Kowas have supersonic hearing."

"Sorry," whispered Squirrel as he tiptoed down the stairs into a room bathed in darkness. Azulfa pulled a feather from under her wing and struck it against her beak. A small blue flame lit the tip, bringing the room into view.

The chamber was like it always was: part kitchen, part dungeon. The stove stood in a corner, as it always did, surrounded by rock shelves stacked with pebbled pots and pans and clay plates. An old wooden candelabra dangled, as it always had, from the ceiling. The heavy wooden shutters on the windows were tightly locked, as they always were.

Squirrel sighed with relief and hoisted himself onto a high bamboo chair at a stone table. On the table was a massive scooped watermelon full of nuts and fruit. A red leather book with frayed edges lay next to it. Squirrel opened the book to the first page and showed it to Des and Azulfa, who had lit the candles in the candelabra.

The page was completely blank except for four words scrawled at the bottom of the page. They read: A *Gift from Me*.

Squirrel felt his heart flutter with excitement. "It's my

mom's old recipe book. I was just using it to make Pretty Piths to give Cheska and Smitten," he said. "But this book must be what the rhyme meant, right? *Find, my son, a gift from me; A puzzle as a recipe.* I have to find a puzzle in here somewhere."

"So what're we waitin' for? A flyin' reindeer?" said Des, jumping into the seat next to him. "Open the book, mate. Let's find this puzzle."

Squirrel grinned back at Des, thankful for his company. He began flipping the pages eagerly, looking through recipe after recipe scribbled in his mother's hand. But there was no puzzle. Squirrel started over. This time, he read each page carefully. But again, he found nothing. He read it once more. No luck.

Squirrel's forehead began to sweat with frustration. This so-called "gift" was nothing more than a recipe book full of nuts and jams and sweets and hams. He was about to shut the book when a loud rumble shook his entire body.

"I'm starving! Looking at all these recipes has got my stomach churning like an empty blender," he said.

Des grabbed Squirrel's paw and jumped out of his seat. "Thank friggin' frog's legs! I've been hungry for ages . . . just didn't know how to tell you."

"I'll whip up something quickly," said Squirrel, happy to

take a break from hunting for nonexistent puzzles. "What do you want?"

"I'll choose somethin'!" said Des. "In the meantime, here's something to whet our appetite."

As he spoke, Des reached into his tuxedo's cummerbund. When his paw emerged, it held two cups of what looked like whipped brown caramel. Though they were no longer fluffy, the contents of the brown spongy cups were unmistakable. They were the scrumptious bark-nut soufflés from Smitten and Cheska's wedding.

Without a word, Squirrel popped the whole soufflé into his mouth and gave in to its crumbly goodness. He forgot everything except for the tingle of the sweet, cinnamony froth on his tongue.

"How can you eat at a time like this? We need to solve this puzzle. I don't think you understand how important it is!" whispered Azulfa, but Squirrel's and Des's hungry bellies had gotten the better of them. Ignoring Azulfa, they savored every last morsel of their creamy treats, and then began flipping through the recipe book for the perfect, hit-the-spot meal. Eventually Des found it—a dish that was sublimely sweet and spicy, one of Squirrel's all-time favorites.

As Des chopped the ingredients, Squirrel heated a large wok. Before Azulfa could properly protest, the two had stewed meat, vegetables, and spices together, so that a tangy aroma wafted through the kitchen. Squirrel grinned. This was definitely more fun than searching for the puzzle.

Finally Azulfa flew to the stove and blew out the fire in one breath. "We can't attract attention to ourselves," she said. "Please understand—they're here for you, Squirrel. They will take you and destroy your cottage. You must be careful or we'll lose everything."

"Sorry, Zulf," said Squirrel.

"Just be careful. Anyway, what did you make yourselves?" she asked, trying to sound interested.

"It smells fantastic," drooled Des, helping himself to the stew. "It's chopped spicy sea urchin with zucchini in a sweet lavender sauce. Yummm," he said, his mouth full of food.

Squirrel nodded. "It's called Peppered Urchin with Zesty Zucchini in Lavender Emulsion."

Suddenly Azulfa snapped to attention. "Squirrel, give me the book," she said so tensely that Squirrel handed it over without asking a single question. He swallowed the bite he was chewing and watched the crow as she read the page over and over again. Her wings began to flap like an overcharged fan.

"Boys, we've found . . ." But before Azulfa could go on, a loud rap shook the floor above them. Immediately Azulfa blew out the candelabra and the room went dark, except for the small blue flame on her feather. She gestured to Squirrel and Des to be absolutely quiet.

The scratchy and screechy voices they had heard at the wedding rang through the silent stone kitchen. The voices were coming from upstairs, right outside the cottage.

"The door won't open," screeched the lady crow. "It's a special lock."

"They ain't in here anywaysh," said Scratchy. "I've been on the lookout."

"We're waitin' here either way, just in case. We'll hear 'em if they're inside. Let's hover around. Can't be riskin' that they slip in under us," said Screechy.

"Shtop tellin' me what to do, you bosshy 'itch."

"I'm gonna listen to the boss, but you do what you like."

Inside the cottage, Azulfa was helping Squirrel and Des climb the stairs silently, using the commotion outside and the carpeted staircase to muffle their footsteps. Once in Squirrel's bedroom, Azulfa lit a candle.

In the blue light, Squirrel's four-poster bed looked like a cocoon of fluff, fur, and fabric. A tall grandfather sundial winked mysteriously from the wall, and a desk squatted lazily under a nook full of books bound in different colors—red, blue, violet, black.

Azulfa walked up to the desk, found a blank piece of moth-wing paper, pulled a quill from under her wing, and scribbled something. She passed the note to Des and Squirrel. It read, *"We must not speak. Try to get some rest."*

Squirrel took the quill from Azulfa and wrote, *"How long will they be outside?"*

"Till dawn."

This time, Des grabbed the paper. *"But, what were you saying earlier? What did you find?"*

Azulfa's lips curled into a sliver of a smile. *"What we were looking for,"* she wrote. Silently she opened the recipe book and flipped till she found a page. It was the recipe for the meal Squirrel and Des had so happily cooked and consumed. She circled the first letter of each of the key words in the recipe title.

The circled letters were: *P-U-Z-Z-L-E.*

Peppered Urchin with Zesty Zucchini in Lavender Emulsion

Ingredients:

1 sea urchin, chopped

1 zucchini, chopped

2 cloves of garlic, finely chopped

1 red pepper, diced

2 shells full of rice juice

½ shell full of ground peppercorn

Salt to taste

5 lavender flowers, crushed

2 shells full of groundnut oil

1 shell full of sugar

Instructions:

First check the ingredients and make sure they are ripe.

Chop the zucchini and urchin into bite-size pieces. Make sure that they are the same size, so they all get cooked at the same time.

In a pot, add salt to water and boil.

Put zucchini cubes in the pot and count till 30. Remove and soak in cold water so that they do not get soggy.

In a wok, over medium heat, fry the garlic until golden brown.

Add chopped urchin and peppers. Turn the heat to high.

Add the blanched zucchini slowly into the wok and stir.

Add in the rice juice, salt, and pepper and stir 20 times.

Now for the second component—make the lavender emulsion:

Mix crushed lavender with the sugar and oil.

Make emulsion by placing lavender, sugar, and oil mixture in a saucepan over low heat till syrupy.

Drizzle the emulsion over the wok-fried urchin and zucchini.

Tip 1: To best enjoy this dish, follow it with a Raisin D'Etty. Try and see for yourself.

Tip 2: Also, the lavender emulsion is very sticky, so you have to soak the pan overnight in water. It is the universal solvent, after all.

Eat with a smile. ☺

6

A Fresh Set of Eyes

The puzzle made no sense to Squirrel. He glanced at Azulfa; her eyes burned blue in the light. Squirrel sighed and forced himself to read the words again.

He massaged his forehead. His brain felt like an iron block, his eyes like lumps of gravel. *I must sleep*, he thought, looking at the soft, yielding bed. Des was sprawled on it, his snores muffled by plump fur pillows. Squirrel pushed Des to the side and collapsed next to him.

Squirrel was about to doze off when he felt the bed sink. He blinked sleepily. Azulfa had scrambled into the bed next to him, closed her eyes, and immediately fallen into a deep sleep. He groaned as he found himself squashed between her thick wings and Des's thick limbs.

I'll never fall asleep like this, he thought, his eyelids fluttering. But, a moment later, he was dreaming of berry pies and bark-nut soufflé and barley ale. The puzzle would have to wait till the morning.

Tucked into the fluffy bed, Azulfa looked as out of place as a hippo stuck to an elm tree.

Wake up, thought Squirrel as he watched the crow twitch awkwardly in her sleep. He began to hop around the room like a jitterbug and gestured to Des to do the same. The pattering of their feet and the pounding of their hearts worked—Azulfa's ears pricked up. She opened her eyes. Success.

Before she could even sit up, Squirrel shoved a note in her face.

The note read: *Is it safe to talk? Are the Kowas gone?* His fur was raw with excitement. Sweat squelched between his toes.

Azulfa lay in bed, blinking at the note. Squirrel felt bad about waking her, but they had no time for sleep right now. He was about to nudge her again, but before he could, the crow yawned, somersaulted out of bed, spread her wings, and floated up to the mustached grandfather sundial. It was just past dawn.

"We can speak. The Kowas meet twice every day, at dawn and at dusk, so they should be gone for a while," said Azulfa with a frown. "This would have been the perfect time to get out of Wickory Wood. But we haven't solved the puzzle yet."

Squirrel smiled. He looked at Des. The dog's cheeks were blown up like a balloon. And, like a balloon letting out a stream of air, Des gushed, "Puzzle. Solved. We solved it. We solved the puzzle!"

Azulfa's eyes darted from Des to Squirrel, who felt himself grinning widely. "It's true, Zulf. We figured it out! Actually, it was quite easy . . ."

"It was not easy!" cawed Azulfa. "I tried everything. Nothing worked."

Squirrel cocked an eyebrow, pleased with himself. Despite the rush they were in, he strutted over to the window, unlocked it, and let the pale yellow sunlight flood the room. Fully aware of Azulfa's impatient eyes fixed on him, he began playing with a big blue book on his desk. Only when Azulfa was hopping from one foot to the other did he start speaking.

"I woke up early this morning. Obviously, I couldn't wake either of you in case the Kowas heard me speak. Didn't fancy being minced to meat pie by your criminal friends, Zulf."

As soon as these words came out of his mouth, Squirrel

regretted them. Azulfa's eyes glinted, her feathery body tensed. "Excuse me?" she said in a harsh whisper.

"Sorr-sorry," said Squirrel, stumbling on. "Anyway, I . . . I decided to have a go at the puzzle. When I looked at the page, I noticed this. See? Three of the words are smudged." He opened the recipe book and pointed to a large stain on the page.

"Earlier I thought it must have been a dribble of oil or emulsion or something. But when I flipped the page over, the writing on the back was fine. Strange, huh? I mean, any liquid should have soaked through the leaf page and smudged both sides, right?"

"So, I got wondering . . . maybe someone smudged the words on purpose. Maybe the smudges are part of the solution."

"That's when I woke up," piped Des.

"Yup. And good thing he did," said Squirrel. "Des noticed that only parts of the words had faded." He passed the recipe over to Azulfa.

Indeed, the letters "sec" of second, "la" of lavender, and "sion" of emulsion were faded.

As Azulfa studied the smudged letters, Squirrel held his breath. He was so giddy his head felt like a kernel of corn just about to pop. Finally Azulfa nodded. "You're right. A different ink has been used to write these letters. It's deliberate. But why?"

"Des figured it out. The part-words can be put together. So 'sec' plus 'la' plus 'sion,' which equals 'seclasion.' That sounds like a word! Now we just need to figure out what it means," said Squirrel, bursting with excitement. "SEC-la-sion. Sec-LA-sion. Sec-la-SION."

"It has a nice ring to it, doesn't it?" said Des cheerily, helping himself to a plump raisin from a bowl on Squirrel's bedside table. He popped it into his mouth. "Hmmm . . . these are delicious. What are they?"

"We call them Raisin D'Ettys. It was my Aunt Etty's recipe. I eat one before I go to bed every night—always have. My mom used to feed them to me," said Squirrel. "But never mind the Raisin D'Ettys, Des. We need to find out what 'seclasion' means. Who can we ask? Where can we find out?"

"We'll figure it out. But you gotta eat some of these first. Didn't it say in the recipe that the Peppered Urchin was best followed by a Raisin D'Etty? Should've done that. Yummy!" said Des, shoving another raisin into his mouth. "Yummy. Raisin D'Ettys in my tummy. Raisin D'Etty . . ."

Des's eyes bulged open like two flying saucers. Staring at a half-eaten raisin, he spluttered, "The *Raison D'Être*! That's why the recipe said it should be followed by the Raisin

D'Etty! It meant the *Raison D'Être*! That's what we gotta do!"

"Huh?" said Squirrel, wondering if Des had gone loopy from the sugar rush. "What're you talking about?"

"The *Raison D'Être*! It's the biggest, oldest encyclopedia. It's got *everything* in it. If 'seclasion' means anything, we'll find it in the *Raison D'Être*!"

"But, Des, the *Raison D'Être* is very rare," said Azulfa. "Where'll we ever find one?"

"I'll tell you where. At my house. We have my great-grandpa's *Raison D'Être*. You know, he was a very important dog in his day. With very important books," said Des with a wink. "Now, let's go."

"Excellent," said Squirrel, bolting the window shut and throwing on his PetPost uniform. He pocketed a few candied Raisin D'Ettys and popped one into his mouth.

As he bit into the raisin, he glanced at Des and a funny thought occurred to him. The only reason he had gotten anywhere on his quest was that Des had an uncanny knack of choosing what to eat.

The sunlight glinted off Des as he hurried down the alley. He was still wearing his tuxedo from his sister's wedding, and he was attracting a fair amount of attention. As he passed the small fish market, a few of the fisherwomen stopped to whistle.

"Late night, eh, Des?" said an old dog as she scaled her fish. "'Tis almost mid-morn, lad! What sorta mischief you'n up to?"

"Juneby, stayin' up late with beautiful girls ain't mischief! It's just plain, catch-a-cat-spank-it-silly good sense. 'Specially if that girl's your stunnin' niece," said Des.

"You rascal," croaked the old crone. "Quit yankin' my tail."

"What fun'd that be? Now, toss me a bite of that delish kingfish, will ya?" said Des, strolling over to the stall.

Squirrel, who was following Des, quickly passed the market. The fisherfolk were all so busy with Des that none of them even glanced at him. The plan had worked: Squirrel had managed to enter downtown Bimmau unnoticed.

Quickly Squirrel turned onto the Prowl Promenade. He glanced back to check on Azulfa. She grimaced back at him: As she passed the market, the chattering went silent. Everyone was weary of crows—and probably more so since last night.

Squirrel plodded on until he spotted the two large rocks on the beach that Des had told him about. He slid between them and waited. Moments later, Azulfa squeezed in next to him. Squashed between the rocks, they watched Des stroll past them and duck into the carriageway of a large house.

"That's Des's house? It's huge," whispered Squirrel, his eyes round with wonder. He was so impressed by the size of the house that he did not notice that the color of the walls had faded from chalk white to dirty eggshell, or that the roof was patched with tufts of grass and straw, or that the pillars were cracking like dry skin.

Azulfa nodded. "It's nothing much to look at now, but thirty seasons ago it was one of the grandest houses in Bimmau."

"Wow!" said Squirrel, eager to see his friend's home. "So what do we do now?"

"Now, Squirrel, we wait."

THE VERZAS AND THE VISITORS

The two rock slabs sizzled like frying pans in the strong morning sun, heating Squirrel's head like an egg. Azulfa's feathers poked his arms, but he stayed where he was. Though he was across the Promenade, he kept his eyes fixed on Des as he knocked on the door of his house.

The door swung open. It was Cheska. She looked nothing like she had the previous evening. Her orange dress was ripped. Her cheeks were streaked with mud. Her wavy hair was wire-straight.

When she saw Des, she screamed, flung her arms around him, and began to sob.

"Easy, sis," Squirrel heard Des choke as he lumbered into the house with Cheska clinging to him. Through the window Squirrel saw Cheska whistle something, and a moment later three more honey-colored dogs in gowns mauled Des, hugging him, cuddling him, scrunching his hair. Squirrel recognized two of them as Aubry and Brioche, Des's other sisters. The third dog, he knew, had to be their mother.

When Des had managed to shrug the ladies off, a group of men gathered around him. An elderly white-and-brown Pug in a tuxedo, with a bow tie hanging around his neck, seemed to spot Des's hurt shoulder, and hurried over to him and began to speak. Immediately a big burly Alsatian, a blond Pointer with glasses, and Smitten helped Des into an armchair.

Squirrel saw Des grin as one sister added cushions to his chair, another poured him a cup of what looked like chunky plum cider, and his mother laid a plate of cinnamon-glazed bones in front of him.

As Squirrel watched Des's family buzz around him like bees on a honey pot, he began to feel something he never had before. His face went tight, but his arms fell limp. His mind was empty, but his eyes began to sting. He was trying to understand this odd feeling of heavy emptiness when he felt a sharp twinge on his arm. Azulfa had just pinched him and was pointing to the window of Des's house.

"Who's that?" she whispered.

Squirrel blinked back the warm wetness in his eyes and focused on the window.

A tall Bengal cat was sauntering over to Des. The cat was a head and a half taller than anyone else in the room. His steel-gray fur framed his face, showing off the highest cheekbones Squirrel had ever seen and a jaw that looked like sculpted iron.

As the cat walked, everyone in the room watched him. Even from across the road, Squirrel could not help but stare at the tall cat whose eyes glistened like silvery moons in the morning sun.

The cat himself seemed easily aware of the effect he was having on the crowd. With a casual smile, he offered a paw to Des. Des shook it, looking very awkward. They spoke for a few moments, and Des showed the cat his wound. The tall cat untied the blue Malmali bandage and retied it properly. Then, after a few more words, he bowed to all of them, and then headed for the door.

As the door swung open, Squirrel watched the tall cat bend over and kiss Des's mother's paw. With a smile, the cat purred, "Mrs. Verza, please think about the Pawshine more seriously. I'll take my leave of you now. My eyes shall be blind, till your beauty they find." And, with that nugget of flattery, the tall cat left the Verza home.

The cat strolled out of the house, his suit rippling over his body. He twirled his cane in one hand and there was a spring in his step.

As he passed their hiding place, Squirrel felt Azulfa's breath grow quick. "He looks . . . he looks . . . regal!" she whispered. Squirrel looked at her and saw that her clear eyes were foggy and she wore a punch-drunk smile on her face.

Squirrel burst out laughing: Azulfa had not seemed the type to be interested in any male, no matter how good-looking. Squirrel was wondering if he could risk teasing her when a whistle from the Verza house stopped him. Des was waving them over.

"Did you find out what seclasion is?" asked Squirrel, scuttling over to him.

"Haven't had a chance yet. They're all just so happy to see me. I guess they were pretty worried. And that muddy fish friend of Zulf's only freaked them out more."

"Hmmm," said Azulfa, frowning.

"Sorry, Zulf. It's just that my family's not used to fish delivering them messages about me," said Des. "Anyway, let's go inside. After Baron Dyer left, I told my folks about last night. They want to meet both of you."

"You told your family about last night?" Squirrel said, almost shrieking. What had Des told them? Had he told them everything? This could be terrible . . .

"Don't fret, Squirrel," said Des quickly. "I didn't tell them about the song you heard. I just said that those Kowas are after you, and we don't know why. My family wants to help. Smitten especially. He thinks it was his fault that the Kowas found you. Anyway, the whole family is waiting, so come on in. We'll look up 'seclasion' in my great-grandpa's *Raison D'Être*. And maybe we'll even get a nibble of lunch." Squirrel noticed that as Des mentioned lunch, he was careful to avoid Azulfa's gaze.

Squirrel felt his shoulders relax as he walked toward the house. He was almost at the pillars when he realized that Azulfa was not behind him.

He turned around. The crow was standing outside, her back so straight she looked as though her feathers had been starched.

"What you waitin' for, Zulf? Come on in! We don't want anyone to spot us here," said Des, waving at Azulfa so energetically his ears began to flap.

But Azulfa did not move. "I'll wait outside."

"What? Why?" asked Des.

"It's best. I am a Kowa, after all," said Azulfa, looking down.

"Don't be as ridiculous as a ribbon-wearing rhino, Zulf!" said Des. "I've already told my family about you and they asked me to invite you in. You helped me. That's all my folks care about."

The firmness in his voice seemed to persuade Azulfa. She entered the house.

But, if Squirrel had looked at her closer, he would have seen that her eyes were welling with something—something that looked a lot like guilt.

Des led them through a brilliantly bizarre living room. Cotton pod sofas and horsehair chaises were strewn about, yellow wood tables crowded every corner, and tapestries of glossy silk draped the walls.

"It's a bit of a mess," said Des, looking embarrassed as he pulled a yak fur stool out of the way.

"It's . . . it's . . . awesome," said Squirrel, looking at a coral sculpture that looked like the top part of a windmill and the bottom part of a tarantula.

"Thanks," said Des with a grin. "I'll show you everything properly some other time. Come. Meet my family first." He led Squirrel into a courtyard.

"This is Cheska, Smitten, Brioche, Aubry, and my mom,

Mello," said Des, pointing to each of the ladies. "This is Squirrel and"—he gave Azulfa a small nudge—"this is Zulf."

Everyone shook paws. Squirrel thought Mello stiffened a bit when she shook Azulfa's talons. But, a moment later, she was thanking Azulfa warmly for helping her son escape. Squirrel rubbed his eyes. Maybe he was just seeing things.

Something soft touched Squirrel's shoulder. It was Brioche. "Dear boy, you must be so tired. And so scared." She smiled kindly.

"And to think you've no idea why the Kowas are after you," said Aubry. "Cheska's wedding . . ."

Cheska's wedding!

A cannonball of guilt hit Squirrel squarely in the face. Wringing his paws, he turned to Cheska. "I'm so sorry, Cheska," he said. "Your wedding was attacked 'cos of me." Squirrel could not believe how thick he had been. He had ruined the happiest day of Cheska's life, and now he was standing in her living room, with all her family petting him as though he were a broken butterfly. He looked down. He wanted to run straight out of the Verza house, into the ocean, and let it swallow him up.

But before he could run, Cheska took his arm. "Squirrel, this is not your fault. Not in a dragon's dream. Those Kowas are evil. There's no excuse for what they did." Her voice trembled.

Smitten put his arm around his wife. He cleared his throat and looked Squirrel straight in the eye. "The whole thing was my fault, Squirrel. I organized this wedding because I wanted the world to see how much I love Cheska. I got too carried away." He looked down. "*I'm* the one who insisted on inviting you so publicly, Squirrel—so anyone and everyone in Bimmau knew exactly where to find you. *I* insisted on having ushers. *I* invited the Kowas. They would never have found you so easily if it was not for me . . ."

Squirrel could not believe what he was hearing. "Sir, no! The Kowas would have found me anywhere. This is not your fault. And thank you so very much for inviting me. It was the most . . . the most . . . magical evening of my life, sir."

"Please call me Smitten. I'm just happy you and Des are okay, Squirrel. And I will help you in any and every way that I can. I mean that." Smitten's deep brown eyes were bright with sincerity. "Anyway, how about some lunch now?"

"Yes, everyone's famished! No one has been able to digest a morsel since Des disappeared," said Aubry, ushering them into a room with just one long, wooden table and at least twenty chairs.

At the head of the table three men were locked in deep discussion.

Squirrel glanced from the females to the males. Though

the ladies were almost identical, their chosen life part-
ners could not have looked more different. There was
Smitten, of course—a handsome cat who looked like a
mini-tiger. Sitting down was a brown Alsatian with a scar
across his left cheek. When Des introduced him as Akbar,
Aubry's husband, he smiled roguishly and his black eyes
twinkled.

The dog sitting next to Akbar was a thin blond Pointer.
He had even features, and the green eyes behind his spectacles were quiet and kind. This was Bobby, Brioche's husband. At the head of the table sat an older Pug. He was
Des's father, Ricky. The soft wrinkles on his face and his
unruly tuft of hair made him look like the most pleasant
being imaginable. He welcomed both Azulfa and Squirrel
with big hugs and asked them to sit down.

"Thank you for helping Despatches home. I hear you've
all had quite an adventure! Don't worry. We won't tell anyone," said Ricky with an easy grin.

"We're a big family; we're used to keeping all sorts of doggone secrets," added Akbar with a wink and such a deep
laugh that Aubry playfully dinged him on the back of the
head with the cantaloupe serving bowl she was carrying.

"Here's lunch," she said as she and her sisters laid the long
table with dishes.

A hungry silence settled over the table as the Verza clan and their visitors dug into a meal of sweet potato and eel porridge, peanut butter and jellyfish sandwiches, and sweet and sour seahorse.

Between mouthfuls, Des asked, "By the way, what was Baron Dyer doing here?"

"Baron Dyer? Was that the tall cat with the cane?" asked Azulfa, wheezing a little.

Smitten, who was the first to finish chewing, answered, "He's my uncle—my mother's brother. He got the Pawshine Club to invite Mello and Ricky to become members. I'm sorry he was so pushy. He's like that sometimes."

"I was shocked by the invite," said Ricky. "After what happened, I never thought the Pawshine would invite us back. The Baron must've twisted his tail three times to get us that invitation."

"But why?" asked Bobby.

Aubry smirked. "Because now we're connected with his family, and he wants us to hobnob with the princey-wincey types. Dogs can never be members of the Pedipurr, of course, but he probably figured we should at least join the Pawshine." She stuck her nose in the air and put on a funny foo-fooey accent. "The Wagamutt's simply *unacceptable*." She bit her lip and quickly added, "No offense, Smitten!"

"You'll have to do better to offend me, sis," replied Smitten, chuckling.

"I wish your uncle had not put in all that effort. He should have known that it was a waste of time," said Mello quietly. "We will not be joining the Pawshine."

"You're members of the Wagamutt?" asked Azulfa stiffly. Squirrel could tell she was trying, rather unsuccessfully, to join the conversation.

"Yes, and it's the best," said Akbar. "No dress code, no drama. Works for me." He pointed to the sleeveless T-shirt and shorts he was wearing.

"You can see that my husband doesn't believe in dressing up much," said Aubry, blowing him a kiss.

A sudden noise ripped through the room, and every pair of eyes darted to Des.

"Oops!" he said, not the least bit embarrassed at having let out a whopper of a burp.

"Son, do try to mind your manners," said Mello. Then, turning to Squirrel, she said, "I'll prepare the guest rooms for you and Azulfa, my dear."

"Don't bother, Mom. We're leaving at dusk. We're only here to find something," said Des. "We can't tell you what it's about, but Mom, can you take out Great-Grandpa's *Raison D'Être*?"

Squirrel flipped through the leaves of the big, old book. Flip, flip, crackle, crackle. His eyes read words he had never seen or heard before: *Buzzling, Cabbledion, Cactus Meat, Cadmuncie.*

"It's arranged alphabetically," said Des.

"Well spotted, Des," said Squirrel, flipping forward.

"Well spotted, indeed! That's me," said Des, grinning as he pointed to the spot on his ear.

Squirrel laughed. Des had a knack for cracking jokes at the weirdest of times. In fact, Squirrel was so busy laughing that he did not realize that he had already reached the letter S. *Sciosys, Scriptex, Seaweed, Seclasion, Sedi-lily.* "Wait! *Seclasion!* It's here! It's a word!"

"Where? What does it say?"

"Des, don't splutter like a dog stuck in a pound cake! Let Squirrel read," said Azulfa.

"Fine, fine," said Des. "Squirrel, read on, mate."

This was it. The meaning of *seclasion.*

Squirrel cleared his throat and began to read.

> *Seclasion is the most advanced way to keep secrets. During seclasion, a memory is "zipped" into the folds of an individual's brain and*

the memory remains hidden there until it is
"unzipped."

Squirrel paused before reading on, more slowly this time.

> To "unzip" and recall the memory, the
> individual must come in contact with a specific
> trigger. The best triggers are liquids. When
> the secret-keeper drinks a liquid trigger, the
> liquid diffuses into the blood and trickles to the
> brain. As soon as the trigger hits the zipped
> brain fold, it tears open the hidden memory,
> releasing it. The process of "unzipping" is oft
> accompanied by brain cramps, spasms, and
> sharp pain.

Squirrel nodded as he read. He had experienced the pain firsthand.

> Seclasion is the best way to keep a secret, as the
> secret-keeper is not even aware of it. The major
> risk with seclasion is that the memory may not
> be uncovered and may get lost forever.

Squirrel let these words swirl in the dusty library. When neither Azulfa nor Des said anything, he read on.

> *Complex memories can be stored as seclasion ladders. In this, multiple memories are zipped onto one another and each requires its own trigger. In seclasion ladders each memory can only be unzipped if the previous one has been released. Seclasion ladders are used to provide one clue at a time.*
>
> *Highly experimental seclasion research suggests that the science can zip up more than just memories.*

Squirrel went silent. His tongue felt as numb as a beached whale.

Azulfa spoke first. "Your mother led us to the word *seclasion* for a reason, Squirrel. I think, somewhere in that head of yours, you have hidden memories you need to crack open."

"In my head?" said Squirrel, gaping. He held his temples and began to shake them. "There is a memory jiggling inside my head?"

"I wouldn't be surprised if you've got one of those ladder-ma-jiggies bobbin' around somewhere up there," said Des, looking at Squirrel with eyes wide open.

"A seclasion ladder? Why would you say that?" asked Squirrel.

"Mate, didn't the song you heard at the wedding say somethin' about you drinkin' three liquids?" asked Des. "Think about it. This whole thing started when you drank the Wedded Wine. It's a liquid—it must've triggered a memory. And, when you drink three more liquids, they'll trigger three different memories in your head." Des scratched his head. "You just need to drink them in order."

Squirrel thought back to the words he had heard at the wedding. His mind stretched and curled like an acrobat, trying to understand the meaning of the words. Even though something did not feel right, he decided to ignore the nagging in his gut and focus on his mother's message.

While the first part of the verse was still a mystery, he had cracked the second part: he had found and solved the "puzzle as a recipe," and now he suspected that he had a seclasion ladder "zipped" up in his brain somewhere.

His mind wandered to the words in the next part of the verse. *Journey; long-lost Brittle's Key; weapon most mighty.* So far, this meant absolutely nothing to him. He frowned with concentration and began to say the last part of the verse aloud. "*So find and sip liquids three; The first one lies with the Queen Bee; It is called Marbled Honey; Go find, my son, your destiny."*

The frown on his face faded. Now, this was better, clearer. He had to find and drink three liquids, but at least his mother had told him exactly where the first liquid was.

"I guess I know exactly what the first drink is. It's Marbled Honey and it's with the Queen Bee."

"But how're we going to find the Queen Bee, Squirrel?" asked Des.

"The Queen of Bees will be in Mellifera—the Walled City of Bees. But it is very far. It'll take us two moons to get there," Azulfa chipped in.

"Two moons? What'll I tell my boss? I've never missed a single day of work in my life," said Squirrel, looking down at his PetPost uniform. He knew that if he skipped work, he would be a deserter slave. He could lose what little he did have—his wages, his house, his life.

As his mind and heart pushed against each other, Squirrel found himself thinking of the message from the wedding again. "This journey supposedly is for me to find three liquids. And, at the end of the journey . . . is a mighty weapon—Brittle's Key."

Des scratched his ear. "The question then is, mate, what in the pluck-a-duck world is Brittle's Key? And, is it really worth all the hassle?"

"Why the glum looks? Did you find what you were looking for?"

Squirrel jumped. Smitten had entered the library and walked over to them. Squirrel was wondering what to say when Des blurted, "Smitten, have you ever heard of Brittle's Key?"

"Nope, unless, of course, it has something to do with Brittle's Map," answered Smitten.

"What's Brittle's Map?" asked Squirrel.

"It'll be in the *Raison D'Être*. Here, let's look it up," said Smitten, taking the leathery book and flipping through the pages. "That's odd . . ." He showed the others the page. A small subscript said: *A special map. For further details look in the* Original Raison D'Être.

Squirrel grimaced. This hunt was becoming harder than forcing a wild goose to lay a golden egg. "Do we know where the *Original Raison D'Être* is?"

"At the Den at the Pedipurr," said Smitten. "It's a restricted section. Only a Lord or a Lady's Clawcrest can access the Den."

"What's a Clawcrest?" asked Des, looking confused.

"A key that opens all the doors at the Pedipurr—like the 'Members Only' door. This is mine," said Smitten, tugging at a blue claw-shaped pendant he was wearing.

"So we need a Lord or Lady's Clawcrest," said Squirrel. A plan began to take shape in his mind.

"You reckon a Lord or Lady'll let us in?" said Des.

"I doubt it. They're very possessive about the Den. I don't even think Uncle Dyer would," said Smitten, frowning.

"What do we do, then? We need to find out what Brittle's Map is," said Des. "We need to figure out if it's worth the hassle."

"I've an idea," said Squirrel. "Smitten, sir, did you by any chance manage to get your wedding presents after the wedding?"

The Pedipurr Revisited

Y ou failed." The two chilling words echoed in the dark
space. The figure speaking adjusted her black, hooded
robe so that no part of her body was visible.

"All you had to do was snatch one weak, little squirrel. I
told you where he would be. And still, that was too much
for you to handle?" she said, twisting her words with disdain.
Her eyes were fixed on a crow with a dented beak, standing
in front of the Kowas.

"We did as ya ordered, Madame; we 'ttacked just as the
guests were about to start leavin'. We 'ad our eyes on him. 'E
got 'way in all the smoke and the firing," said Dented Beak.

Another voice, a grating, scratchy voice, chimed in uninvited. "I told the bunch of yoush that the shmoke wash a dumb idea. I told ya . . ." He fell silent as the hooded lady turned her head toward him.

When she spoke this time, her words were as smooth as butter. "The smoke was a dumb idea, was it?"

"Yesh, 'courshe! We losht 'im, didn't we?" replied Scratchy, his voice brimming with confidence. "A real shtupid idiot musht've come up with it," he finished, obviously happy to slander his boss, Dented Beak.

"A stupid idiot?" said the hooded figure, her voice prickly.

"Yesh, ma'am," said Scratchy.

"The 'shtupid' person who insisted on using smoke was me." As she spoke, she got out of her seat and strode up to Scratchy. Before the crow could move, she put her paws on his neck and began to squeeze it.

The crow's eyes popped out of his skull and his eyeballs rolled up. With a thud, he fell backward and lay there—a heap of dirty black feathers on the stone floor.

"He's not dead. But I promise you idiots this: when your friend wakes up, he won't be quite as quick to speak his empty mind again," said the hooded lady. "As for the rest of you, while you work for me, failure is not an option." She removed a long, thin leather whip with a fanged tip and lashed it around.

Whippsht. Whippsht. Whippsht.

The sound of leather as it sliced the flesh off the Kowas' backs rang through the cave. "Now, fix your mistake. You go back and plan, scheme, kill . . . whatever it is you do. But find that squirrel for me. Follow him. Find out his every move."

Dented Beak cleared his throat. "But . . . but . . . Madame, the orders were to bring him in . . ."

"Shut up! If I tell you to follow him, then you follow him. Who gives the orders, you or me?" she yelled, swiveling her whip in his face. "Do as I say, or you will have to answer to the Colonel himself. And, trust me, you beakbrains do not want to do that."

Tring-a-ling-a-ling, tring-a-ling-a-ling.

In the gathering dusk, the Grand Hall in the Pedipurr wobbled as though the walls were made of raspberry custard. Squirrel heard a scraping, a chattering, and a flurry of paws pattering on the floor. The evening classes at the Pedipurr had just ended, and the students were about to rush out.

"Quickly, you two, go hide behind the two busts on that side, by the Lion's Library," said Smitten.

Squirrel darted off, a crate very similar to the one he had taken to Smitten's wedding somehow balanced on his shoulders. Though no one ever paid him much attention, he certainly did not want to be seen today. After all, he was being hunted by the Kowas. He had to remain invisible.

As he ducked behind the bust of a big marble lion, Squirrel was glad for two things. First, he was glad that Azulfa had decided to run some errands instead of coming with them to the Pedipurr. After the attack at the wedding, a big black crow like her would have stuck out like a suckling pig in a vegetable patch. Second, he was very glad that Smitten was with them.

When Squirrel had shared his idea with Des, Azulfa, and Smitten, the cat had insisted on helping them. "You don't need to tell me anything you don't want to, Squirrel," he had said, "but I am going with you to the Pedipurr. I meant what I said earlier—I will help you in any way that I can." And now that he was at the Pedipurr, Squirrel was very glad that Smitten was a man of his word.

Just then, a row of Pedipurr school kittens marched into the hall, humming what sounded like their latest lesson: "Polished Pussycats Purr; Only Muddy Mousers Meow."

Squirrel peeped from behind the bust. He always enjoyed watching the Pedipurr kittens with their crisp purple uniforms and their glossy fur. As they bickered with one another, Squirrel began to recite their names and addresses under his breath, a little game the mailman Squirrel liked to play with himself to sharpen his memory. He was doing very well—until he was completely stumped by one kitten.

The kitten had fur the color of caramel and a nose like a marshmallow—soft and round. Her black hair could have been strands of wavy licorice, and she kept licking her pink plumlike lips.

Squirrel's chest went warm and fizzy, like a hot bubble bath.

The kitten was not traditionally pretty, like Cheska. Nor did she have the striking beauty of Lady Blouse. Yet, Squirrel could have stared at her all day—and he would have—if Smitten had not come up behind him and said, "Come. She's waiting for us in the Library."

Ignoring Smitten, Squirrel asked as casually as he could, "Who's that kitten? The new one?"

Smitten smiled. "Marchyse Bonbete. She's fetching, for sure, but I've heard she's bad news."

"How could *she* be bad news?" sighed Squirrel, not realizing he was speaking out loud.

Des grinned and began to sing, "Squirrel's-got-a-kitty-crush, kitty-crush, kitty-crush. Squirrel's-got-a-kitty-crush, and-I'd-better-get-one-too . . ."

Squirrel felt the blood rush to his cheeks, and he wished

he could dissolve into the lion bust next to him. Thankfully, Smitten interrupted Des's teasing.

"Come on, you two! She'll leave and then we'll have no way into the Den." As he spoke, Smitten opened the door to the Lion's Library and entered, dragging Des along with him.

As planned, Squirrel waited before picking up his crate and walking over to the Library door. As he waited, he stole one long look at Marchyse Bonbete. Then he glanced at the S branded on his arm, frowned, and ducked into the Lion's Library.

The Lion's Library was a lofty, circular room that always smelled like the crispest of autumns. Stacks of leafy books stood in semicircles and split in the middle to make room for a white stone table. Lady Blouse sat at the table, tapping the tabletop with her sharp, manicured claws.

Squirrel glanced at Smitten and Des, who were waiting in the bend of a shelf, pretending to browse some books. Readjusting his crate, Squirrel walked toward Lady Blouse.

"Dahling, I was beginning to think you weren't going to show up," said Lady Blouse, getting up from her seat and kissing the air around Squirrel's cheeks.

"I could never let you down, m'lady," said Squirrel with a

grin that he did not have to force. "Here they are! Six Pretty Piths. All for you."

"Excellent, dahling! I can't wait to try these. It'll make me prettier," she said.

Squirrel looked at the sleek black cat. She wore a yellow silk dress that brought out the flecks of gold in her eyes. This time he could not stop himself from saying, "How could you possibly get any prettier, Lady Blouse?"

"What a charmer you are, Squirrel! But, as my mama, Countess Quattrine, used to say, 'A kitty can never ever be too pretty,'" said Lady Blouse, taking the crate from Squirrel. "Now, let's see if these Pretty Piths work."

Squirrel watched in wonder as Lady Blouse lifted her dress above her right leg and removed an ornate bone knife from a garter. With a surprisingly fluid flick, she sliced the wooden crate clean open. She reached inside and picked up a wrinkly yellow mango and cradled it. Slowly, lovingly, she brought the mango to her lips and sunk her sharp teeth into its soft, sweet flesh.

Squirrel watched the juice trickle down Lady Blouse's pink lips as she bit two big chunks of pulp off the mango. And then, just as she was about to take one more bite, her lids dropped shut, her body went as limp as a sock, and she fell forward, flat on the marble table.

A moment later, the beautiful Lady Blouse was snoring like a flugelhorn.

Des ran out of his hiding place, with Smitten behind him. "It worked!"

"I feel awful, but there was no other way to get into the Den. Dipping the Pretty Piths in Skullcap Tea was genius, Squirrel," said Smitten.

"I'd never even heard of Skullcap Tea. How'd you know it'd put her to sleep?" asked Des.

"It's in my mom's recipe book. I've been drinking this tea forever to help me fall asleep," said Squirrel.

"I'm gonna get the recipe from you," said Des, grinning. "Imagine what I can do with Skullcap Tea. If I slip this tea into my parents' evening whisker-y, then I can spend each sunset at the Wagamutt playing Dodge Bull or Truth or Bear . . ."

"Des, perhaps you should hatch your schemes after we get what we need," said Smitten. "We need to find Lady Blouse's Clawcrest. I wonder if she wears it around her neck." Gently Smitten lifted Lady Blouse's head off the table, checking for a Clawcrest around her neck. But it was bare. Des opened her piranha-skin purse and shook his head. No Clawcrest.

"She has the Clawcrest with her. She must've used it to enter the Pedipurr," mumbled Smitten. "But where could it be? We're running out of time."

Squirrel had a tickle of an inkling he knew where it was. His heart pumped as he lifted the right side of Lady Blouse's dress and checked the garter in which she had kept the bone knife. Sure enough, tucked into it was a claw-shaped black-ivory nugget. Carefully he removed it and gave it to a shocked Smitten.

"How d'ya know 'twas there?" asked Des, his eyes forming two big Os.

"I saw her take out the knife to open the crate. Just thought that maybe she put her Clawcrest there too," said Squirrel, trying to sound nonchalant, though his heart still hammered. "But we must move. Let's go find the *Raison D'Être*."

9

ꝾNTO THE ꝽEN

Smitten pressed his head against the stack of books at the very back of the library. His pointed ears perked up in concentration.

"Sounds empty," he said, knocking on the frame. "With a whisker of luck, we'll get in and out undiscovered. We just have to be very quiet."

Squirrel tiptoed around Smitten. If he got caught trying to break into the Den, the Pedipurr cats would flog him to a pulp. So he waited, as mum as a mummy—until he saw Smitten lean against the book stack. It began to topple over like a massive domino.

Squirrel's heart sank as the shelf fell belly-up, threatening to rattle the entire library. The stack, however, did not crash to the floor. Instead it swung all the way across the floor silently, and opened onto the mouth of a stone staircase.

A knot of nerves tightened in Squirrel's body as he followed Smitten onto the narrow staircase lit with feather torches. He shut his eyes; his lungs grew heavy; his chest itched with the familiar pangs of claustrophobia. "Is this the only way to the Den?"

"It is," said Smitten as he walked sideways down the stairs. "At least your shoulders are thinner than ours, Squirrel. Otherwise, you'd have to walk like us."

"Seriously, mate. It's making me as dizzy as a lizard chasing its own tail," said Des, bumping into the wall as the stairs curved.

Squirrel mumbled, focusing on the uneven steps before him. He could not wait to get down.

Unfortunately, the situation did not get much better when Squirrel got off the last step. The landing at the bottom was barely big enough for him, Des, and Smitten together, and Squirrel found his head locked in the nook of Smitten's armpit. He wiggled himself out only to have his face squashed against the mouth of a stone tiger carved into the wall.

"What now?" gasped Squirrel, trying to fill his lungs with air.

"Here." Smitten pointed to the tiger's eye. Squinting, Squirrel realized that the black pupil of the carved tiger was actually a scooped-out hole.

There was a flurry of movement as Smitten jammed Lady Blouse's Clawcrest into the hole and turned it. A loud thud shook the walls; the tiger's mouth swung open; and Squirrel felt himself go wheeling forward till he lay as flat as a pancake on something soft and lush and warm.

Squirrel was in a large room carpeted with golden deer hide, which looked even more golden in the light of a dozen oil lamps. Glossy sandalwood panels clad the walls and curved into a gentle arc on the ceiling, filling the room with the smell of spring and spices and spruce all at once.

Squirrel breathed in and pushed himself off the floor. To his left, he saw a row of silk couches and coral tables. To his right, he saw three chambers, each curtained by a cascade of shimmery peacock feathers. And, in the center, he saw a towering wooden cabinet, planted in the earth like a giant tree trunk. The cabinet was filled with books; Smitten was standing in front of it.

"Squirrel, over here," said the cat as he opened the cabinet. He blew the dust off the rows of books, scanning the titles till he pulled out a book that looked larger than Squirrel's rib cage. He began to turn the long, grasshopper-wing pages delicately. He stopped.

"It's here," he whispered.

"Where?" said Squirrel and Des together, pouncing on the book. Each pulled it toward himself, almost ripping the page in two.

"Easy, boys! Together, shall we?" said Smitten. He adjusted the book, and together the three of them peered at the old page.

Brittle's Map is a string of words more powerful
than a thousand swords. It speaks of slaves
and of how they came to be: of how they were
stripped of a name and bound, so they could not
act free. The gist of the Map of Brittle is that
a slave is the lowest critter; he is property to be
traded and sold to the highest bidder.

Slaves do not have the "Right to a Name"—
they cannot be their own person, lay claim
to their home, or have their own fame. If a
creature does not have this right, he is forced to
work for a master so he can sleep at night. For

*only a master will pay a no-name a cent, and
that is the only way a slave can make rent. And
if a slave goes bad and deserts his master, he
will lose everything all the faster. For without a
name a creature is nothing—he is just beholden
to whoever is his king.*

*But the Code of the Jungle states that the bonds
of slavery can be broken if the words in Brittle's
Map are spoken. The one who reads Brittle's
Map has a power true: he can free any slave,
and he can force anyone to become one too.
Brittle's Map tells how to find anyone's name,
and how to take it away just the same.*

Squirrel flipped the page. His body trembled like a bay leaf
in a pot of boiling water.

*So, if the map is used by those colder of heart,
slavery could reign in every part. To preserve
freedom and what is true, Brittle's Map has
been split in two. The first is the map carved in
marble pure, warmed by sun and wet by shore.
The second is a coded key, hidden where none*

*can ever see. The key makes the map make
sense and it becomes readable hence.*

*The clues to the key are seclasioned in one
mind so that the key only he can find. But first
he must prove his heart and mind are strong
and that he will do no wrong. And a word of
warning I will give for he who wants to surely
live. The thing he should always know is that
the key is sought by many a foe. The easiest
way to protect the key is to leave it rest and let
it be. For if he does not unlock Brittle's Key, the
secret of the map will die with him and me.*

Squirrel scrunched his forehead. Since sunrise, he had learned more than he had over the entire thirteen seasons of his life. He had learned about seclasion. He had learned about the Map of Brittle. He had learned about a key to the map. And now he had learned he could possibly get his freedom . . .

"There is a powerful map that can make me . . . make me . . . a free creature? It can give me a name?" He looked at Smitten, blinking in confusion.

Fragments of thought spun in his head, like the dancing

lights in a disco ball. "But Brittle's Map is lost. And the clues to the key have been hidden . . . *in my mind? In my head?*"

"It seems so," said Smitten, his eyes blinking seriously. He put a paw on Squirrel's shoulder. "Squirrel, you have a decision to make. Do you want to take the risk and find the key? Or would you rather forget all about it, and go back to your life?"

Squirrel thought for a moment. His life was fine, he supposed. He was a slave, but he earned wages and had a roof over his head. A cozy, comfortable roof. He could just forget about the map and the key and do what he was supposed to do—serve Bacchu for the rest of his life. "I'm not sure. It sounds like finding Brittle's Map may be like walking the plank and not knowing if you're jumping into a sea full of sharks or goldfish." He decided not to mention the other doubt that had been nagging him like a splinter in his paw.

Des jumped up. "But, if you don't find the key, it's going to be lost forever. The map will be lost forever!"

"But . . . but if I go to find the key, I'll be a deserter. I would have deserted my boss. How will I pay rent? How will I live?" said Squirrel, aware that his voice had gone up three decibels.

Des scratched his chin. "Mate, I reckon whoever left you the clues thought you'd be able to find the key. And if you do find the key *and* the map, you don't need to pay rent anymore. You can claim your right to a name and live in your cottage—as a free creature."

"But I only have clues to Brittle's Key—not Brittle's Map," said Squirrel. "I'll lose everything if I don't find the map. I'll be homeless."

As Squirrel spoke, he thought of his cozy tree cottage in which he had lived his entire life. Then he thought of Bacchu. He thought of Bacchu stealing his Mud Milkshake. He thought of Bacchu throwing his beret at him in Malmali's studio. He thought of all the times Bacchu had called him a mind-numbingly stupid rodent, or a red pimple, or a waste of fur . . .

Something began to tick in Squirrel's tummy—a quick tick, an urgent tick. It grew stronger and stronger until his entire body began to shake.

"The thing is, though . . . I want to be free," whispered Squirrel. He gulped and his voice grew louder. "I don't want to be a slave. I've never wanted to be a slave. I never had a choice. Now I do. I'll use whatever wages I've saved. I'll find a place to stay. I'll figure it out. Somehow . . ."

"Mate, don't worry about that. You can always stay with me till we figure it out," said Des. "With Cheska gone, we'll have plenty of space. I'm sure Mom and Dad won't mind.

They miss their daughters and would be happy for some company."

Des put his arm around Squirrel, and Squirrel felt his narrow shoulders grow wider. Maybe, just maybe, he could do this.

"That's true, but there is something else," said Smitten, lowering his voice and frowning. "What if the Kowas know that you're the one with access to the key? What if that's why they're after you? If they find the key, who knows what they'll do. They could make everyone their slaves. Imagine. It would be . . . chaos." He wrung his tail. "Squirrel, the only way to stop them is to find the key first."

Squirrel looked down. Somewhere, deep in his rib cage, something small had begun to flutter. He could find a long-lost key. He could stop a band of villains from getting to it first. He could find his own name. And, maybe, maybe he could be a bit more than just the PetPost slave.

He looked up at his two friends. "I'm going to go try to find the key. And then, I'll find the Map of Brittle."

Des whooped and hugged Squirrel, and then did a cartwheel that ended up with him flat on the floor, his legs twisted outward in a wonky W. The dog did not seem to care. He continued to grin like a crazy clown and began to sing, "We're gonna find Brittle's Key. First we're off to the Queen Bee, to beg her for some Marbled Honey, and then . . ."

"And then, we shall see," said Smitten, ushering them out of the Den. "Now we need to get out of here. If we get caught, the only place we're going to is Dimbuck Prison."

They darted back to the main library, careful to cover their tracks. Thankfully, Lady Blouse was still snoring.

Squirrel went up to Lady Blouse. He was just lifting her skirt to replace the Clawcrest when he heard footsteps coming toward him. Shoving the Clawcrest into her garter, he dashed over to Smitten and Des's hiding spot. He peeked to see who it was; it was Baron Dyer, Smitten's uncle.

Squirrel and his friends did not wait to see more. As quickly as they could, they crept out of the Lion's Library and left the Pedipurr. Once outside, they broke into a sprint, running all the way to the Verza house.

Squirrel was running so blindly that he ran smack into something black, and tough, and bristly.

"Ouch!" yelled Squirrel, rubbing his eyes. As his vision adjusted to the late evening light, he realized that he had run straight into Azulfa, who was also just returning from her errand.

"Whoops! Sorry, Zulf," said Squirrel, his legs turning to putty. Azulfa had never looked so incredibly angry.

"You're as blind as a blond bat, Squirrel," she began, wincing as she rubbed her body.

"Sorry. But it could not have hurt that much! Now listen to our news," burst Squirrel, launching into the full story of what they had learned. He told her about Brittle's Key. He told her that they had to leave for the bee city of Mellifera immediately. He even told her that Smitten knew the shortest way to get there, since he had gotten the wax paper for his wedding invitation from Mellifera itself. He told her everything—except for the fact that they had almost let themselves get caught by Smitten's uncle. After all, why anger the crow further? Especially when she seemed to be in a spectacularly bad mood.

"Lady Blouse, wake up. Lady Blouse. Natasha, Natasha! Wake up." The sound of her first name uttered in that husky voice did the trick. She awoke and looked straight up at the sculpted face of Baron Dyer. She checked her reflection in the silvery mirrors of his striking eyes.

The Pretty Pith had worked. Somehow she had become more beautiful: The slight signs of her forty seasons were gone, her eyes shone like green chandeliers, her cheeks were tight and silky, her body young and supple. And, best of all, for the first time ever, Baron Dyer was looking at her with a trace of admiration. His perfect lips curled into a smile.

Lady Blouse caught her breath. She had longed to see that look on his face since she knew the difference between male and female.

"Oh! I must've dozed off. Thank you for waking me," said Lady Blouse, tousling her fur. She leaned forward, letting the light strike her in all the right places.

"At your service," said Baron Dyer, bowing deeply. "Is your husband traveling again?" He twirled his cane casually, but his eyes sparkled with interest.

"He is," she replied, her body tense, her heart throbbing.

"His loss is my gain," said Baron Dyer with a smile, his white teeth glittering like delicious sugar cubes. "Would you accompany me down to the Den, Natasha? Maybe we can have a smoke or something?"

Lady Blouse took the muscular arm he offered. He looked down at her and she lowered her lashes. If Pretty Piths could make this cat notice her, she would make Squirrel make her one for every single day of her life.

They climbed down the narrow stairs that Smitten, Des, and Squirrel had used only moments before. Lady Blouse felt dizzy as Baron Dyer's tall frame leaned over her in the darkness. She wondered what he wanted. Her body tingled with the thought of what would happen on the other side of the stone door.

When they reached the cramped little landing with the carved tiger, she slowly hiked up her dress, so that he would be able to catch a long look at her garter and her legs. It worked.

Baron Dyer leaned over and whispered in her ear, and she began to tremble. As she pulled out her Clawcrest, she was too excited by the Baron's breath on her neck to notice that her Clawcrest was in a completely different position from when she had placed it there.

THE WALLED CITY

They bid a quick farewell to Smitten, Cheska, and the rest of the Verza clan, and then took off.

They flew to Mellifera. Azulfa insisted on carrying Squirrel and Des, but by the second sunrise, her body seemed broken. Her black feathers were streaked with white, her wings drooped, and the muscles of her back were as stiff as stone.

Squirrel was wondering how much longer Azulfa could go on when he felt the crow lurch and plunge downward— tumbling toward a gushing river.

"YAAAAOOOO," Squirrel squealed as they crash landed on the riverbank.

Des, on the other hand, seemed least bothered. He got to his feet; his nose twitched like a rabbit's, and he rubbed his belly. "D'you smell that?" he asked, inhaling deeply. "It smells sweet and syrupy! Like . . . like . . . *honey*!" He stuck his tongue out to taste the air.

"This way," said Des, running straight. "Follow me."

Squirrel took off behind Des, but as his feet hit the dry red soil, he was surprised how difficult it was to run on it. The soil was grainy and rough—very different from the moist, brown earth in Bimmau.

Squirrel was so busy trying to avoid the rough clumps of mud that he banged his head straight into something— something hard, strong, and full of holes. It was a wall, and it was glowing like warm amber.

Rubbing his head, Squirrel hoped neither Des nor Azulfa had seen him squash his already funny-shaped head even further. Luckily, they were both too busy examining the wall itself to notice him.

"The wall's made of six-sided bricks. Perfect hexagons," said Azulfa, pointing to rows of hexagonal cells sitting precisely on one another. She grabbed the wall and tried to shake the lattice. It did not move. "Hexagons make any wall very strong."

Meanwhile, Des was peering into the hollow cells. A flame danced on a wick in each waxy nook. "A little candle is carved into each cell. That's how it's glowing like marmalade."

"Great, but how d'we get to the other side of the wall?" said Squirrel, trying to push the wall with his back. He did not have time for walls, or hexagons, or candles. He just wanted to find the Marbled Honey, rip the clue from his brain, and go on to his next drink.

Hoping the hexagonal bricks would give way somehow, Squirrel banged his body into the wall again and again. But the wall stood there, sturdy as steel.

"Squirrel," whispered Azulfa, grabbing him. "Stop! Stop doing that!"

The urgency in Azulfa's voice made Squirrel stop. But before he could realize what was going on, a cool shadow fell across his face.

Squirrel looked up.

Six tall, muscular bees with square jaws and wide, strapping shoulders towered over him. They wore metal helmets and silver mesh tunics and carried shields. Sharp, spearlike weapons hung from their belts.

"What izz your buzinezz in Mellifera?" asked the first bee, stepping forward.

Squirrel choked—out of both fear and surprise. Though he could have sworn the big, scary bee was a male, the voice that spoke was soft and sweet.

He took a closer look. Each of the soldiers had a screen of long hair under her helmet and hints of curves under her armor. They were all female.

"We need to meet your Queen," said Azulfa, flying up behind Squirrel and squaring her wings. "We must get some Marbled Honey from her."

The bee looked at Azulfa with her round, unblinking eyes. Then she looked at Squirrel and, finally, her eyes settled on Des. She looked at the dog for a long moment and then softened. "Wait here pleazze."

With the other five soldiers following her, she stomped over to the side and began to speak in a soft, buzzing language. The whole while the bee kept her eyes on Des—who seemed to be getting mighty uncomfortable.

As the bee marched back, Squirrel could not stop staring at her legs. They were carved of pure muscle. He gulped; he did not want to get on the wrong side of this Amazon of a bee.

The bee came and stood before them, the bulk of her being towering over Des like an iron column. Then she smiled. "I zhall take you to Queen Apize."

"Ma'am, we wouldn't want to bother you. If you could just tell us where to go, we'll find the Queen ourselves," said Squirrel, not wanting an escort.

"We cannot let vizzitors into our city unezzcorted," said

the bee. "My name izz Nizza. You will follow me." As she spoke, Nizza raised her shield and, all of a sudden, her voice melted into a throaty song.

"Davaaz uzzaq abiz, Zust ho lim lim, Zunder banaz lapiz, Khuzza jo zzim zzim."

As she sang, the other bees unfolded a bridge as bright as an orange peel. Nizza marched across it, into the city, obviously expecting them to follow her.

Squirrel looked at Azulfa, then Des, wondering what to do. But one look at their resigned expressions made him realize they had no other choice. They would have to let Nizza lead them to the Queen. So, with a sigh, Squirrel marched off behind the big, scary bee—into the walled city of Mellifera.

As soon as Squirrel entered Mellifera, he said, "Ms. Nizza, could we go straight to the Queen? We're in a bit of a rush."

"You muzzt wait till Court to meet her. Till then, you will be with me." While speaking, the big bee looked only at Des. Squirrel noticed that her stern eyes had melted into heart-shaped goop.

With a smile, the bee batted her small, stubby eyelashes, and placed her chunky hand on Des's back. Then she began to gently putt him forward, as though he were a delicate golf ball.

Nizza led them through a garden of large, speckled flowers with bees skidding from bud to bud, past a group of wax pillars that melted gently into a golden pool with bees cooling the wax with their wings, and through a bevy of bees polishing pink apples till they shone like star rubies.

Squirrel was marveling at the strange, golden, buzzing city of Mellifera until he saw Des stop and point to a row of oversize, golden, hexagonal pumpkins. Each pumpkin had a door and a window carved into it. "Are those some sort of giant Howl-o-ween decorations?" Squirrel noticed that Des was squirming uncomfortably. He presumed this was because Nizza's hand was resting heavily on his lower back.

"Howl-o-ween? We don't have time to zelebrate that wolf fezztival here in Mellifera. Thoze are our apartmentz— we call it the comb. Thoze beez are repairing a home that melted in the zun." She pointed to a line of bees wearing loose pajamas, T-shirts, and bandannas. Each bee had a mirrorlike bowl full of gooey wax strapped to her tummy.

The bee in the front of the line reached into her bowl, shoveled the wax into her mouth, and began to chew. She put her mouth to the ramshackle apartment and blew. Out came a waxy bubble.

Using just her mouth, the bee flattened the waxy bolus, spun the ball into the broken wall, and repaired part of the cell. When she was done, she moved to the back of the line. Another bee, with a fresh pail of wax, moved to the front and began chomping on her wax gumball.

"So they make the entire comb with their mouths? Can you do that too?" Des asked Nizza.

Nizza smiled and struck a pose that Squirrel guessed was supposed to be appealing. Unfortunately, she ended up looking a bit like a circus chipmunk. "I can't do that. But I can do many other thingzz with my lipz. What about you?" she asked, puckering at Des.

Des began to cough as though he had a moth stuck in his throat. "Ms. Nizza," he managed, "the only thing I want to do with my lips is *eat*."

Moments later, they were stuffing their faces with rhododendron lamb, honey chicken, pollen potato gravy, fried paprika petals, and zingy grasshoppers. A round of dessert followed.

"A-plus," said Des, licking the last creamy crumb of his nectar cheesecake till his plate sparkled. The only things that twinkled more were Nizza's eyes as she watched Des lick his plate.

Squirrel, too, had finished his meal and was looking around the buzzing bazaar.

"What's that?" he asked, pointing to a row of wax columns. Behind the columns was a squat, very official-looking beehive.

"That izz our Bank and Mint. That izz where we make our money," answered Nizza, staring goo-goo-eyed at Des as he belched the letters of his name.

"Your money?" said Squirrel. "You don't use gufflings here?"

"Of courzze not. We uze zalikz."

"What 'bout bizkits? Gromms?" asked Squirrel.

Nizza shook her head.

"But . . . I don't have any zaliks. How do I pay for this meal?" asked Squirrel.

"The bank will change your money to zalikz, of courzze," said Nizza, giving Squirrel a look that made him feel as stupid as a stuffed turkey. "You and the crow, go change the money. I'll stay with him." She put a finger on Des's spotted earlobe and stroked it.

"Ummm . . . be right back," said Squirrel, getting up with Azulfa and trying very, very hard not to laugh at Des's desperately uncomfortable face.

Squirrel shoved his paw into his bulging pocket.

"I got one thousand zaliks for just one bizkit! One thousand!" he announced to Des. He dumped a fistful of golden wax coins on the table and said, "There. Paid. Now let's check out the rest of your Grand Bazaar."

They wandered down a winding alley until a building shaped like a flying bee caught Squirrel's attention. "That's the BuzzEx building!" he said. As a slave to the owner of the PetPost Mail, Squirrel had always admired the speed at which the BuzzEx worked.

"It izz," said Nizza. "That izz where we zend mezzagezz to other citiezz. We can get a mezzage to any place fazzter than the zun takez to zet."

"Excellent!" said Des, his ears perking up a little bit. "Soon as we get the Marbled Honey, I'll send a message home. Smitten told me to let 'em know where I'm off to next. They worry less when they know where I am."

"Izz thizz Smitten your girlfriend?" demanded Nizza, her body bristling.

Politely Des explained that Smitten was his brother-in-law. Squirrel was impressed by how well Des was handling this crazy bee—especially when she looked as angry as a bull in a rodeo.

When Nizza had been mollified, she led them past a waterfall where a dozen wide-winged male bees lounged about idly, sipping pollen beer and tanning themselves. Squirrel thought that the men were comparing wing size.

"Those are the first men we've seen here," said Azulfa.

"Yezz, they're the dronez. We don't have much uze for men in Mellifera. Their only purpoze izz to mate with Queenzz from far-away citiezz. We ourzelvz prefer foreign men." She tried to lick Des's ear, but the dog shrank away from her, his tail between his legs and his cheeks burning a flamingo pink.

They ambled along the marketplace till Squirrel felt something yank his arm. Des was dragging him away from Nizza and Azulfa toward a shop. The mannequins in the window were covered in armor from head to toe.

"Really want to get myself one of those bee spears, mate. Plus I need a break from that bulky, sulky, licky bee. Eeefff, gross!" said Des, shivering with disgust as he ducked into the store.

Chuckling, Squirrel followed. He knew he should tell Azulfa and Nizza that they were taking a detour, but what was the harm? They would only be a moment.

Squirrel entered the store. Immediately he wished he had not. Torrents of white light bounced off the polished armor and hit his face. He shut his eyes, wondering if he had somehow landed on a star.

When he finally got used to the brightness, Squirrel saw Des rummaging through a pile of weapons—iron-ore

140

shields, arrows made of porcupine needles, barkwood clubs, and whips of twisted lion hair. He looked around. No store attendant was in sight, but he noticed a flight of stairs leading upstairs. The attendant must be there, he guessed.

"I can't seem to find that spear Nizza's carrying 'round," muttered Des, pulling out a dresslike mesh tunic. "Ooooh! Look at this, though. A rhino-skin vest! And matching rhino horn-boots and helmet. I'll try these on," he said, slipping the tunic over his head and somehow squeezing his paws into the knee-high boots. He put the helmet on and picked up a shield to check his reflection. "So, whaddya think?"

"You look like a silver bullet!" said Squirrel, half-impressed and half-appalled by the sight of the silver-clad Despatches Verza.

"Why, thank you," said Des, bowing deeply. As he dipped, the helmet shot off his head and smashed into the wall. *Clank.* In slow motion, Squirrel saw the cannon-of-a-helmet ricochet off the wall and hit a mannequin square in the neck. *Clank. Clank.* In horror, he watched the fully armored mannequin tip over and crash to the floor. *Clankitty, clankitty, clank.*

Squirrel held his breath. For a moment there was pin-drop silence. Then he heard a rustle above and a distinct flutter of wings coming from the direction of the stairs.

"'Elp me get out of this rhino straitjacket," squealed Des as the fluttering got louder.

With a wiggle and a wriggle, Squirrel freed Des from his silver casing, and they bolted out of the shop. They ran back to Azulfa and Nizza. Nizza looked rather cross.

"You were not zupozzed to go anywhere wizzout me," said Nizza, her hands on her hips. "Where were you?" Suddenly Nizza did not look like a doting dodo at all. Her jaw was clenched and her eyes flickered red.

"In . . . in . . . there," said Des, pointing to the store. He looked as terrified as Squirrel felt.

"The one where that loud crazzh juzzt came from?" asked Nizza tightly.

Squirrel knew he could not get out of this. He looked down and nodded. When he looked back up, fear clutched him. Nizza was gripping her spear tightly. Her eyes bulged out of her skull.

Azulfa inched over to Squirrel and Des and put a claw on each of them. Squirrel could feel her get ready to launch into flight, but a ground-shaking rumble made her lose her balance.

The noise was coming from Nizza. She was shaking violently from head to toe.

IT'S ALL IN THE FAMILY

Squirrel knew he was going to die. Any moment now, Nizza's spear would pierce him as if he were a cube of soft cheese. Squirrel clamped his eyes shut and waited.

When nothing happened, he forced himself to peek at Nizza. He was shocked at what he saw. "Nizza, are you . . . are you *laughing?*"

Sure enough, Nizza's body shook like a baby's rattle. Fat, guttural chuckles burst from her mouth.

"What's so funny?" asked Des, hopping out of reach of Nizza's spear.

Nizza clapped her chunky hands in glee. "You knocked zomething over in the Armory?" When Squirrel nodded slightly, she said, "Hope it wazz zomething big. That'll teach Zebi!"

"Who?" asked Azulfa, relaxing her grip on Squirrel and Des.

"Zebi runzz the Armory. Zhe izz a zoldier bee, like me. But zhe failed her zoldier examzz three timezz. *Three timezz!*"

"Obviouzzly, zhe couldn't guard Mellifera, zo Queen Apize made her the keeper of the Armory. And now Zebi thinkzz zhe wazz hired for the Armory cozz zhe izz better than everyone. Zhe flutterzz and putterzz around like a mini-Queen! Good you dezztroyed her store. Maybe now zhe'll underzztand zhe izz juzzt a zhopkeeper!"

"Well, Zebi just got taken down a notch or two, or rather a mannequin or two," said Des. "Had no idea how hard it could be to find a spear like yours!"

"But you can't buy one of theze! It'zz my ztinger. It'zz a part of my body," said Nizza, shaking her long spear till it shimmied in Des's face. "My ztinger izz very big compared to the other beezz. Zebi'z ztinger izz zo narrow and weak-looking, it could be a worm!"

"You really hate Zebi, don't you?" asked Squirrel, a bit amused.

"Hate? No. I couldn't *hate* Zebi. Zhe izz my zizter, after all," said Nizza with a shrug.

"Your sister?" asked Des, detangling himself from Nizza, who had managed to link her trunklike arm through Des's.

Nizza grabbed Des again—this time so forcefully that it looked like Des's arm might pop right out. "'Courzze zhe's my zizter! In Mellifera, only the Queen can have children. Zhe choozes a mate, matezz with him, and layzz thouzzandz of eggzz. You zee, we're all related. Even Zebi."

"And the Queen mates with . . . ?" asked Azulfa.

Nizza looked at Azulfa as though she were as dumb as a dust mite. "With a drone from another town, obviouzzly! Every few zeazonz, the Queen takezz her mating flight from the top of the Parthenog. The firzzt drone to catch her will be her mate. But only the fazztezzt and zmartezzt will catch the Queen. After all, thizz drone fatherzz the next generation of Melliferanz. He muzzt be fit. And, after he matezz with the Queen, he will die."

"That's ridiculous," said Des, hugging his body tightly. "The drone is willing to die just to mate?"

Nizza looked at Des, heaving her chest forward so that it almost struck Des's jaw. "Mating with a good bee izz alwayzz worth dying for."

"But what happens when the Queen falls in love?" asked

145

Squirrel quickly, trying to distract Nizza before she began licking Des again.

"The Queen of Mellifera doezz not fall in love. Zhe muzzt mate with only thoze worthy of her, and after their time together, the drone muzzt die. There izz no room for love. Not for her."

"All our Queenzz have followed thizz law." Nizza paused, and when she spoke again, her voice was a whisper. "All exzept our current Queen."

"The Queen fell in love?" asked Squirrel, who was in the mood for a hot cup of brewed gossip.

"Zhe fell in love with a drone from a faraway land. Every day, they walked around the Parthenog arm-in-arm, chatting about honeycomb zcienze and pollen art, dizcuzzing hive politicz and bee warfare."

"What happened to them?" asked Squirrel.

"Well, Queen Apize had a difficult choice. Zhe could mate with him, but then he would die. Or, zhe could keep him at a ztinger'z length, but never have him completely. Our Queen thought and thought and thought. Finally zhe made the only mizztake zhe hazz ever made: zhe choze not to mate with him.

"Zhe made him her chief zcout. Thizz way he wazz far

enough from her not to tempt her, yet cloze enough zo zhe could zee him often. The arrangement worked very well. But, one day, when the Queen called him, he did not come. Zhe called again and again, but he did not come.

"Rumor hazz it that he zaw another Queen from a faraway land in her mating flight. He could not rezizzt hizz natural inztinct. He chazed the Queen down and mated with her. He died right after.

"Queen Apize wazz heartbroken. But zhe learned from her mizztake. They zay zhe carved out a poem on two zpezzial ztonez—ztonez that he got for her from zome dizztant land. They zay that the poem remindzz the Queen that zhe muzzt ztay zztrong and never fall in love again."

"What does the poem say?" asked Squirrel.

Nizza shook her head. "No idea. Zhe hid the ztone in the Bone Tomb acrozz the river, away from prying eyez. No one ever goezz there."

"No one ever goes to the tomb?" asked Des. "Not even to visit the dead?"

"No. It izz zcary!" said Nizza with a shiver.

Then and there, Squirrel decided that he would never go to the bee mortuary. He was going nowhere near a place that made a broad, strapping soldier like Nizza shiver.

"Nizza, it looks like a giant version of your stinger," cried Des, bending backward to look at a tower that pierced the bubble-blue sky.

"That izz the firzzt time I've ever heard the Parthenog dezcribed like that."

Squirrel looked up at the long javelin of a building, wondering how he would get to the top. The tower was made of wide bands of orange and white wax, which looked as slippery as an eel. A glassy mango-shaped lake surrounded the tower.

"Is this where we'll meet Queen Apize?"

"Yezz. The Queen'z court izz the chamber at the top," said Nizza. Turning to Des, she said, "Wrap your pawzz around my waizt and I'll carry you up. The crow can take the zquirrel."

Squirrel thought Des would hesitate, but the dog just shrugged his shoulders and obeyed the bee. As Des hopped onto Nizza, Squirrel thought he saw his friend grin a little.

Squirrel chuckled as he got onto Azulfa's back; Des had begun to enjoy Nizza's attention.

He was still laughing when Azulfa launched into flight, but as the wind's whoosh hit his face, and his feet kicked the air like scissors, his laugh turned into a long, frightened squeal. Until—thankfully—he felt Azulfa land with a jerk.

They had landed in a glittery hexagonal chamber full of puddles of pink and purple. Bees were muddling dried petals into the water, making the airy room smell of roses and lilies. The syrupy air pressed against Squirrel's fur—full of wax, of nectar, of honey.

"Thizz izz the Court of Commonz in Mellifera," said Nizza. "Anyone can bring a problem to Queen Apize here. Zhe lizzens to each one herzelf and judgezz it. You can azk her for Marbled Honey here."

A tremor of excitement shot through Squirrel's belly. He was here! He was moments away from meeting Queen Apize and asking her for some Marbled Honey. He was moments away from his next drink. His next clue. His next . . .

"Pssst! Mate. Watch where you're going!"

Des had grabbed Squirrel just before he walked into a circle of bees kneeling on the floor, all staring at a throne shaped like an unfurling flower. It was encrusted with bright little wax balls that shone like a million mini-suns. The throne was empty.

Nizza came up behind Des, grabbed his arm, and led him to a gap in the circle. She sat down, tucking her shins under her thighs like all the other bees. She motioned to Des, Squirrel, and Azulfa to do the same.

"How long'll the Queen be?" asked Squirrel, trying to keep his feet from going numb under the weight of his tail.

"We muzzt wait," said Nizza. She folded her arms in her lap and stared at the empty throne.

Squirrel's leg muscles burned with the stretch, and his head was frothy with impatience. When would this Queen come?

He was about to say something when Des beat him to it. With a loud noise Des rolled over and muttered, "Just can't sit like that." He stretched his legs out behind him and let out a relieved "Aaah!"

At that very moment, there was a buzzing rustle and all the kneeling bees rose in one swift motion. Squirrel managed to scramble to his feet just in time. It took Des a bit longer.

Then a troupe of bees in straw skirts flitted into the room, swaying together. In synchrony, they spun round and round, their arms swishing about their bodies gracefully.

And then, without realizing it, Squirrel too was spinning. Like leaves in the wind, his arms lifted to his sides automatically, twirling and swishing as they never had before. He looked around. Des, Azulfa, Nizza—and all the others in the circle—were twirling as well.

Squirrel tried to stop himself, tried to control his muscles, but he could not—he was on autopilot. He looked at Des and Azulfa, and could tell by their expressions that they were as surprised by their pirouetting as he was.

They danced faster and faster—till the crow, the dog, and Squirrel were spinning like tops in a tornado.

"What's going on?" Squirrel whispered.

Nizza shook her armored body till she looked like a robot having a seizure. "Zhe izz coming," she said with a jiggle. "Queen Apize izz flying in now."

12

A DANCE AND A DRINK

A streak of gold descended on the sky; the smell of night-blooming jasmine filled the air. The Queen landed and fluttered her wings.

She was taller than the other bees. Her violet eyes glinted against her fair skin, and her lips looked like flower petals. A petal blouse showed off her flat stomach, and a dewdrop tiara crowned her forehead.

The Queen smiled at her court and then began to shimmy her belly with graceful vigor. Along with her, everyone in the court began to shake their bellies.

As his stomach wiggled in ways he could not imagine, Squirrel felt Des nudge him in the side.

"Hey, check out the stinger on that royal hottie. It's longer than Nizza's and it's curved," said Des, who seemed to be blissfully enjoying the belly shaking.

"But, Des . . . why are we belly dancing?" asked Squirrel as his stomach rolled in and out.

"When we're around Queen Apize, we danzz like her. Her body zendzz chemicalz that make uzz all danzz," answered Nizza. "It izz called the waggle danzz."

"Are we gonna dance throughout?" asked Squirrel as a cramp gripped his abdomen in protest.

"Not exactly," said Nizza, sketching the number eight with her hips. "We ztop when Queen Apize ztopzz." Squirrel held his belly, hoping the Queen was almost done with her waggling. He watched as one of her attendants shimmied up to her and gave her a crystal goblet full of white cream. The Queen smiled. Squirrel thought her smile was prettier than spring, yet he was sure he would enjoy it more if he were not dancing like a drunk octopus.

"What's she drinking?" he whispered to Nizza, watching the Queen swig the goblet.

"Royal Jelly. The Queen izz fed Royal Jelly all the time. Now, zhhhuzh! Court izz about to begin."

One of the Queen's attendants buzzed, "I prezzent Queen Apize of Mellifera. The Court of Commonz izz now in zezzion."

Still swaying her hips, the Queen walked up the steps and sat on her throne. As soon as she sat, everyone stopped swaying.

It had not been a moment too soon. Squirrel's tummy felt like a bowl of knotted pinecones. He was not sure if the knots were because of the dancing, or because of his nerves.

"Now, boyzz, you will zee how wize our Queen izz," said Nizza. She looked almost as proud as when she was showing off her stinger to Des.

Squirrel watched two bees stand up. The first had a delicate face painted with makeup. Her yellow suit clung to her body like a peel, and a purple flower was pinned in her primped hair.

The other bee wore the same uniform, but her jumpsuit fell about her frame like a pair of overalls. Her face was sharp, with keen brown eyes. She bowed and began to speak.

"Queen Apize, I am zorry to zay I witnezzed a violazzion thizz morning."

"You have my attention, Zizter Izzak," said the Queen. "What infringement did you witnezz?"

"While taking my roundz of our gardenz, I zmelled zomething different. It wazz . . . it wazz . . . the zmell of frezh baby zap. A flower bud had juzzt been plucked." Sister Izzak paused as a murmur of protest ruffled the courtroom. With a stern nod, she continued, "And then pretty Zizter Eulia came flying around the corner. Thizz murdered young flower wazz in her hair." Sister Izzak gestured to the guilty bee beside her.

Queen Apize looked at Eulia, her gaze long and steady. "Izz thizz true, my zizter? Did you pluck a youngling flower from our gardenz?"

Sister Eulia kept her eyes fixed on the ground. Her thoroughly rouged cheeks grew redder and redder. "I'm zorry . . . It wazz juzzt zo . . . zo . . . pretty."

"Your Majezty, thizz izz a crime mozt zevere," piped Sister Izzak. "Flowerz belong to the hive—to all of uzz. Zizter Eulia haz ztolen. Zhe muzzt be punizhed." Sticking out her lower lip, Sister Izzak stared at the Queen.

Squirrel watched the Queen, whose face was as still as marble. She simply blinked and nodded. When she spoke, her voice tinkled through the open-aired Parthenog like a wind chime.

"Eulia, my zizter, your punizhment izz to wear thizz carnazzion in your hair, not juzzt today but all through zpring. Alzzo, you are banned from the gardenz till zummer."

"But, Queen Apize, that izz not enough! Zhe will not learn anything!" said Izzak, shaking her head like a furious fan.

"But zhe zhall learn, Zizter Izzak," said Queen Apize patiently. "The flower will wither. It will die and grow ugly. But Zizter Eulia will ztill keep it in her hair azz a reminder that individual vanity izz uzelezz. Good only comezz from zerving the colony."

The Queen took a sip of Royal Jelly and continued, "Becauze zhe izz banned from our gardenz, Zizter Eulia will long to zmell the zweetnezz of our living flowerz, to zee their vibranzy, to fly among their living graze. Zhe will realize that not a zingle flower izz beautiful. It izz the entire living garden, the act of pollinating, of giving life to flowerz, of working for the good of the colony, that izz truly beautiful. Zhe will realize that the community muzzt come firzzt. Thizz izz my royal ruling." She clasped her hands together and brought them to her forehead. Her voice melted in the air.

As a much-appeased Sister Izzak bowed, an attendant stepped forward and said, "Queen Apize will hear the next caze. Who zhall zpeak?"

Nizza nudged Squirrel. "You're next."

Squirrel felt his heart jump to his throat. He got up and shuffled to the center of the room and waited for the Queen to say something.

Queen Apize picked up the cup of Royal Jelly and sipped it slowly. "What izz your purpoze here, guezzt?"

But Squirrel had gone numb. He had been so excited about speaking to the Queen that he had not thought of what to say. Was he supposed to tell her about the zipped memory? Or about seclasion? Or about Brittle's Key? What was he to do? His mind had turned to mush; only one sentence came to mind. "I need a cup of Marbled Honey," he blurted out. His knees wobbled as he spoke.

The Queen stared at him; her violet eyes made his fur sizzle. "You want a cup of Marbled Honey?" she whispered.

For a moment, Squirrel was so scared that he almost threw up everything he had eaten. But then he thought of the key to Brittle's Map, of slavery, of his name, of his freedom. What was the point of being free if he could not think or speak clearly?

He breathed in, focusing on what he wanted to say. He looked into the Queen's fiery eyes. "Your Majesty, I have come all the way to Mellifera for your Marbled Honey. I hope not to leave without it. Just a small cup of it should do. In fact, even a sip . . ."

Queen Apize lifted her wing and flapped it gracefully. "I have the Marbled Honey, my guezzt. But whether I give it to you or not dependzz on the anzzer to thizz quezztion: Why do you want it?"

Squirrel had to use all his strength to push down the panic

in his throat. Scooping all his thoughts together, he said, "I want the Marbled Honey because . . . because . . . the honey brings me closer to finding something. Something that I must protect. For the good of my community. As you just said yourself, Your Majesty, the community must come first. And I need this honey to help protect mine."

The Queen's mouth curled into a soft smile. "You zpoke well, guezzt. I'll give you a drink of Marbled Honey. But making Marbled Honey makezz me weak. Hence, it izz only fair that I make you weak too. Do you agree to thizz?"

"Agreed," said Squirrel. He would have traded his left eyeball for some Marbled Honey.

"Good," said the Queen. She drew her stinger straight and walked up to Squirrel. Before Squirrel could react, the Queen jabbed just the tip of her stinger into the meat on his palm. Squirrel yelped as a hot sting shot from his arm to his heart. Blood bubbled out from his palm and dripped onto the white marble floor.

Then, as Squirrel's knees went weak and the strength drained from his arms, Queen Apize said, "Now I zhall mix you a batch of frezh Marbled Honey."

She swiveled her wings, and her attendants began to scurry like mice in a cheese shop. One bee conjured a curved, frosty marble slab and laid it in Queen Apize's lap.

Another held a blue petal pitcher and she tilted it, pouring brown syrup into the icy marble dish. A third bee handed a dainty, lollipop-like object to the Queen. All eyes were on the dish. All except the Queen's.

Queen Apize's eyes were closed. Her pretty face contorted with pain. She began to shake. Then she brought her hands to her milky white neck and began to stroke it. Her lower lip curved, forming a perfect O. Then she blew a stream of soft gold vapor into the marble dish.

When she was done, Queen Apize picked up the lollipop-ish ladle and dipped it into the dish.

His palm throbbing, Squirrel watched as the Queen stirred slowly till the lollipop dissolved into the dish. The syrup became thick and went from brown to a shimmery gold.

Looking as though she might collapse any moment, the Queen lifted the ladle. A big dollop of golden gel fell back on the marble slab. The Queen smiled weakly. "The Marbled Honey izz ready."

Squirrel watched as one of the Queen's attendants rushed forward and took the marble slab off her lap and poured some creamy Royal Jelly into her mouth. Only after the Queen seemed to regain her strength did the attendant ladle the honey into a wax goblet and hand the cup over to Squirrel.

Squirrel did not wait. He drank the Marbled Honey down.

He did not have even a moment to relish the sweet, chilled drink.

A zap and a crackle ripped from the back of his brain all the way to the front. A terrible pain seized his head, blinding him, choking him. He fell on the floor, shaking as though an electric current was sizzling him alive. The only thing he could feel was a deep unzipping—as though his head were being cleaved in two. And then, as it had done before, his mother's voice sang to him—cool aloe to his badly burned brain.

> *Now, my son, as you proceed*
> *Find stolen stones that you now need*
> *Two slate-blue stones from a tomb*
> *Buried close, in a white-bone womb*
> *Then, my son, with haste you go*
> *To where the tea leaves thickly grow*
> *Nestled in the hills of heart*
> *Lies your own journey's second part*
> *Pluck ten leaves from richest soil*
> *Mix in water, and bring to boil*
> *If you brew this tea, you've learned*
> *To give what you have newly earned*
> *Return what has long been stole*
> *For that, my dear son, is your role*

When Squirrel came to, he realized that Des and Azulfa had propped him up and Nizza was fanning him with her wings. Actually, Nizza was fanning Des with her wings, but Squirrel was a lucky beneficiary of the cool air as well.

It took a moment for Squirrel to speak. He thought through the words he had just heard in his head. Finally he looked straight at Nizza and gulped, "I really hope that there is more than one tomb around here."

They sat in Nizza's cell in the comb in silence. Azulfa was stretching her body, Squirrel was pouring over a tattered military map that Nizza had given him, and Des was scribbling a letter to his family on a dry-leaf scroll, with Nizza blowing butterfly kisses to him from across the room. They were biding their time.

Much to Squirrel's dismay, the only tomb nearby was the big, white tomb in the mortuary across the river. The Bone Palace, as it was called, was the same place Nizza had called too creepy for words. Yet, it sounded like the tomb with the slate-blue stones. First, it was the only tomb close by. Second, it was white. Third, it was made of bone. However, there was a problem: Queen Apize had forbidden anyone living from entering the tomb.

Squirrel did not want to go to the tomb anyway, and he

really did not want to disobey the Queen's order. But he knew he had to. So, as soon as Nizza left to find Des a waxy heart memento, he announced, "I'm going to break into the Bone Palace. I'll go alone. The stones have gotta be there."

"You're not going there alone. Of course we'll go with you," said Des, his smile wavering only slightly.

Azulfa nodded. "We'll go in the middle of the night. There'll be less chance of being spotted." Squirrel and Des agreed, and returned to their tasks.

Taking a break from his letter, Des looked over at Squirrel. "Any luck with what your mother meant by the 'hills of heart'?"

"Perhaps . . . have a look at this," said Squirrel, pointing to a range of hills on the eastern edge of the map. The name "Darling Tea Hills" was neatly lettered below.

Squirrel continued, "My memory said, *'Go to where the tea leaves thickly grow; Nestled in the hills of heart.'* It seems to match, doesn't it? Darling is a tea estate. And the 'hills of heart' fits with the hill station of Darling. Whaddya think?"

Des grinned. Even Azulfa almost smiled. "It must be Darling Tea Hills." She looked at the map and seemed to make a few mental calculations. "I can get us there by our next sunset, I think."

"Excellent!" said Des, pumping his fists. "Let's just wait for the sun to start snoring. Then, first stop is the Bone Tomb. Next, Darling Tea Hills."

Squirrel forced a smile at Des's enthusiasm. But he himself could not help questioning this mission. His freedom would not come easily; and this journey seemed to be riddled with danger. A part of him felt like running home. His life was comfortable enough, even though he was a no-name slave. But deep down, something in Squirrel began to bubble. He wanted to find his name. He wanted to be free.

So he steeled himself. "Des, finish your letter and drop it off at the BuzzEx office," he said. "Then, we should rest before we go to the Bone Palace. Who knows what we'll have to deal with there."

A GREAT THEFT

He is right outside Mellifera," said the Colonel. "I know exactly where. And he is not alone."

"I shall find Squirrel, sire. I promise you. I shall find him and his friend," said the Madame.

"I don't care for your promises, Madame. Just go. Find Squirrel. I shall not tolerate any more of your mistakes. Do you understand?"

"Yes, sire," said the Madame as she bowed deeply and scurried out of the cave before the Colonel could growl again. She had to find Squirrel. Luckily, the Colonel had told her exactly where to look.

"*Davaaz uzzaq abiz, Zust ho lim lim, Zunder banaz lapiz, Khuzza jo zzim zzim.*"

Squirrel heard Nizza's voice fade away as the bridge to Mellifera banged shut, with him, Des, and Azulfa outside. A tendril of fear gripped Squirrel—he had to raid a tomb, and a tomb that scared the wings off every bee in Mellifera.

Through the darkness he looked at Des and Azulfa. At least Azulfa's strong, muscular presence was something of a comfort. She did not look scared. Instead she seemed to be in her element as she skulked along the shadows of the great, orange wall.

Squirrel darted from shadow to shadow, until—just as suddenly as it had appeared in the morning—the walled city of Mellifera fell out of sight and became a piece of the past.

Squirrel faced the present. In the moonless night, it was just him, his two friends, the darkness, and the gush of an angry river. He hurried toward the sound of the water and stopped when they reached a wide riverbank. Squirrel gulped.

"We'll have to wade through it," said Azulfa, confirming Squirrel's fears. "I don't want to fly because the soldier bees might catch sight of us."

"Well, let's just get it over with, then," said Des, looking at the churning white water.

Azulfa went first, her strong wings cutting through the fierce stream easily.

"It's shallow—just wade across slowly," she said as Des slid into the water and paddled across.

Des pulled himself out of the water and gestured at Squirrel. "Your turn, mate."

Squirrel tried to smile back, but he knew his face could not have been convincing. Taking a deep breath, he slid into the water, pressing his feet into the riverbed. Carefully he began to waddle through the water.

Just when he reached the smack middle of the river, the muddy floor below his feet began to dissolve. He tried walking faster, but it was too late. The riverbed caved and Squirrel felt himself getting sucked into the current.

Wildly Squirrel tried to grab anything—a straggly rock, a strong weed, a stray log—anything that would keep him afloat. But his paws only gripped fistfuls of slippery water.

"Sink . . . sinking," he cried as unwelcome gulps of icy water shot down his throat.

Through the gush, he heard Des's voice. "Mate, it's not deep. Sink your claws into the bedrock."

Squirrel tried, but he had no footing. He just kept getting pulled into a whirlpool of white froth. Desperately he looked at Azulfa and yelled, "Help!"

But the crow did not move. She stood there, watching Squirrel with empty, glassy eyes.

As his head got pulled under the water's surface, Squirrel realized that Azulfa was not going to do anything. He was going to drown. Right here. Outside Mellifera . . .

Splash!

Squirrel felt the water crush him. Then, suddenly, two paws gripped his skull and yanked his head. Squirrel's face broke the water's surface.

Streams came jetting out of his frozen nose and mouthfuls of cold water spluttered out of his mouth. Blessed air filled his lungs, and he became vaguely aware that he was moving. When he stopped, he was on the solid riverbank, with Des's paws around his head.

For a moment he just lay there, next to Des, breathing heavily. Finally Des said, "That could have been a very watered-down way to go, mate."

As Squirrel realized that Des had jumped in and saved him, he managed a wet smile. It faded quickly. Azulfa was looking at him. Her eyes flashed with something he could not quite place.

"Come boys, let's go. We can't afford to dillydally," was all she said, and she swiveled on her foot, stalking off into the velvety purple darkness.

"It creeps me out, and we haven't even gone in yet," whispered Squirrel, staring at the rusted wrought-iron gate.

"Don't worry, mate. I'll be right behind you," said Des, swallowing loudly. Azulfa cawed in agreement.

Squirrel nodded gratefully. With a deep breath, he swung the gate open. It creaked noisily.

"Here goes," said Squirrel, squinting. He spotted something that looked like a massive glowing white onion and broke out into a jog. "Over there. Let's get this done quickly."

Swroooosh. Fush. Swrooosh.

As Squirrel's feet landed on the ground, millions of dust particles swept into the air. He closed his eyes and almost tripped over a mound. "Be careful, the ground is uneven," he said, coughing.

"I can barely keep my eyes open," said Des, shielding his eyes with his paws.

"That's not necessarily a bad thing," whispered Azulfa, her low voice sounding even lower through the dusty haze.

"What do you mean?" asked Squirrel, rubbing his eyes. He looked down.

A bony hand with discolored blue fingernails lay there, sticking out of the soil.

Squirrel gagged as he flung his foot over a dusty mound. But just as he was about to break into a run, his back foot got caught, and he flew nose-first straight to the ground.

A heavy, musty stink hit Squirrel. He opened his eyes and a scream died in his throat.

He was lying on the bare body of a dusty, dead bee, his nose on a decomposing shoulder. The bee's skin was torn, showing her rotting flesh. Parts of her body were wrapped with a tattered old cloth; others were sickly naked.

Squirrel jumped up, his fur cold with disgust. He heard the brittle bones under him shatter. He felt sick. He had been trampling on thousands of moldy bee corpses, hidden under a thick layer of gray dust.

"NO!" said Des, retching as he saw the gross gangly bees.

"We must be quiet," whispered Azulfa, jumping over a skull. "Let's move." She grabbed both Squirrel and Des and pulled them toward the white tomb.

They drifted into an edgy silence, broken only by the crackle of bee bones under their feet. When they reached a raised, translucent platform, they stopped. On it was a hexagonal white structure with a big onion dome.

"This is it," said Azulfa, stopping at the bottom of a flight of stairs.

"Well, let's go," said Squirrel, taking the steps two at a

time. The white steps were not cool as he had expected them to be. They were hollow, almost warm. He turned around to say something to the others, but they were not behind him. Instead Azulfa was holding Des back with a powerful wing, preventing him from following Squirrel up.

"What's going on?" asked Squirrel, feeling uneasy.

"We'll keep watch," said Azulfa. "You go in, fetch the stones, and come back out."

Squirrel nodded and slowly walked toward the upside-down bulb. Did he want to go alone? No. Especially since he might be entering a small, enclosed area. But Azulfa was right. Someone needed to keep watch. So Squirrel ignored his fear and claustrophobia and went in.

"Get the slate-blue stones. Get out. Get the slate-blue stones. Get out," Squirrel chanted to himself, trying to swat his fear away. He walked into the grim shadows on the far side of the white-bone building. There was a slit in the wall. Sucking in his stomach, Squirrel wriggled sideways through the opening.

He found himself on a ramp. It spiraled all the way down to the dark pit of the earth. The rest of the space was a hollow wind tunnel.

Squirrel looked up. The white dome sent ghostly shadows shimmying into the abyss. He blinked as a silvery form that looked like a bee playing the cello floated toward him and then piddled away into the darkness.

He rubbed his eyes. *Just focus,* he told himself. *Two slate-blue stones from a tomb; Buried close, in a white-bone womb.*

Squirrel frowned. *Buried close, in a white-bone womb.*

It sounded as though he had to go down the ramp, into the womb of the Bone Tomb. His gullet snapped shut like a matchbox. His heart rattled in its cage. Sweat beads squeezed out of his cold temple. Claustrophobia.

"I'm not going to give in to this. I'm not going to," said Squirrel aloud. Oddly, hearing his voice in the funnel of the tomb was calming.

"I'll just keep talking to myself," he said as he started walking down the ramp. "I'll just keep breathing and talking to myself."

"Thank goodness for that dome. At least there's a smidgen of light . . ."

He stopped.

In front of him, on the ramp, was a white, rectangular box. On it lay a bee, embalmed in wax so that she was preserved perfectly. She wore a purple gown and a peaceful expression. Her reddish hair, adorned with a silver circlet, cushioned her head. A plaque read: QUEEN MARIUM.

Squirrel moved on. A few steps down the ramp was another white table with a dead Queen on it. Her eyes were wide open, a scared expression on her face. Quickly Squirrel went farther down. Every few feet, he saw a wax-caked Queen of the past. He gulped; he was in some ghoulish museum of the dead.

Squirrel forced himself to keep going, but the image of the corpses made him tremble. The truth was this: For the first time since his journey began, he was truly scared. He did not want to be alone in here.

And now that he was alone in the dark tomb, the nagging doubt that he had been pushing to the corner of his mind crept back and took hold of him.

The thing is, Squirrel knew he was not supposed to be on this quest. Not yet. He should have heard his mother's first message later in his life—when he was older. Specifically, when he was married. After all, it was the Wedded Wine that triggered his first memory. And Wedded Wine, he knew, was only drunk at one's own wedding. Perhaps Squirrel was not equipped to handle this journey. Perhaps he was too weak to be facing these dangers. Perhaps he was too young to find Brittle's Key and Brittle's Map. Perhaps he was not ready to discover his name and get his freedom.

"I should keep talking. The more I talk to myself, the better I feel. So if I want to talk to myself, I will," muttered Squirrel, trying to distract himself.

"I'll deal with this one step at a time. It's pitch-dark down there, but I can see right now. That's important. I must keep going. And I must look out for any stone that could be a shade of blue or gray . . ."

As he spoke, the ramp leveled under Squirrel's feet. He was on flat ground.

Despite the darkness, Squirrel's blue eyes cut through the shadows. He was in a small white crypt. In the center of the crypt he saw a rectangular white trunk, similar to those on which the corpse Queens lay. On the trunk was a single blood-orange blossom and two gray-blue stone plaques. The stone plaques had two halves of a poem etched on them.

He read the poem aloud, trying to focus on the words instead of the small, enclosed space.

Love

I have learned

Is the alchemy most potent

A drop lets copper shine like gold

A look sweetens bitter into honeyed dew

A kiss transforms night to the sunniest noon

But this cursed alchemy is a reversible boon

A fight shatters a whole into fragile few

A memory loses its warmth till icy cold

Until passion and love are latent

And all that is earned

Is wisdom.

Squirrel realized this must have been the poem that Queen Apize had written about her ill-fated love. Unfortunately, he could not appreciate it because the walls, the floor, and the ceiling seemed to be shrinking in on him, crushing the breath in his lungs. He fell to his knees, choking. Claustrophobia squeezed his neck.

"Keep talking," Squirrel said, battling spasms of nausea. "This must be 'the earth's white womb.' Now, where're the stones I'm looking for?" He looked at the walls, but they were pure bone—all smooth and white.

He crouched on the floor and felt around. Nothing.

"What if the stones aren't here? What if they've been moved?" Squirrel whispered, his heart spinning like a top in his chest. He closed his eyes. He was about to start hyperventilating when he heard something that zapped every thought from his mind. Two voices sliced through the tomb.

"Well, whaddya reckon 'e'd be doin' here?" came one scratchy voice.

"We don't care, dumdum. We just have to check," came a screechy answer.

Squirrel went as still as the dead Queens. He would have recognized the voices anywhere: It was the two Kowas who had been looking for him at the wedding and stalking his tree house. How had they found him here? In a tomb outside Mellifera?

Clak. Clak. Clak. Footsteps slapped against the ramp, echoing through the hollow tomb.

Squirrel knew he had to hide. And fast. They would reach him in a few moments, and then he was as good as gutted and stuffed. Frantically he fell to his knees and began to crawl silently toward the white table.

He reached the trunk in the middle of the room. There was a small gap between the floor and the raised white platform. Squirrel wedged his shoulder into the gap and, with a squirm, he shoved his foot into the crack. Curling his paws beneath the rectangular table, he pushed with all his might. Slowly, silently, the table lifted just enough off the ground. Squirrel rolled through the gap, and the table dropped with a soft thud.

Damn! A soft thud might as well have been a loud boom. The Kowas, with their supersonic hearing, would be upon him like flies on fruit.

He was hidden, but there was that crack. He needed to find something to cover the slit. Not knowing what to do, he reached out and grabbed the two stone plaques with the poem on it. Squirrel quickly lined them against the gap so that he was completely hidden. He waited, not daring to breathe.

If he was discovered, he was dead.

"I tell ya there 'ash definitely a noishe," Scratchy said.

"'Course there was a noise, idiot. I was here too. You think I'm deaf?" said Screechy.

Squirrel gritted his teeth to keep from groaning. The Kowas were pelting down the ramp. Squirrel could hear their sharp claws scuffing the white floor on which he lay.

"Well, whoshe to know? You could be deaf. It wouldn't be the firsht thin' wrong with ya."

Screechy did not answer. The tomb was silent except for a pair of footsteps walking toward the white stone casket under which Squirrel lay like a marinating piece of meat.

"Eeaaoo. Donouchme," came a shrill squeal.

"Garrrh. I can't shee a darn thin'," said Scratchy.

"You gruntin' gargoyle. If you ever try 'n grope me in the dark again, I'll poke your eyes out," came the earsplitting response.

"Shut it, you vain vixhen. I ain't tryin' to touch ya."

"Eeeek, let's just drop it. There's no one here. Let's just . . . What was that?" said Screechy, her voice climbing even higher.

Squirrel cupped his mouth to stop breathing, but it was no use. He was sure that they could hear his pulse pounding. He put his face against the gray stone, hoping the stone would muffle his breath. And in that moment of dark fear, he really saw it.

The stones were not gray; they were dull blue. Actually, they were slate blue! And the stones were buried in a white-bone womb. His memory had told him that the stones were 'stolen,' and hadn't Nizza said that the Queen's poem that was etched on special stones was taken from some distant land?

Squirrel's heart pounded even louder. These *had* to be the stones he was looking for. Right there in front of him. Right there within his reach. Right there, under the beaks of two killer Kowas.

"Shorry, just had to let out a squelch of gas. Now shtop wastin' time and let'sh get outta here. It'sh too dark. There ain't no way he could be 'ere. I'm shure he'sh in Mellifera."

"Oh, you hell-smell! That's gross. I'm outta here." And with that, Squirrel heard Screechy's and Scratchy's razor claws scrape the ramp as they took off.

Squirrel waited till the birds had left before taking a full, deep breath. What had happened to Azulfa and Des? Why hadn't they stopped the birds? Something was horribly wrong . . .

Worried about his friends, he tucked the two slate-blue stones with the poem on them safely into his PetPost belt and pushed hard on the underside of the table. As he hurried up the ramp, his head spun like a mill. How did those

Kowas know where he was? Where were Des and Azulfa? And could these two stones with the poem actually be the stones he was looking for?

Not a single star pierced the blanket of night, yet Squirrel could see quite clearly. In fact, he realized, he was lucky that he could see better in the dark than the Kowas. Otherwise they might have found him.

Just then, he saw a floppy-eared figure patrolling the platform. He recognized him immediately. It was Des. At least he was all right. But what had he been doing all this while?

Des ran over to him. "You sure took your time in there, mate. Must say, it's been no fun walking around this morgue alone. Did you get the stones?"

"Where were you? And where is Zulf?" said Squirrel, not bothering to respond. He wanted answers first.

"We split up. Zulf went to check out that side, and I'm guarding this side."

"Well, you've been doing a lousy job," spat Squirrel.

"Huh?" asked Des, looking confused.

"I had a couple of visitors in there," said Squirrel.

"Whaddya mean? The bees caught you?" Des's big brown eyes were full of concern.

"It wasn't the bees. It was the Kowas."

"WHAT?"

"You really had no idea?" asked Squirrel softly. His brow collapsed into ripples. A deep frown weighed down the tips of his mouth.

"Of course not!" protested Des. "You think I'd let them in without a fight? I'd at least have barged in to warn you! They definitely didn't enter from this side, mate. I've been on the lookout. Honestly, I have!"

Squirrel looked at Des and knew that his friend was telling the truth. He began to think—if Des had really been watching carefully, and if he had not seen anyone, then . . .

"Aaaaaaaah." The groan came straight from Squirrel's belly. His knees buckled and he fell on the floor. "I've been so, so stupid!"

"Squirrel, what's going on?" asked a low, cold voice from behind them.

Swiveling, Squirrel saw Azulfa walking toward them. She looked surprised.

"Squirrel was just telling me that he had—" started Des.

"I was just annoyed with myself for not taking one of those feathers you keep lighting with the blue flames down there. It was really dark," Squirrel butted in.

It was not the best cover-up, but he looked at Azulfa defiantly, daring her to challenge him. She looked back at him, her beady black eyes blank. Finally she said, "Yeah, I used the last feather that I could light in your kitchen. We should have saved it, though. Some fire light could have been useful in there."

Des, who was watching this exchange with a bewildered expression, began to sputter. Thankfully, before he could say that Squirrel had not been talking about light at all, Squirrel shot him such a bullet of a look that the dog shut up.

"So did you get the stones?" asked Azulfa, her eyes searching Squirrel's body. Squirrel thought he saw her feathers bristle as they rested on his belt, where he had tucked the stones.

"I did," said Squirrel with a curt nod.

"Good. Well, should we carry on, then?" asked Azulfa.

Squirrel nodded and turned his back to Azulfa. While his paws tied the strong petal rope Azulfa had cut from Cheska's wedding tent around his waist slowly, his mind whirled. He had to escape. He and Des had to get away—as far away as possible. But there was nothing he could do just yet. First he had to get to the next potion. He had to get to Darling Tea Hills safely.

So Squirrel turned around and flashed Azulfa his most disarming smile. "How long will it take us to get to Darling, Zulf?"

Squirrel's friendly smile worked. Azulfa's narrowed eyes

182

relaxed and she said, "Till next nightfall, I think."

"Great! Well, I'm starving and grumpy," said Squirrel as an excuse for his prior brusqueness. "We'd better have a quick nibble before leaving. Anyone for some candy?" As he spoke, Squirrel reached into his pocket and produced a fistful of the Raisin D'Ettys he had been carrying around.

Greedily Des grabbed four and stuffed all of them into his mouth. Azulfa used her sharp talons to lance two. "Thank you," she said.

"Alrighty, now up, up, and away," said Squirrel, pulling his face into such a wide smile that his cheek muscles began to ache. But he kept the expression plastered on his face. He could not let Azulfa catch on to the fact that he had discovered the truth about her. Right now his life depended upon keeping up appearances.

HILLS OF HEART

The Madame kneeled before the Colonel, her head bent. "Colonel, we couldn't find them in Mellifera," she whispered. Yards of black silk covered her head, stretched all the way down to her toes, and formed a clothy pool on the floor. Through her veil, her yellow eyes were fixed on the mess of fabric. "Squirrel wasn't where you said he would be."

Even though the Colonel's eyes were also covered, the Madame could feel the hot fury in his stare. Her fur bristled and her tail twitched like a grasshopper.

"Madame, I got my information from the best source—

someone who is *with* Squirrel. I told you where to find him. I told you when to find him. So how did you and your pathetic birds let him escape?"

"Colonel . . . I . . . I . . ."

"Madame, I'm not interested in excuses," he hissed. "Can you do what I hired you to do or not? Can you find out where he is going next?"

"Yes, sire," she said, bowing so low that her wet nose touched the floor.

"Good. And, Madame, I have someone else on the job too. So if I hear one more yarn-brained excuse, you'll be sorry. Understood?" he said, filing his claws against each other.

"Yes, sire." With a choked sob, the Madame crawled out of the cave.

"There's nothing here!" exclaimed Des, his neck wilting in dismay.

Squirrel's throat trembled with frustration. They had flown all day, without stopping, without eating, without speaking. The violent sun had scorched their fur; cruel air pockets had somersaulted them through the sky, tossing their empty stomachs into their throats; the thin air had made their eyes feel like dry rocks. And why had they gone through it all? For nothing.

Squirrel watched Azulfa. She was perched on the edge of a barren hilltop and was swinging her shoulders to get her blood flowing to the tips of her wings. Her beak was pursed and her bushy eyebrows were narrow with pain. Ordinarily, Squirrel would have felt sorry for the tired, old crow. But not now. Right now he was happy she was suffering.

Azulfa must have felt the chill in Squirrel's gaze, for she turned around, her beady black eyes spearing Squirrel's cool blue ones. Quickly Squirrel looked away, his heart pounding. He had just realized how unsafe it was for him and Des to be stuck on an empty hilltop with a muscular ex-Kowa, who probably wanted to wear his head for a crown and his fur for a coat.

"I don't see any tea estates here!" groaned Des, kicking at the parched yellow earth.

"Maybe we misread the map. Or maybe Azulfa flew too far ahead," Squirrel said, happy to blame the crow. He squinted into the dusk, wondering where to go next.

"We're in the right place," said Azulfa, the treble in her voice shaking the loose rock on which they stood.

"How do you know that?" asked Des, massaging his mouth and cheeks. He had not chewed a morsel of food all day, and his jawbone seemed to ache from disuse.

"Look at that tunnel over there," said Azulfa, pointing to

the valley at the base of the hill on their right. A passage had been punctured through the sandstone hillock.

"There is a carriageway!" cried Squirrel as he saw two tracks snaking from the valley to the tunnel. A sign of civilization at last!

"Let's go," cried Des, jogging toward the valley. Squirrel was at his heels, bounding clumsily down the rocky hill.

"STOP!" yelled Azulfa.

"Why?" asked Des impatiently.

"Don't tread so heavily. The rock is weak; your steps could easily cause a landslide. Look," she said, banging on the stone. As she banged, the hill groaned and shook.

Massive chunks of orange rock and rubble came pelting toward Squirrel and Des. Just before they were pulverized to a bloody mince, Azulfa lifted them off the ground and careened wildly through the air toward the tunnel in the valley.

Squirrel's heart spun with confusion. What was Azulfa playing at? First she had warned them against the landslide. Then she had started the avalanche that almost minced them to nothingness. And, finally, she had swooped in and saved them. He could simply not figure her out: If she wanted him dead, why did she keep saving him?

They entered the dim tunnel. And there, in the darkness, Squirrel saw the whole ugly truth.

Azulfa wanted the key to Brittle's Map for herself. Since the clues to find the key were clipped to his brain, she needed him alive. But . . .

Squirrel gulped. As soon as Azulfa got Brittle's Key, she would dispose of him faster than a dirty diaper.

"Now, this looks more like it," said Des, his ears perking up.

Squirrel stopped thinking about Azulfa long enough to look around him. He stood in a valley of rolling green hills combed into neat, terraced rows; plant saplings were pruned to precision; and a grid of canals made the soil dark and moist. A big birchwood sign had "Darling Tea Hills" carved into it.

"My navigation must be better than you thought. Perhaps you should trust me more, Squirrel," said Azulfa, a steely glint in her eyes.

Squirrel avoided the bait. "Well done, Zulf," he said, forcing a smile. This was not the time to dwell on Azulfa and her motives. She would not hurt him while she still needed him; so, for now, he was safe. Instead he needed to find the next trigger. He looked around at the dark, moist earth. He had to be close.

"Squirrel, what are we looking for again? What exactly did the memory say?" asked Azulfa.

Squirrel considered ignoring her, but decided to answer.

The truth was that he was not sure what to do next and he could use Azulfa's help.

"It said: *Nestled in the hills of heart; Lies your own journey's second part; Pluck ten leaves from richest soil; Mix in water, and bring to boil.*"

"We need leaves from the richest soil?" asked Azulfa, a frown pinching her brow.

"It appears so," said Squirrel. Darn, even she was finding this tricky.

"Well, let's find someone who lives in Darling," said Azulfa. "We can ask them where the soil is the richest."

"Yes. And we can also ask them where to find some grub," said Des. "You remember how the bees kept saying community comes first? Well, I think my motto is food comes first." And, with a chuckle, Des led the way to find his next meal.

On the other side of the hill they met their first residents of Darling Tea Hills. Four field mice were chatting as they trimmed a hedge. They wore colorful patched clothes, smeared with soil. Oversize grass baskets were strapped to their backs.

"Oye, oye! Hello there!" said Des, trotting over to them. With a smile, he extended his paw to the man mouse closest to him.

The mouse did not take his hand. Instead he stared at

Des, his jaw dropping. Awkwardly Des turned and offered his empty hand to the other mice. But all of them simply stared at him through their slanted slivers of eyes.

Finally the first male took Des's paw and shook it timidly. Des seemed surprised. Squirrel realized why—the mouse's palm was covered in pebblelike calluses.

"How you do?" asked the mouse, speaking slowly, enunciating each word.

"Very well, thank you," said Des. "I'm Des, and this is Azulfa and Squirrel."

Squirrel smiled at them. Though they did not look old, their faces were covered in the supple wrinkles caused by long labor in the sun. They were short—a head shorter than Squirrel. Yet he was sure that one punch from any of them would leave him flat on the earth, eating dirt. Their wiry bodies looked as tough as nails.

"I Khoy, and this Luleen, Sonny, and Vida," said the mouse, pointing to the other mice beside him.

As Squirrel shook hands with the mice, their brown faces cracked into wedged smiles, showing off large white incisors. They gripped his red hand with such happy vigor that Squirrel felt his knuckles bruise.

"What you do in Darling Tea Hills?" asked Khoy eagerly. "You are first visitors I ever see."

"We are in search of a particular leaf that grows here," said Squirrel.

"You search tea?" asked Khoy. "I tea tender; I know much about tea crop. I help you . . ." And then he added quickly, "If it please you, only."

"That would be great! Could you tell us where the soil is the richest?" asked Squirrel. His lungs swelled with hope.

"But all soil rich here. We have six hills in Darling. All same quality," Khoy answered, shaking his head.

"But some soil must be the most fertile?" Squirrel insisted, his hope deflating like an air mattress.

Khoy looked at his three mice friends. They all looked away. Luleen stared at a leaf in her hand. Vida pretended to scratch her brown arm. Sonny flicked some wet dirt off his pants. It was obvious: none of them wanted to disappoint Squirrel by confirming Khoy's news.

"I sorry, but it all the same . . . all very good soil. That why we have tea plantation here," repeated Khoy, struggling to find the best words he could.

Squirrel frowned. He could not possibly pluck leaves from every area in this ridge and boil them with water. He had to be missing something.

"All right, well, we'll figure it out. Now, is there anywhere we can go and get some food?" asked Des. His stomach churned so loudly that the four field mice took a hurried step back.

"Yes, food. I take you to Prospect Point?" said Khoy with relief. He was obviously happy to oblige his guests.

"Yes, you take us," said Des with a grin.

"Good. We take train," Khoy informed them. "Look, here it come now."

Squirrel looked down the carriageway. He could not help the "oh" that fell from his mouth when he saw the train heaving toward them.

It was nothing more than a six-wheeled open-air cart, pulled by two field mice. The rickety box-on-wheels rattled down the road till it stopped with a jerk a few feet from them.

The mice who were tugging the cart along stared at Squirrel, Des, and Azulfa.

"No scared. These nice folk. I take them to Prospect Point," Khoy told the train conductors. As he spoke, Khoy thrust his hind legs out and leaped into the old, wooden cart. He then helped Des and Azulfa aboard. Khoy was turning around to help Squirrel when Squirrel decided he would try to jump into the cart too.

Copying Khoy, Squirrel pushed his legs and leaped, feeling himself lift off the ground. The wind made his cheeks flap as he went hurtling through the air straight into the train. He was about to fall on Khoy, but the mouse ducked just in time.

"That was fun!" wheezed Squirrel.

"Yes, you a good jumper," said Khoy with a wide grin. "You stay in Darling. You help us for our crop."

"You never know. I might have to," said Squirrel with a smile. Though it was a joke, Squirrel could not help thinking that if he did not find his name and get his freedom, and if he had to return to Bimmau as the PetPost slave, he might actually be better off hiding in the remote tea hills of Darling than facing the well-known vengeance of Bacchu Banoose.

Khoy giggled. "Yes! Darling very nice. Now, everyone grip side."

Squirrel obeyed. It was good that he did—as the uneven stone wheels began to spin and the cart rattled down the path, Squirrel's body began to jiggle violently.

"I . . . feel . . . like . . . I'm . . . being . . . electrocuted," said Des, his voice quaking with the motion of the carriage.

"You've obviously never been electrocuted, have you?" said Azulfa.

"And you have?" retorted Des jokingly. But the crow's grave eyes smashed the laughter out of his face.

They fell silent, letting the loud rumble of the cart scratch their eardrums. Sighing, creaking, gasping, the train inched up the hill, passing acres of rolling tea plantations.

"Look at how many mice are working in the fields," said Squirrel in awe. Even in the late twilight, hundreds of mice were patting, pruning, and picking the tea crop.

"Yes, and look how shocked they are to see us!" said Des, waving at the workers.

"Oh no! They are actually encouraging you," scowled Azulfa.

Sure enough, the workers were waving back at Des excitedly, some using both their hands. They broke into thrilled applause as Des began to juggle three scrunched-up Raisin D'Etty wrappers. When a huddle of children ran up to the train, Des leaned over to give them brushing high fives, as though he were some sort of a celebrity.

"The children enjoy you," said Khoy with a merry chuckle that only seemed to deepen the scowl on Azulfa's face.

Squirrel smiled at Des's theatrics, but he himself was too preoccupied to join in. He stared at the clay and the crop, trying to make sense of the land. Unfortunately, his untrained city eyes did not understand soil in the slightest.

"You interested in tea crop, Mr. Redtail?" asked Khoy.

"Ummm, yes," stammered Squirrel, who had never been called either Mister or Redtail before. "I was just wondering about the leaves: they all look exactly the same."

"Yes. All the same," said Khoy, bobbing his head. "We have only one plant, but we make four types of teas."

"How does that work?" asked Des, who stopped playing celebrity long enough to join the conversation.

"In spring, we pluck first batch of tea leaves. It called first flush, and this tea is . . . how do you say . . . airy. In summer, we pick second flush. This tea full of flavor and is gold color. In autumn, there is autumn flush. This smell nice and light."

"And during rain, we have between flush tea. It dark and strong. It poorest quality. Should be called toilet flush." He beamed, evidently pleased with his joke.

"I never knew that tea could be described like that," Squirrel was saying when Des yelled, "YAAAAY! I can smell something. I'm pretty sure food is close by."

"Yes, we almost at Prospect Point," affirmed Khoy. "We close to highest point in Darling now."

Squirrel looked around. He could not believe how high the train had brought them.

Rattle, rattle, bang, bang. With a final shiver, the train stopped.

"Train cannot go up there, Mr. Redtail," said Khoy, pointing to the top of the hill.

"What's up there?" asked Squirrel. The apex of the clay hill looked like it had been squashed flat by a powerful thumb.

"Rule of Rodentia. It is where our Micetros meet. It is our parliament, Mr. Redtail."

"Who are Micetros?" asked Squirrel merrily. He was still tickled by this new nickname.

"The Micetros are our leaders. We choose thirteen best mice in Darling. They become Micetros," answered Khoy. "They sit at Rule of Rodentia every day—from first ray to last ray of sun. The Micetros decide how to govern Darling."

"My uncle Tupten is Micetro," continued Khoy, puffing up with obvious pride. "He sits in Rule of Rodentia too. Now we go past it to Prospect Point. Follow me," he said, skipping up the steepest part of the hill. Des, excited about food, ran off behind Khoy, and Azulfa unfurled her wings and flew above them.

Squirrel looked from his tired legs to the steep hill and groaned. He would have done anything to have wings right now.

SOMETIMES WARM,
SOMETIMES COLD

Carved out of the hill, Prospect Point bustled with activity. Some mice loitered about on weathered stone chairs, chatting. Others sat on low black stools, quaffing down pints of twig ale and acorn wine.

Squirrel reached up to touch a misty cotton puff of a low-hanging cloud. It dissolved in the cool wetness of his palm. He saw the mice look at him curiously and giggle. Apparently, the news that three foreigners had come to Darling had reached the top of the hill before they had.

Khoy looked at them shyly. "You like Darling Tea Hills?"

"Love it! I'm a little color-blind, but I gotta say that the scenery is absolutely fantastic," said Des.

Squirrel nodded. The misty periwinkle sky, the plush green slopes, and the rippling leaves made Darling look like the backdrop of a sweet dream.

Khoy beamed with his big, rectangular teeth. "We sit here, yes? We get good view, then," he said, pointing to a nearby table that looked like it was made of something black and compressed, like coal.

"Sounds good," said Squirrel. He plopped down and put his legs up on the high table, relishing the stretch down his hamstrings. He was very happy to be seated, and even happier at the idea of a hot, hearty meal.

"Anyone else feeling a little chilly?" asked Des, whose fur was standing at attention.

"It get cold at night here. You wait, I go get ale and some quilts," said Khoy, bounding out of his seat.

"What a nice guy," said Des, straining his eyes trying to peek at the food on everyone's plates. "I can't see much. It's getting dark."

"Yes, I've been wondering about that," said Azulfa quietly, staring at the sky. The sleepy sun was slipping into the valley, hijacking the last rays of light.

Garrrrarrrrr.

"Oops," said Des with a sheepish smile. His hungry stomach was making a ruckus.

Right on cue, the waitress materialized at their table. She was a young field mouse with a twig pen in her hand. She was trembling with excitement. "Hello. I bring you order?" she asked, shaking as she spoke to them.

"Huh?" asked Des, puzzled.

"I think she wants us to order," said Squirrel, nudging Des. Turning to the little, nervous field mouse, he smiled. "What are you serving today?"

The waitress looked flustered. Stammering, she said, "Today . . . today . . . we have . . . have cheeses, nuts, worms, fruits, berries, butters . . ."

At that moment Khoy returned with three woolen quilts and four mugs.

"Why don't we just let Khoy order for us," suggested Squirrel.

"I happy to order for you," said the mouse, plonking a full glass of frothy brown ale in front of each of them before speaking to the waitress in a squeaky foreign language. As he spoke, he gestured animatedly, using his teeth and hands.

"I ordered," said Khoy. "Now you wear blanket to keep warm and drink pinecone ale." He helped each of them cocoon themselves in the quilts.

"Where's your blanket?" asked Squirrel, who had noticed that Khoy's large rectangular teeth were chattering a little.

"I no need. I be fine. I go without coat in winter, too."

"Well, that very brave of you," said Des seriously, rubbing his shoulders. "I cold. When I hungry, I always get cold."

Squirrel smothered a grin; he knew that Des thought that by copying Khoy's way of speaking, the mouse would understand him better.

"Very hungry," Des continued to grumble until the waitress came up to their table, her arms balancing five trays. Quickly she arranged the stone platters on the table along with wooden knives and forks.

"Enjoy dinner," she said with a small curtsy before scampering off.

"Yum, this looks amazing," said Squirrel, digging into the colorful dishes before him.

He dipped corn in butter and gnawed at it until nothing was left but green husk. He helped himself to a pomegranate and orange salad, dripping with herb dressing. Nibbling wedges of cheese, he savored their nuttiness. He sucked the slippery worm with barley mince dry and gobbled the mixed nuts and berries, relishing the salt and chili pepper.

With a belly full of bliss, Squirrel licked the last morsel of food from his stone plate. He decided to try to make these dishes for himself when he returned to Bimmau. His own cooking was fine, and perhaps almost good, but this food was new and tickled him. Perhaps, if he ever got his freedom from Bacchu Banoose, he could cook this for others in Bimmau . . .

Squirrel's happy thoughts were interrupted by the sight of Des's face. The dog was wearing a deep, disappointed scowl.

"Des, what's wrong?" asked Squirrel between mouthfuls. "You didn't like the food?"

"Well, it is all very good, but nothing here is cooked. I wanted something hot," said Des, his voice getting whiny.

"We no cook here," said Khoy with a chuckle.

"What do you mean?" asked Des, his blanket dropping off his shoulders.

"We no cook. You need fire to cook. We don't have fire," answered Khoy simply. And, after dropping that bomb of information, the mouse got back to chewing his raw dinner.

"So . . . you have no heat. Or light?" asked Azulfa, pointing to the sky, which was already a deep navy blue. The only light came from the large-faced moon and the glowing stars.

"How do you manage at night?" asked Squirrel.

"We survive," said Khoy with a pleasant smile.

"So you've never had fire?" asked Azulfa.

"Oh, we had fire. But it went away," said Khoy.

"And where did the fire go?" asked Squirrel, utterly confused.

"When I was younger, we have fire. We used to have Flame Flints of Rodentia. They were two stones that gave us fire. In middle of Rule of Rodentia, our parliament, we have big stone basin for fireplace. Every day, Micetros rub stones together and make fire. All mice go and get fire on their torches from there.

"One day, suddenly, the stones disappear. We never knew where the stones go. But, after that day, no more fire. No more light. No more heat. No more cooking. And no more visitors. Darling become like old days again," finished Khoy.

"Someone stole your fire?" asked Des, beginning to cough.

Khoy just nodded, blinking sadly.

"That's terrible," said Squirrel, shaking his head. These mice were so friendly, so hardworking, and they lived in a difficult climate. How could any heartless creature steal their source of warmth and comfort?

"Does not matter now. We do fine," said Khoy, pulling himself together. "Now you all finished dinner?"

"Yes," they chimed, and Khoy waved at the waitress. She came over carrying their bill.

Squirrel saw the small piece of paper and panicked. He had been so busy eating that he had not even considered how he would pay for their meal. What if they did not accept guf-flings, bizkits, and gromms in Darling? What would he do?

"Uhm, Khoy, how much is it? I have gufflings. Do you think they will accept . . ."

Khoy looked horrified. His thin, wispy eyebrows shot up to his hairline, and his large muscular jaw stuck out. "You no pay!"

"What do you mean?"

"You no pay! None of you pay. You are first visitor in Darling since fire go away. I treat!" said Khoy, rattling around in his patched pocket.

"You must let me pay," protested Squirrel. "I have money. I can give you—"

"No! Now you no talk of this," said Khoy. With that, Khoy opened his wallet, shook out every last coin in it on the table, and bought Des, Azulfa, and Squirrel dinner.

"So all the mice families live in their own burrow?" asked Des, yawning loudly.

"Yes, we all have own burrow. This is burrow that me and my wife built," said Khoy proudly, pointing to a round door in the rocky slope of the mountain. He inserted a notched pebble into a hole and jiggled till it clicked. Pushing the door open, he said, "Tonight you sleep here. I help you find richest soil tomorrow." So saying he led them down a long, dark passage.

As he walked down the narrow stone tunnel, Squirrel breathed slowly, trying to forget his claustrophobia. Luckily, after a few steps, the passage widened into a large den. Two big, circular windows pierced the wall, letting the silver moonbeams stream into the room.

The room was bare and simple; yet, it had the happy smell of having been lived in. A fur rug was strewn across most of the stone floor. Dewy green plants clumped in the corners gave the room the smell of fresh rain. The scent reminded Squirrel of his own tree cottage. Despite the nip in the air, a happy warmth spread inside him.

To the side of the den was another chamber. It had a simple sofa, a coffee table, and a long dining table with twelve seats carved entirely from solid black coal. Sitting at the coal dining table were four young mice, each wearing a pair of old, woven-leaf pajamas.

"Hello, family," said Khoy, giving each of his four children a pat on the head. A round-faced mouse with big black eyes under her bonnet burst into the room, carrying a large stone cauldron. Khoy ran to her, took the heavy pot she was carrying, and put it down on the table.

"Thank you, my dear," she said with a sweet smile, giving

Khoy a small peck. She took a wooden ladle out of her apron and began to scoop large helpings of green goop into the four stone bowls in front of the children. Only when she was done did she notice that her husband was not alone.

"Oh my!" She dropped the ladle to the floor.

"Cheesewedge, these my friends. They stay with us tonight. We prepare three rooms for them?" Khoy asked his wife.

"Yes, yes! I so sorry. I no see you earlier. Please come here. Sit down. I go bring you drink," said Khoy's wife, dropping a quick curtsy to her guests before disappearing into the kitchen.

The four children beamed at their guests and pushed their plates away, obviously happy not to be forced to eat the pea-pod pulp.

"Friends, sit. I go make bed for you. You all tired," said Khoy, springing up.

Squirrel sat next to the children. They were looking at him.

"You red," said one of Khoy's daughters with a small giggle.

"Yes, yes, I am," said Squirrel, smiling at the little, whis-kered mouse.

"I like red," said the young girl shyly, hiding her face in her hands.

"Awww . . . isn't she just the cutest thing ever?" said Des, groping his way toward Squirrel. "Wow, I can't see a thing!"

Squirrel was surprised—he could see quite clearly. But before he could say anything, a loud crack shook the walls and a bolt of light blinded their eyes.

"What was that?" asked Des, his voice just a bit shaky.

"Thunderstorm," answered one of Khoy's sons. "Sky get angry and we have many lightnings and thunders." The mouse gave a grave nod with his little berry-shaped head.

At that moment Khoy returned, carrying three blankets. He handed one to Azulfa, one to Des, and the third to Squirrel. "Children, today you in one room, okay? It is special day: we have guests. You all sleep in room with the twins."

"Twins? You have twins as well?" asked Squirrel happily. He loved twins. The idea of sharing everything with someone else, of never being alone, had always amazed him.

"Yes, but they still in crib. You see, newborn mice are blind. They cannot see anything," explained Khoy.

"Well, I got nothin' on them," grumbled Des, who had finally groped his way to the coal sofa.

Khoy's wife entered the room again, this time carrying a tray with three cups of brownish water. "Hibiscus water?"

Squirrel had a sudden brain wave. He jumped out of his seat and went over to Mrs. Khoy.

"Please let me help you with that," he said, taking the tray from her. With his back to the others and under the cloud of darkness, he slipped his hand into his pocket and took out the piece of Skullcap that he had used to make the Pretty Piths for Lady Blouse. In a flash he dropped the whole thing into one of the cups and waited a few moments for it to dissolve. He turned around and handed the cup to Azulfa, who drank the tea in one large chug. She would be out for a long time.

Squirrel gulped his water down and then did a pretend yawn. "Thank you so much for everything, Khoy. I think I will go to sleep and we will think of how to find the rich soil tomorrow."

Squirrel lay awake in his coal bed, tucked in a warm blanket. Everything in this dark room smelled of coal. In fact, he was surprised by how much coal he had seen in Darling.

"I shouldn't get distracted. I need to solve this fast; I have no time," said Squirrel to himself.

He repeated the words from his memory. *"Pluck ten leaves from richest soil; Mix in water, and bring to boil; If you brew this tea, you've learned; To give what you have newly earned; Return what has long been stole; For that, my dear son, is your role."*

Squirrel almost started to cry. There was yet another obstacle. His memory had said that he had to boil the water.

207

How could he do this if there was no fire in all of Darling?

Desperately Squirrel rehashed everything he had learned about Darling Tea Hills and the mice. He had to be missing something. He listed everything that had struck him: the friendly mice, their hard work, the tea flushes, the Micetros, the coal, the stolen fire . . .

Suddenly Squirrel's eyes lit up like two slate-blue torches. He swung his legs, feeling around for the bed. Coal! Fire! The answer was coal and fire! Yes, that was it!

A roll of thunder pealed loudly. Squirrel hopped out of bed and hurtled toward the door. He knew what he was supposed to do.

LET THERE BE LIGHT

By the time Squirrel got to the Rule of Rodentia, it had stopped raining. He stood outside the circular stone structure, watching the wet tea plantation yawn sleepily as the sun kissed the sky good morning.

Too fidgety to stay in one place, Squirrel decided to take a walk around the stone building.

The Rule of Rodentia was carved completely out of the hill's weathered gray rock. The rotunda had no roof, and Squirrel could not help thinking that the structure was challenging the elements, standing tall in the face of the sun, the cold, the mist, the hail. Everything about the stone building was strong and true, softened only by the age-old work of moss.

Squirrel hurried around the Rule of Rodentia, hugging himself to keep warm. He checked the sky; the morning sun blinked back at him sleepily. He picked up his pace as he heard voices chatter on the other side of the stone. The first session must be starting in parliament.

Jittery, Squirrel paused and patted his bulging pocket. The two stones from the Bone Tomb with the poem carved on them were carefully tucked away in his belt. He took a deep breath and crossed the threshold.

The Rule of Rodentia was an amphitheater of old days. Stone bleachers ran along the pillars, cracking into rubble. Enterprising blades of grass had spread on the rocky surfaces, providing a soft cushion for the thirteen Micetros settling down around a circular, central pit.

As Squirrel walked down the narrow aisle, he felt thirteen pairs of brown eyes stare at him. Drawing himself to his full height, Squirrel walked onward, trying to introduce a bit of a swagger into his step. He wanted to appear confident. And tall.

He walked up to the Micetros. Not knowing how to greet them, Squirrel bowed.

"Micetros, I have an offer for you," said Squirrel, reciting

the words he had been practicing since he hopped out of bed.

The Micetros broke into squeaky murmurs.

"Who is this red creature?"

"What offer?"

An elderly Micetro, sitting in the middle, cleared his throat. The others went quiet. He rose. He looked at Squirrel for a long time before speaking.

"I am Micetro Tupten. I hear you stay with my nephew Khoy," he said. His light brown eyes and gentle, crumpled face smoothed Squirrel's nerves.

Squirrel said, "Yes, your nephew has been an incredible host."

"We hear that there are strangers in Darling, but we no believe. No stranger in Darling for more than I can remember," said a female Micetro with a happy clap. "Where you from, stranger?"

"I come from Bimmau County."

"What is your purpose in our hills? You come from big city of Bimmau. What you need in our faraway tea town?" asked Tupten.

Squirrel took a deep breath. *Come out with it*, he told himself. He just hoped they would believe him. "I have a proposition for you, Micetros of Darling."

"What is it?" asked Tupten, looking at Squirrel curiously.

"I have something that you want. Something that will help all of Darling. But, in return, I want you to tell me where your coal mines are," said Squirrel clearly. While he spoke, he looked each Micetro directly in the eye, holding his neck as firm as he could.

Squeaky mutters rang through the amphitheater. Tupten spread his arms. This time Tupten's tone was not kind. "Coal mines are our best-kept secret. They are our one richness. It is all we have. We no tell anyone. Specially not outsider." His eyes did not budge from Squirrel's face.

Squirrel stared back at the old field mouse. "I've an offer you can't refuse."

"We no take kindly to blackmail," said Tupten, his voice beginning to quake with anger.

"I am not trying to blackmail you," Squirrel said quickly. This was not going well at all.

"Then what?" asked a stern-looking Micetro.

"I want to give you something. Something that was taken from you long ago. In return, I need to know where the coal mines are."

Silence. Finally one Micetro asked, "Why you need our coal?"

"I don't need coal. I need tea leaves," said Squirrel, whistling with frustration.

"Leaves?" asked Tupten, obviously confused.

"Yes, I need ten tea leaves, plucked from the soil where the coal is mined," said Squirrel. He desperately needed to convince the Micetros that he was not trying to steal their coal.

Tupten considered Squirrel's words. He asked quietly, "What you have for us?"

The other Micetros jumped up in protest. "We no negotiate." "We don't ever tell." "Never."

Tupten spoke over the protests, "Friends, I no suggest we tell him. But we find out what he has at least. It called good business."

The Micetros grumbled, but let Squirrel speak.

"I have the Flame Flints that were taken from you," said Squirrel boldly, reaching into his pocket and producing the long gray-blue stones. Now he had to hope he was right.

His words were met with shocked silence. All eyes were fixed on the two stones.

Eventually a gray-haired she-mouse spoke, "He lies. There is writing on them. Our Flame Flints were plain."

Squirrel ignored the angry squeaks of the Micetros and handed the two gray stones to Tupten and said, "Try it, sir." He was almost sure that these were the flints stolen from Darling. That is why his mother had wanted him to go to the Bone Tomb; that is what she meant by *If you brew this tea, you've learned; To give what you have newly earned; Return what has long been stole; For that, my dear son, is your role.* She had led him to the Flame Flints, because she knew it would allow him to make tea.

With trembling hands, old Tupten struck one stone against the other. A baby spark fizzled on the tip of the stone. Excited, Tupten struck them against each other harder. This time a sinewy flame jumped into the cold air.

"These are Flame Flints," cried Tupten, wonder sketched onto his little, pointed face. "I no believe, but they are Flame Flints. Thank you. You are . . . you are . . . red fire angel."

Squirrel bowed, humbled. Warmth rushed through his being, and he knew it had nothing to do with the fire. Not only had he fulfilled part of the memory, but he had also given the gift of fire back to an entire community. He was about to ask to be taken to the coal mines again when someone spoke. It was a shriveled little mouse with big yellow eyes.

"How you have this?"

Squirrel was prepared for this one. "I found them on my travels. They were hidden in the earth. And I found instructions to return them here." It was a vague version of the truth. Then, swerving the conversation, he asked, "Now will you tell me where the coal mines are?"

Tupten looked straight at Squirrel and, without blinking, said the most surprising word Squirrel had ever heard.

"No."

"No?" cried Squirrel hoarsely. He had been sure the exchange would work.

"No, we cannot. We no give you our biggest secret. But . . ." Tupten held up his hand to quell the protests that were visibly shaking Squirrel's larynx. "But I have idea to repay debt. I first consult with other Micetros. You go outside, take a look around, and come back. We do voting."

Squirrel had no choice but to agree. Outside the rotunda, he kicked himself hard. He had given them his secret weapon without securing his part of the bargain. That was the stupidest thing he could possibly have done.

When he was done thoroughly berating himself, Squirrel reappeared before the thirteen Micetros, his face red with anger. But as soon as he saw Tupten's smile, he relaxed. "We vote and we all agree. We owe you big debt. We shall take you to coal mine and you go pluck your leaves."

Squirrel grinned like he never had before. He would find the leaves. He looked at the Micetros. They were kindling a fire in the stone basin.

A fire. Squirrel would be able to brew the leaves in hot

water. He could not wait another moment. "So you will take me to the mines? Can you take me now?"

It was not impatience; it was urgency. He had to be back before anybody woke up. At least he had thought to drug Azulfa with a cube of Skullcap, so she would sleep much longer than anyone else.

"We give you whatever you want. We owe you biggest debt of all. But only thing is we cannot let you see how to get to the mines," said Tupten apologetically.

"So how will I get there?" asked Squirrel, confused.

"I take you there. But you will wear this," said Tupten, handing Squirrel a dark-green reed blindfold. "Now put it on. I will lead you there."

The sun was up when Squirrel returned to Khoy's burrow. Yet as he tiptoed through the hall, the stone walls shook with the sound of snores. Everyone was still asleep. Squirrel sighed with relief.

He felt bad about leaving without saying good-bye to Khoy and thanking him and his family for their hospitality, but he could not risk waiting any longer. He had to escape Azulfa, and this was his best opportunity.

Squirrel went to the room that the Khoy children had given him and began looking for something to scribble two quick notes with. A blanched ream of leaves sat on the coal desk, but there were no pens or pencils anywhere. He wanted to scream—if he did not act fast, everyone in the house would wake up.

Panic gave Squirrel an idea. He reached into the sack of coal that Tupten had given him as a reward, pulled out a small piece of coal, and hurriedly wrote two notes.

Tiptoeing across the hall, Squirrel slowly opened Khoy's bedroom. Khoy and his wife were huddled together in the cold. They were sleeping without a blanket.

Squirrel thought back to the warm blanket that he had been huddled under all evening and realized that, on top of his incredible hospitality, Khoy had also sacrificed his own warmth for his guests.

As quietly as he could, Squirrel placed the bag of coal that Tupten had given him as a reward in the corner of Khoy's room. On top he placed his note of heartfelt thanks and good-bye.

Squirrel crept out of the room and down the hall. He entered another room. It shook with snores. He saw Des, wrapped snugly in his blanket, looking completely at peace.

Gently Squirrel shook his friend. Des awoke with a start. Before the dog could grumble his protests, Squirrel put a finger to his lips and shushed his friend.

Noiselessly he pulled out the second coal-scribbled note and handed it to Des. Des opened the letter.

Des, don't say a word. I don't want to risk waking Azulfa up. We must get out of here immediately. Azulfa has betrayed us. I've drugged her, so she will sleep for a while longer. Enough to give us a head start. We must move now.

Des was now sitting in his bed, wide-awake. He gestured for something to write with, and Squirrel gave him the piece of coal.

Quickly Des scribbled, *What about the memory?*

I got it. I'll explain everything later, wrote Squirrel.

Des looked into Squirrel's honest, blue eyes and nodded. Taking the coal crayon back, he scribbled, *I'm with you. But where are we going?*

Squirrel inhaled sharply, jotted five final words, and placed the coal on the bed. He handed the note to Des.

Des read it and his eyes became as round as coins. The note fell out of his paw onto the floor.

The five words read: *The Desert of Blood Kings.*

17

THE FERRY

I don't know about this," said Des as he watched a muscular python slither through the water. Her yellow eyes darted over to Des, who stood on a gently rocking boat.

"She looks hungry," whispered Des as the python darted her tongue in and out of her mouth with a bloodcurdling hiss. Her bottom jaw unhinged and opened so wide she could have gulped Des down.

Des stepped back just as the snake lurched forward. Her glossy body sailed right past him and landed on the muddy riverbank. There was a fraction of a tussle, and two frog's legs disappeared into her mouth, leaving a line of bluish blood on her jaw. The python then slunk back into the river, giving Des a cruel wink as she slid past the ferry. Des shuddered.

"Did you see that?" he asked.

"Yeah. Try not to look at her," said Squirrel. He himself was staring at the two strong gavials, with their hard, horny skin and their flat, hammered heads. Their tails whipped around in the water, propelling the boat.

"But why'd we ditch Azulfa? She may not have betrayed us, mate. I mean, I know she's a cranky ol' bird, but she's mighty useful to have around," said Des, eyeballing the river, trying to find the snake.

"I'll explain later," Squirrel said, looking away. He did not feel like talking about Azulfa yet.

"Fine, but can you at least tell me what the memory said? Do we know where in the desert we need to go?"

Squirrel looked around. The raft was empty save a monkey, who was so engrossed in a game of cards with himself that it was highly unlikely that he was aware that a uniformed Squirrel and a patchy dog were in the same raft as him. It seemed safe to speak, but Squirrel dropped his voice anyway.

"It said,

> Go, my son, to arid land,
> Where kingly ghosts roam on red sand

221

In a town that speaks of gold
Find a wise woman, tall and old
Back to back she hunts for game
Her spring is rare, and has much fame
Tell her what it is you seek
Don't be too brash, don't be too meek
She will think, and she will chew
Her questions will be chosen few
She will guide you to the brink
Of learning where lies your last drink
But guide is all she can do
The answer, son, must come from you."

Squirrel yawned as he finished speaking. Except for the first two lines of the verse, nothing else made sense to him. "So what do you think?"

Thought lines creased Des's forehead. "I agree, mate, the first two lines have to be the Desert of Blood Kings. That's the only dry land with ghosts of kings. But I've never heard of red sand. And how do we find this tall old lady? What do we do?"

"We do what we've been doing so far. We just keep putting one paw in front of the other and keep hoping for the best," said Squirrel as he yawned and let the wobbly boat rock him to sleep.

The Madame entered her bedroom. She was still cloaked, but had removed the veil covering her face. Her flat, gray features were scrunched in worry.

She dumped herself at her desk and flipped through the pages of the *Bimmau Meow*. She skimmed the news: "Asteroid Shower Expected This Half Moon," "Lady Natasha Blouse Still Missing," "Dog Union Revolt Against Biscuit Price Hike" . . .

She crumpled the newspaper and tossed it on the floor. She was too preoccupied to focus on anything. She looked out her window at the orange morning sky, and her brow furrowed further. She had heard all of nothing. If she did not find out where that stupid Squirrel was going, the Colonel would scratch her out as if she were a vermin-infested rat.

If she could just discover who the Colonel was, then perhaps she could find some way to defend herself. But she did not have a smidgen of a clue. And, what was worse, she was certain he had figured out who she was, despite the swaths of black cloth she wrapped herself in.

A hiss drew the fat cat's attention. Slithering toward her was one of her spies—Narva the python.

For the first time in half a moon cycle, the Madame smiled. "Any news?" she asked, opening the window to let Narva in.

"Yesss, Madame. Ssquirrel isss on the Gavial Raft with the dog. I sssaw them. They were going to the Desert of Blood Kings," hissed the snake.

"Do you know where in the desert they are going?"

"Sssorry. The voices were too sssoft."

"Hmmm . . . no matter. Now you go back, Narva. And find out what you can about where that red splinter-in-my-behind is, and what he's up to."

Narva the python hissed and her tongue darted in and out of her mouth. "Madame, you have a bonusss for me." It was not a question.

"Yes, yes," said the Madame, flicking her paw. "There should be a piglet fattening himself in the garden."

"Thank you, Missss." The python bobbed her head and slid out of the room.

The Madame watched as Narva slithered down the orchard toward her unsuspecting young prey. Slowly her thick body circled the pig. By the time the pudgy pink pig realized he was in danger, it was too late. Narva wrapped her body around him, squeezing him tightly. Only when the pig's body went limp did Narva swing her jaw wide open and gobble him up—fresh, pink, and juicy.

The Madame looked away and let out a purr. Snakes were sickening, but they were excellent informants. And Narva had been particularly useful. She rose from her seat and put on the black cloth that covered her face. With a small shiver, she stalked off to the cave to find the Colonel.

At least, this time, she had good news for him.

The sun pulsed in Squirrel's eyelids. He pressed his lashes together, trying to squeeze out the morning light. His neck was stiff, and his narrow shoulder blades throbbed as his back pressed against hard planks. Trying to get comfortable, he rolled onto his stomach and toppled off the bench, face-first on the damp ferry floor.

"Hmmph," he grunted, rubbing his body as he sat up and opened his eyes. He blinked.

The river, which had been wide with lush green shores when he had fallen sleep, was now barely wide enough for the Gavial Raft to plough through. The banks were lined with the thinnest strip of grass, balding into miles of dirty yellow sand.

"Of all the Confounded Canine Conundrums! This sand's not red! Where's the red sand?" Des was awake, and leaning over the ledge of the raft so far that he could almost touch the bank.

"It'll be here somewhere," said Squirrel groggily as he hoisted himself onto the bench next to Des.

"But which way should we walk? This place is as empty as the sun's surface," said Des. "Should we ask that monkey?" The monkey was sitting in exactly the same position, playing cards, as he had been when Squirrel dozed off.

"No, it's too risky," said Squirrel. After Azulfa, Squirrel had decided not to confide in any more strangers. Not only his life, but also Des's, depended on them remaining as quiet as possible. "We have to find the sand ourselves."

Des's face puffed up like a dumpling. He was going to speak, but Squirrel looked so firm that he gave in. "Okay, your call. We'll figure it out when we get off the Gavial Raft—which is now, it seems."

Sure enough, the stream had dwindled into nothingness. This was their stop.

"Let's go," said Squirrel. He got up, dropping his and Des's fare of four bizkits into a tin jar by the door. As the wooden squares tinkled against the tin, the gavials lifted their jaws and the door to the ferry swung open.

"Squirrel, let me pay for something at least," said Des, reaching into his pockets and pulling out a tiny purse that could not possibly have held more than three bizkits.

"You crazy? Look at all you've done for me—I mean, you're in the Desert of Blood Kings, for parrot's sake. The least I can do is pay for you."

Des looked down at his tiny, almost-empty purse and nodded. "Well, all right. But please let me pay for something . . . at some time."

Squirrel grinned back. "You got it! Now, let's go find this red sand!"

"Tell me this, Madame, how is this good news?"

The Colonel's voice was so cold that it made the beads of nervous sweat freeze into icy drops on the Madame's fur. She shivered under her cloak, but hoped that the Colonel could not tell. She could not appear weak.

Steadying her voice, she said, "Well, we know he's in the Desert of Blood Kings."

"And how big is that desert?" The Colonel's words were poisoned darts. "How do you propose to find a midget of a squirrel in such a large desert?"

"I . . . I . . . I . . ."

"SHUT UP, YOU FAT FELINE!"

The Colonel's fury erupted like dark lava. He sprang out of his throne and pounced on the Madame, pinning her against the wall. His razor-sharp claws pierced her fat shoulder, and she screamed as a stream of sticky blood trickled down her fur.

When the Colonel spoke, his voice was nothing more

than a soft hiss from under his mask. "Madame, I'm giving you two more moons. If you don't find out what that red rodent is up to by then, your fat body will be a piece of flat, fleshy roadkill. Do you understand?"

For a long moment he continued to pierce her with his claws, and she knew that he wanted nothing more than to mince her like meat at that very moment. But, eventually, he relaxed his grip, snarled, and strode out of the cave.

Madame watched as his tail whipped angrily against his black cloak and, for the first time, pure regret filled her fat belly. She could not believe how eager she had been when the Colonel had first approached her, how badly she had wanted to squash the PetPost Squirrel into nothingness. But now, as she clutched her bloody shoulder, she understood how dangerous her alliance with the Colonel had become for her. Even one slight misstep, even a hint of a faux-paw, and she would probably end up as a gray rug in his living room.

The realization slapped the Madame on her flat face. She removed the veil from her face, and her yellow eyes narrowed. She would not let this so-called Colonel threaten her. She had to protect herself . . . starting right now.

A DESERT AND A DEER

Squirrel and Des trudged through the scorching desert. The landscape had turned from muddy yellow to pretty gold, and the sand had become soft under their heels. But it was peak afternoon, so it was too hot and they were too lost to appreciate the scenery.

"Okay, Squirrel, enough's enough," burst Des. "I'm not taking a step more till you tell me what happened with Zulf." Des's breath had such force that a cloud of sand flew off the ground straight into his eyes.

Squirrel sighed. "I guess this is as bad a time as any to tell you."

"You think," grunted Des, fluttering his eyelids like moth wings to get the sand out.

Squirrel understood Des's frustration. Their furs were basted in sweat, the scorching sand had made their heels peel, they had no food, their throats could have been coated in rock salt—and they were no closer to red sand or kingly ghosts.

"Des, remember when I went into the tomb outside Mellifera? Two Kowas knew I was there. They came looking for me."

"How'd you know that they were looking for you?" asked Des. "I thought it was a coincidence . . ."

"Des, the Kowas were talking about me. Someone had told them to look in Mellifera, specifically in the Bone Tomb. And who could it possibly have been? I mean, the only people who knew about the Bone Tomb were you, me, and . . ."

Des shook his head. "That's hardly conclusive, mate!"

"When I got out of the tomb, Azulfa was looking at me as though she were shocked to see me out of there alive."

"That might've just been one of her funny expressions. I mean, Azulfa can throw some real odd looks, can't she? I can't read her face at all," said Des.

"No, I'm sure she hadn't expected me to come out of the cave," said Squirrel. "And why're you defending her?" He felt himself getting annoyed at Des for the first time.

"I'm not . . ."

Squirrel went on. "How do you explain the Kowas coming into the tomb? You didn't see them come in, did you?"

"No, I didn't. If I had, I would have come in to warn you, or at least helped you fight those thugs."

"Well, if you didn't see them, then Azulfa must've, right? Especially with her supersonic hearing," said Squirrel, looking at Des as though daring the dog to challenge him.

"Good point," said Des slowly, scratching his head.

"I just can't believe I didn't see it sooner," ranted Squirrel, springing up. "Azulfa's been watching me from day one . . . maybe even before the wedding. She led the Kowas to my tree cottage, she didn't save me when I almost drowned, she set up a trail to the Bone Tomb, and she would have had them show up in Darling." Squirrel paused, taking in a breath of the hot, dry air.

"But why didn't she just kill us? Or at least, deliver us to the Kowas like little sacks of meat," said Des. Despite the heat, Squirrel thought he saw Des shiver.

"Because of the seclasion ladder. Once Azulfa realized that I'm the only one with the clues to Brittle's Key, she needed to keep me alive. That's the thing with seclasion, right? No one can find the clues except for me. If I'm gone, the trail is lost," said Squirrel, the words leaping from his mouth like trapped frogs. "But as soon as we found the key, she would've lobbed our heads off. She's a baddie, Des!"

Des crumpled his patched ears as though they were used paper napkins. "You're right. Good thing you shook her off our trail. You think there's any way she could find us here?"

"I don't think so," said Squirrel, frowning. "The only one who knows where we are is Tupten. And he promised me that he'd never tell anyone I asked for directions to the desert—"

"Who's Tupten?" asked Des.

"Khoy's uncle. He's a Micetro. He's the one who told me to use the Gavial Raft to get to the Desert of Blood Kings. We can trust him. He owes me big. I think everyone in Darling owes me big . . ."

"Owes you big? How?"

Squirrel told Des about the Flame Flints of Rodentia, how he had found them in the Bone Tomb, and how he had returned them.

When Squirrel was done, Des whistled. "Mate, that's incredible. Absolutely bon-a-hide crazy! I can't believe I missed all this! I feel like we've been on two different journeys. Not fair, mate."

"Hey, it wasn't all fun, you know. In fact, I don't think any part of it was . . ."

"You escaped the Kowas, you met the Micetros, *you gave*

fire back to a city . . . ," jabbered Des. "We've unzipped two memories; only got one more special drink to go. And it's in this desert somewhere. We just need to know in which direction we should walk!"

"Where you wanna go?"

Squirrel turned around so quickly that his knees almost buckled. That was not Des's voice.

His eyes darted everywhere, searching for the speaker. But the only person in sight was a very confused-looking Des.

"Who was that?" asked Des.

"I thought it was coming from that direction. But there's no one there," said Squirrel.

"You don't think . . . Nah . . . Impossible," started Des.

"What?" said Squirrel.

"You don't think . . ." Des flushed. "You don't think that was the voice of a ghost, do you?"

Squirrel stared at Des. It couldn't be a ghost! Could it?

"Isn't the Desert of Blood Kings famous for ghosts?" said Des, his eyes darting around like a pinball. "We both heard the voice, and there's no one here except for you, me, and the desert." Des gestured wildly at the sand around him.

"I don't know. I guess the Desert of Blood Kings is known to be haunted. . . . It's possible it was a ghost," said Squirrel, not liking the words coming out of his mouth.

"Oh! Gimme a break, you 'yperactive ninnies!" pelted a strange voice, catching Des so off guard that he yelped and jumped toward Squirrel.

"I ain't a g'ost!" said the voice, scudding like a boomerang through the hot, grainy air.

"Please show yourself," said Squirrel, pulling the last of his courage from somewhere under his gall bladder.

Sure enough, two gnarled black horns and a shadowy face appeared on the top of the tallest sand dune.

"What now?" murmured Des as a muscular copper deer appeared on top of the hillock.

The deer grunted and trotted down the dune. The deer's left cheek was covered in scars, and his eyes were as hard as stones. He looked much more like a fox than a deer—a fox with a set of sharp, scary horns.

"Umm . . . hello," said Squirrel, who was sweating as though he were in a sauna.

"So you lost or 'umthin'? Where d'ya two gerbils think you're goin'?" asked the fox-deer, with a leer so deep it seemed to be hewn into his face.

"We're looking for red sand," said Des, too busy keeping his eyes on the deer's squiggly horns to beat around the dunes.

"Red sand? So the sun's boiled your brains, 'as it? Red sand . . . rubbish!"

"Rubbish?" gulped Des.

"Ya not familiar with rubbish, pipsqueaks? Ya know . . . garbage? Trash? A pile of ferret feces! There ain't nothing as red sand!" said the deer.

Squirrel and Des just stared at each other. It was hard to tell who looked more disappointed. Finally Squirrel said, "We need to find a town in this desert."

"An' why should I 'elp two buffoons who've gone 'n managed to lose 'emselves in the Desert of Blood Kings?"

"We have money," said Des.

"Money?" The deer stopped with a sudden jerk. His cheeks tightened, and the leer slid straight off his face.

Squirrel smiled. Apparently, Des had guessed the magic word. "Yes. We can pay you," Squirrel said with a casual shrug.

"How much?" asked the deer, his beady black eyes narrowing.

"Ten gromms," said Squirrel.

"Gromms, huh? So ya're from Bimmau?"

Squirrel nodded. "Do we have a deal?"

The deer seemed to consider the offer. Then he lowered his head so that his sharp horns were just inches from Squirrel's face. Squirrel was sure that the deer could slice him and Des to shreds in four easy movements. "Twenty gromms, nothing less!"

"Ummm . . . that's a bit much, isn't—"

"Take it or leave it," snorted the deer, his eyes thinning to slits.

"Oye! That's highway robbery!" said Des, but Squirrel just blinked. He didn't want to be bullied by the deer, but they needed his help.

"I'll give you the money if you can get us to where we need to be," Squirrel said.

"And where's that, gerbil?"

"*And* you stop calling us gerbils," added Des.

The deer looked at Des and sneered again, but this time Des stuck out his own chest and gave the deer a curt nod. After a long battle of looks, the deer turned to Squirrel and muttered, "Fine, now where d'ya need to go?"

"We're not sure. We need to go somewhere with red sand . . ."

"I already told ya, you deaf dodo, there ain't no red sand here!"

"Hey, how 'bout no more name calling at all, huh?" chimed Des, his paws clenching.

"Let's try to be civil," said Squirrel, looking from the deer to the dog. "I was saying, we need to go somewhere with red sand that is haunted by ghosts of kings. Can you help us?"

"Don't tell me you're goin' g'ost hunting!" said the deer,

but his expression was not quite as scornful as it had been earlier.

Squirrel ignored the tingle in his tail and said, "Is there any place that could fit that description? Is there any town in these parts with kingly ghosts and red sand?"

The deer spoke slowly, as though calculating the gromm value of each word. "My town's the only one with a 'istory of kings. Some idiots 'ave claimed that they've seen g'osts there."

Squirrel ruffled the fur on his arms, trying to be patient. "Any other towns have ghosts?"

"Other towns 'ave g'osts, sure. But mine's the only one where there are g'osts of kings," said the deer. "But, for the tenth time, the sand ain't red."

"Is it maybe a bit orange?" asked Des hopefully.

"It's the same color as my bottom. Plain, pure gold," grunted the deer, turning around and sticking his backside in Des's face.

"All right, all right! We may as well go there and check it out, what do you say, Des? How far are we from your town?" asked Squirrel.

"Close enough. I'll take ya. You payin' me now or w'at?" asked the deer.

"We'll pay you when we get there," said Des, jumping in.

"All right, dog."

"The name's Des. And this is Squirrel."

"Good for you," said the deer. Then he grunted, "I'm Snear of Gandgoon."

"Gandgoon . . . is that the town we're heading to?"

"Yes, now 'urry up. I don't 'ave all day," said Snear, trotting off with Des and Squirrel trying to keep up with him.

They walked in thick dry silence until Snear asked, "But whaddya need in this town?"

"We're not looking for anything; we're looking for someone," said Squirrel, staring straight ahead.

"Who?"

Snear's curiosity made Squirrel a bit uneasy, but he answered anyway. "A friend of my mother's. Just want to pay my respects," said Squirrel, trying to be as vague as possible.

"Ah! Ya've come all the way to the Desert of Blood Kings searchin' for a friend? Just to pay your respects? Lemme tell ya one thing, you'll find no friends 'ere!"

"Whaddya mean?" asked Des.

"This ain't no nice land of friendship and butterflies. It's harsh. We live for ourselves. We steal. We play. We gamble. A friend's a friend one day and an enemy the next—that's our way . . . And that's the way of anyone who 'as been in the desert for a while."

239

His laugh was coarse, and hard, and jabbing, and it made Squirrel's fur bristle.

Then the deer said, "If there's one thing to know 'bout the Desert of Blood Kings, it's that nothin'—absolutely nothin'—is as clear as it seems."

Though Snear was decidedly nasty, Squirrel was glad for his help. Even before the sun had begun to set, Snear had led them past the dunes to an endless plate of flat sand. "It looks like a golden pancake," Squirrel said.

"This is the Basin of Bodies. It surrounds Gandgoon."

"The Basin of Bodies? Why's it called that?" choked Des, his tail twitching nervously.

"'Ere, on this very sand, the bloodiest battle in known 'istory took place," whispered Snear, scooping a fistful of sand in his palm. "Ages ago, Gandgoon was ruled by the King of Gazelles, King Bereste. Everyone who lived 'ere was royalty. Under Bereste's rule the city grew. Gandgoon was full of silk and sacks of spices. They say that the city smelled of cardamom."

"Sounds yummy," said Des with a wistful smile as he rubbed his tummy.

"Gandgoon got richer and more merchants came to the city, but Bereste's only son, Prince Bari, got mighty mad. 'E was sick of the noise the traders made in 'is city. So, one morning, 'e summoned all the merchants to the town square and dunked the traders' faces in yellow turmeric powder. After 'e had 'umiliated them, 'e kicked them out of the city and told them never to return."

"'Course, when King Bereste found out, 'e was furious with Bari and 'e apologized to the people of the city on behalf of 'is son. But the damage was done."

"How so?" asked Squirrel.

"Bari didn't realize that one of the traders 'e had 'umiliated was the cousin of the Mud Warrior Jackal. When the Jackal found out, 'e was as angry as a pot of boilin' oil. 'E wanted to teach all of Gandgoon a lesson. So 'e and 'is army attacked. They killed every creature on the battlefield. Then they pillaged the town and looted everything."

"What about the women?" Squirrel asked.

"The womenfolk killed themselves in grief. Just like that, in one sunset, the whole of Gandgoon was wiped out. Finished. And this place—the Basin of Bodies—is where the battle took place. This entire patch of land was a pile o' corpses. The sand was all bloody . . ."

"The sand was bloody?" asked Des.

"Didn't I just say that?" snapped Snear.

"But if the sand was soaked with blood, it must've . . . been red, right . . . ?" said Des, his voice trembling.

"What kind of moronic question is that? 'Course it was red!" said the deer. "Now 'urry up!"

But Des did not budge; he just stood rooted in the flat sand. "Red sand," he whispered hoarsely to Squirrel. "Red sand! Red, bloody sand! It fits. The town must be Gandgoon!" Des grinned so widely that his smile almost challenged the big, bright, late-afternoon sun. "And it's the only place that has seen the ghosts of kings wandering around. It must be this place."

Squirrel scratched his furry chin. "I hope you're right, Des. I really do. I guess we'll know soon enough. If Gandgoon speaks of gold, we'll know we're in the right place. That's the next line of the memory."

"Did someone say gold?" Snear stood a leg's length from them, his ears pricked to attention.

"No, Squirrel said he could use something cold . . . you know, to drink . . . ," said Des quickly.

"Hmm . . . well, come along, whiners," said Snear, turning around and trotting off.

"STOP CALLING US NAMES!" bellowed Des.

"Yea, well, don't 'old ya breath. Anyway, we're almost there, so you wanna pay me now?" said Snear, licking his dark, scabby lips.

"Is that all you can think of? Money?" said Des.

"In case you didn't know, money's useful, you turnip. Plus, it's Blackstubbs season." And before either of them could ask what exactly Blackstubbs was, Snear pointed to the distance and said, "Well, it doesn't matter. There it is. There's Gandgoon!"

A Tricky City

Squirrel cursed under his breath. It looked as though someone had punctured the sky, and was pouring oily darkness onto an entire city. Everything was dim, and gray, and black.

Though Squirrel's body clenched with warning, he followed Snear toward the dark city. He looked over to check on Des. The dog was jogging right beside him.

The sight of his friend's face, wrinkled with worry and determination, gave Squirrel a burst of courage. With a deep breath he plunged straight forward, into the blackness of Gandgoon.

Moments later, Squirrel found himself in a mess of dark alleys. He shivered as the shadows that looked like gigantic bats flung themselves at him. His throat constricted as the musty smell of old cloth and older sweat fell on him. He pinched his nose and stepped forward, letting the pulsing darkness of Gandgoon gobble him up.

Snear was waiting for them in front of the alley, his tail whipping from side to side.

Whippppsht. Whippppsht.

The sound of the tail slicing through the air made the S branded on Squirrel's arm prickle. He thought of his boss, Bacchu. Of the whip that he had threatened Squirrel with many a time, but never actually used. Now that Squirrel had done the unthinkable and deserted Bacchu, he did not think he would be so lucky. If he returned to Bimmau a no-name slave, he was certain Bacchu would not hesitate to lash him properly a few times.

That is, if he managed to return to Bimmau *alive*.

"There you are. I thought you were trying to gimme the slip," said Snear, bringing Squirrel back to the hot, dry, dark present.

"I wish," mumbled Des, shrinking into a pit of shadow.

"Don't 'ell me you pair of papayas are scared, are you?" said Snear with a deep smirk.

"Of this? Bah," said Squirrel, lying as loudly as he could. He did not need Snear to know he was so scared that he could have wet his only pair of pants. "Now, let's see what your Gandgoon is all about."

"Oh bleedin' bladders!" said Des as they ducked behind a smoky wall.

They might as well have walked into a nightmare. Dark tents hung everywhere, like hulking bodies of ghosts. Worse, they were packed with terribly unpleasant things: angry skulls, scowling deer heads, cards made of graying bone, and whips that looked like snakes. Customers pushed each other out of the way, clacking, yelling, and haggling. The air smelled of old mildew.

"'Kay, we're here. Cough up the thirty gromms," said Snear, pushing a desert cat out of his way.

"Nice try. But it was twenty gromms," said Des. "We agreed on twenty, and that's what you'll get." As Des spoke, Squirrel pulled him out of the way of a charging bull with mad red eyes.

"I could've bet my bottom that it was thirty . . . ," said Snear.

"It was twenty," said Squirrel firmly, giving Snear four mud patties, each worth five gromms, from his pouch. "Here, take it . . ."

But the deer did not move. He just stared at Squirrel's money pouch as though it were a newborn unicorn. Finally the deer reached out his hoof and Squirrel dropped the money into it.

"You know, Squirrel, if you 'ave cash, you could front me some. I'll play some Blackstubbs for you. I'll double it and you keep 'alf the profits. What say you? Easiest gold you'll ever make." Snear's voice was now sickly sweet. His eyes did not leave Squirrel's pouch once.

"No, thanks," said Squirrel, quickly tucking his pouch away.

"Think. You don't 'ave to do a thing," said Snear, stepping out of a shadow and lowering his voice. "Just sit and watch. In fact, why don't you just give me that pouch of yours and I'll go to the tables. You go enjoy Gandgoon. Find your mother's friend. By nightfall your pouch will be twice as heavy."

"Snear, I'm not giving you even so much as half a gromm more," said Squirrel, who just wanted to get his memory and get out of this sinister city. "Not unless you tell me where I can find the woman I'm looking for."

"'Ow much?" said Snear, his black lips throbbing with excitement.

"Mate, this may be a bad idea," whispered Des to Squirrel. "I mean . . ."

"I know, Des. But who else will we ask?" whispered Squirrel. As Des's shoulders drooped, Squirrel turned back to Snear. "Ten gromms. For one answer."

As he spoke, Squirrel watched Snear's scarred face twist into the oddest expression imaginable. The flesh of his cheeks began to lump together, his eyes squinted, and his forehead stretched like a Japanese fan. It was as though the muscles of his face were being yanked in all directions by invisible wires. Squirrel had to stifle a gasp as he realized that this was Snear's version of a smile.

"Agreed," said Snear.

"We are looking for a tall, wise woman who fits this description: *Back to back she hunts for game; Her spring is rare, and has much fame.*" He crossed his paws, hoping the deer would give them an answer.

Snear listened, scratching his head. His lips twitched, but he said nothing.

"You have to answer us to get paid," said Des, hopping like a jitterbug from one leg to another.

Snear shook his horns and grunted, "I know who you're looking for. She sits right there, in that blue tent. But I would not go to meet her if I were you."

"Why not?" asked Squirrel. "What you playing at now, Snear?"

"Don't believe me? Read the sign for yourself," said Snear.
Sure enough, outside the tent, a big black sign read:

The price to enter here
Is higher than you may think
I take every cent in your pocket
But give you Gandgoon's best drink
And once you drink this splendid thing
No matter what you've seen or read
You will be so entirely happy
That you will lose your head

Squirrel rubbed his eyes. This lady had "Gandgoon's best
drink." This was it!

They were just about to dart into the tent when Snear
yanked Des back. "Where you going? You owe me ten
gromms, you pus-filled poodle."

"Here, here! Take your ten gromms," said Squirrel, handing Snear the cash. He was almost one foot into the tent
when Des pulled him back.

"Not so quick, mate," said Des. "Read the sign. It says she
will take every cent in your pocket. Shouldn't we think this
through a bit?"

Squirrel thought his friend was suffering from heat stroke.

"What's there to think about, Des?" He did not bother keeping the hysteria out of his voice. "Think of what we've been through. What do a few gufflings matter now?" He tried to break free of the dog's paw, but Des's grip was steady.

"Listen. It's just . . ." Des lowered his voice so that only Squirrel could hear him. "Maybe it makes sense for us to hide your pouch out here somewhere. Let's just take my pouch inside. That way we lose less money."

Squirrel stopped struggling. Perhaps Des had a point. They could try making do with one pouch. He looked around. No one was near them. Even Snear had turned away and was trotting off into the hodge-podge of darkness. The extra ten gromms had given him quite a spring in his step.

"Okay, let's bury my pouch right here," said Squirrel. He shoved his pouch into the sand and covered it quickly with a heap of dust. Des had just marked the spot with the last Raisin D'Etty wrapper from his pocket when Squirrel's patience dried up.

"Done! Now in we go!" Squirrel pulled Des into the tent. He was ready to get away from the still-scorching evening sun. He was ready to meet this woman. He was ready for the last drink.

Kneeling on the floor was a gazelle sharpening a sickle. Blades of every shape and size—pocket daggers, spears,

double-edged knives—lay spread out around her like a peacock's tail. A sign that read HUNTING EQUIPMENT was propped beside her.

Squirrel took a small step toward the lady. She had a pair of swordlike horns sharper than any of the blades on the floor, yet her face was delicate. Her hide looked old, yet her body was knotted with muscles.

"Sorry to bother you, miss, but we've come all the way to Gandgoon looking for you. We need a portion of your special drink."

The gazelle looked up at him. Her eyes were a baby pink—the color of a baby rose, of a baby's cheeks. She lifted herself off the floor and leaped over her arrangement of blades. She smiled. "I'm Wipsara. And pray tell, what are your names?"

"I'm Squirrel, and this is Des," said Squirrel, inhaling deeply. The tent smelled wonderfully different from the rest of Gandgoon—of dewy flowers and vanilla. He let the smell seep into his lungs, his stomach, his entire being. It filled his senses like a warm lullaby.

"The drink I have is Cactus Meat. I'll give you some, but I need my fee first." She lifted her hoof, which had been hollowed out. Presumably to collect money.

Squirrel's feet began to sink into the sand. "Sure," he said,

252

gesturing to Des. He was too intoxicated by the smell and her eyes to say anything more than that.

"I'm assuming you each want to purchase one?" she asked.

"Yes, please," said Des, emptying his wallet into her hoof. He then waited as Wipsara patted him down to make sure he had not hidden any change anywhere on his being.

"Okay, what about your payment?" asked Wipsara, turning to Squirrel.

"Uhmm . . . I have no money," said Squirrel as Wipsara patted him down as well.

"Then only one of you gets the Cactus Meat. Who will it be?" asked Wipsara, flicking her sickle between Squirrel and Des.

Des cleared his throat. "Squirrel," he said. His stomach rumbled so loudly it could have been rolling thunder. Poor, hungry Des.

Crick. Crick. Crick.

Squirrel turned toward Wipsara. She had picked up a cactus stem and was shaving the thorns off it with a skill that would have made the fiercest of panthers proud. She lifted the naked, plump, oval stem and sliced it open. She then handed it to Squirrel, her pink eyes twinkling.

Squirrel did not wait for a fraction of a moment. Thrusting

his paw into the stem, he scooped out a palm-full of clear, succulent meat and sucked the gel-like paste down. It was cool and thick and salty and bitter. It was ointment to his insides.

He shoveled another fistful of the meat into his mouth. When he could not scoop out any more, he put his lips to the stem and squeezed the empty, fleshy cactus into his mouth, trying to catch every last dribble of the gel.

As he licked his lips, a current ran through Squirrel's being. But it wasn't the painful current he had expected. Instead he felt like he was melting—into a puddle of warm plum cider. His eyes grew droopy and his mind began to swirl. He felt his lungs fill with the smell of vanilla, and petals, and fresh mist.

Squirrel let his eyes fall on Wipsara, who was now looking back at him, smiling and blinking. He saw a flash of silver sparkle somewhere around her. It was like magic. Another flash and Squirrel realized it was her sickle, which she was flicking from one hand to the other. He smiled broadly as she sauntered toward him.

She stood a butterfly's length away from Squirrel, her eyes glowing like pink pearls. Then she whispered, "Now you must pay me my real price."

In slow motion, Squirrel watched Wipsara's smile turn

into a hungry growl. Her baby-pink eyes turned the color of a hungry tiger's gums.

He watched as her supple body went tight. He watched as she raised her sickle above his head, poised to lob it off in one clean swoop. And all Squirrel could do was stand there. Planted like a pumpkin. Smiling stupidly. Waiting for Wipsara to bring her sickle down on him.

Then it all happened. A billow of dust. A flash of silver. A sharp yelp. A burst of blood. And, then, a familiar scream. "Mate! Run!"

Squirrel's brain sparked to life. Somehow his head was still on his shoulders. He did not know how, or why, or what had happened. The only thing he could trust was Des screaming, "Run!"

So he did. He ran from Wipsara. He ran from the spring of her hind legs. He ran from her blood-pink eyes. And, most importantly, he ran from her sickle.

DESOLATE AND DESPERATE!

Though he knew he shouldn't, Squirrel paused for a moment, stopping to look at where he had buried his money pouch. His Raisin D'Etty wrapper was still there. His pouch was not.

"It's gone," he said, noticing hoof marks that looked a lot like Snear's in the sand.

"Now's not the time, Squirrel!" shouted Des, pulling Squirrel along. "Just keep running."

Only when they got to a noisy market did Des stop. Squirrel turned to Des. "What happened in there?"

"Your eyes went glassy," said Des, huffing for breath. "Then

I saw . . . *oof* . . . her swing that sickle toward your head . . . *whoof* . . . and I knew she was going to attack us."

"But what saved me? How come I'm not . . . dead?" gulped Squirrel.

"I grabbed a spear from the floor and threw it at her. I got her in the shoulder. Just in time too," said Des, still panting. "It was the Cactus Meat. As soon as you ate it, your eyes turned to rubber. Thank the dogs above I didn't eat it."

Squirrel's heart pounded. He had almost let himself be decapitated by Wipsara. He breathed in, trying to focus on what was going on around him.

A small desert lizard was creeping up the stall on their right. As soon as the shopkeeper, a stout goat, was distracted by some customers, the lizard snuck his long tail into a box on the counter and flicked a silver jewelry case off it. It fell straight into his sinewy arms. He clicked his tongue happily and crept away.

Des, who was watching the scene as well, shook his head. "It's an evil town, mate. A town of thieves."

Squirrel nodded and reached into his empty pocket. "I almost got killed. We got robbed. We have no money. And we're stuck in a desert. How did this happen?" Big, fat drops of frustration threatened to drip down his cheeks.

"I don't know . . . ," said Des, plonking his bum on the sand. He buried his face in his hands. His stomach churned loudly.

They sat there, squirrel and dog—desolate and desperate—in the middle of the desert, watching the inky night set in. A big python slithered past them, but they were too tired to notice. They heard a coyote screaming "Cold towels for sale!" but they could not buy any. They watched a herd of goats playing an intense game of Blackstubbs, but they had no money to gamble. They smelled the salty, smoky smell of crisping bacon, but they could not afford any.

They sat in numbing silence. Until Des broke it. "Don't worry. We'll find her." His voice drooped with false hope.

Squirrel could not get himself to speak. His mind was too busy kneading the words of the last clue, trying to figure out where he had gone wrong. Arid land, kingly ghosts, red sand, a town that speaks of gold. Gandgoon fit the description. But he had not found the tall, wise woman. Maybe she was not around anymore . . .

Des interrupted his thoughts again.

"Squirrel, maybe we should get some water. After all, we may have a long journey ahead of us. We've come all the way here. . . . We might as well try to get some water."

Squirrel frowned. "The water will probably cost us more

than both of our livers put together. And we don't have a gromm on us."

"But if we don't drink some water, there won't be a journey, mate. We'll become two dried-up prunes. We really need water." Des jumped up and grabbed the first creature who passed them. It was a stork wearing a tattered turban.

"Sir, may I ask you a question?"

"Quick, dog. Quick. I got bidness that needs attendin'," said the stork.

"Can I get a drink of water here somewhere? Without paying any money?" he asked.

The stork frowned. "'Ow much sugarcane you been chewin', dog? Everyone who comes to Gandgoon knows you can find water for free only at the Oasis Spring."

"So we can just go there and get the water?" said Squirrel, his cheeks stretching with hope for the very first time.

"No!" said the stork, looking at Squirrel as though he were a mute muppet. "You gotta convince the guardian of the spring to let you have some. And she be old and she be nutty. You have to play her for water. Only if you beat her will she let you have a sip."

Squirrel did not care. His throat was as dry as burnt toast. He needed water. He would do anything right now to see this nutty old woman with the spring.

Suddenly Squirrel's eyes brightened. "SPRING!" he cried. *"Her spring is rare, and has much fame! Her spring!* We thought her spring meant someone's walk. But what if it's talking about the spring of the oasis?"

Des curled his paw around his ear and stared at Squirrel. "Mate, aren't we just grasping at straws?"

"Well, it's possible, isn't it?" said Squirrel, desperate to cling to this idea. "And the woman is old, too. We should go there at the break of dawn."

"But Squirrel, we don't know if the lady who guards the oasis is tall. Or wise. Plus how is she possibly hunting for game if she's guarding the oasis?" said Des.

Squirrel paused, looking his friend straight in the eye. "I know I may be wrong. But Des, what else do we possibly do?"

"They're in Gandgoon, sir," said the Madame.

"You are sure about this, Madame?"

The Madame tilted her chin up. "My source has confirmed it."

"What is he possibly doing there?" said the Colonel, pressing his fingers together.

"Sire, I don't know why you fail to recognize that the PetPost Squirrel's skull is nothing more than a bucket of melted dung. He probably forgot what he was doing and went to make a quick buck in Gandgoon. I really think you're handling this all wrong! If you know what you're looking for, why can't we just go ransack his tree cottage and get what you need?"

The Colonel was silent for a moment. When he spoke, his voice was the chilliest whisper. "Madame, do you presume to insult my intentions? Or my intelligence?"

His words hit her like ice picks, crumbling her sheet of confidence. "Sire, I was just saying that maybe you could tell me what you need. I could fetch it for you."

"Madame, I will say this once. NEVER question me. Or my methods. Do you understand, you fat, gray beanbag?"

"Yes . . . yes, sire."

"Now get out of here."

As the Madame left the cave, her face burned. Today, she decided, she would not go straight home. Instead she squeezed herself and her belly into a dark hollow just outside the cave so that she was perfectly hidden. She waited.

The Colonel had called her fat and gray. He knew who she was.

She frowned; she was not safe anymore. She had to discover who the Colonel was, what he was after, and what he could possibly want with the PetPost Squirrel.

Just as Madame Sox was planning how to follow the Colonel

home, she heard a familiar voice. She pressed her ear against the wall.

"We know he's in Gandgoon. Shouldn't we just catch him there?" said the voice.

"We could. But he might not have found it yet." This was the Colonel.

"Even then, we might as well capture him. We can make him find it," said the mystery voice. "Imagine if we find the Key of Brittle. We can break Bimmau—we can make it what it's supposed to be."

"We shall. As soon as we get our paws on Brittle's Key, we can use it to take back all of Bimmau; everyone else will serve us—the way it used to be. We will be the masters, like we ought to be. And we can make anyone we want our slave. Brittle's Map will force anyone and everyone to obey us. The first one I'll enslave is that Sox. She is annoying, sure, but she does her bidding with singular determination. She'd make a good slave."

"But, Colonel, you're sure Squirrel will find the key?"

"I think he will. But, if I know anything about the Keepers of the Key, like old Mr. Falguny, it is this: They would have disguised the key as something else. In fact, Squirrel may not even know that he has it. That is where our chief advantage lies," said the Colonel.

"How sublimely tricky! But, I confess, I cannot help wondering how on earth that little red creature was left such an incredibly important thing?"

Mrs. Sox, hidden in the corner, with her flat face sweating with worry, wondered the exact same thing.

MAKING FAMILY

Squirrel wandered down a sandy lane that glowed like a silver ribbon in the dark morning. Though he had not slept at all and had made it through the night without a sip of water, he was more alert than ever.

As they walked toward the oasis, the dark blue skin of night peeled off the sky. Cotton balls of clouds clotted the horizon, broken with orange scars. The sun rolled into the sky. In the light, Squirrel saw a big dune. Shimmery white ripples of reflected water danced across the sandy surface. His throat gurgled.

"Now, that's more like it," woofed Des happily. "Water!

Yes, Squirrel, I think that today might be a much better day than yesterday."

Squirrel smiled. Today, he hoped, would be a better day indeed.

Squirrel hiccupped with excitement. He was standing next to the oasis, outside a tall white tent, waiting to meet the guardian of the spring. The sound of the water, slurping happily, tickled his ears. He was about to enter when a voice boomed from inside.

"Xerice, please! I need a barrel of water!"

A lady spoke. "Good sir, how long have you known me?"

Squirrel hiccupped harder as he saw a long shadow creep up the tent wall; the shadow began to bob up and down like a giant air puppet.

The loud voice yelled back, "Too long!"

"Have I ever given water to anyone without losing at Making Family first?" asked the lady.

The loud voice harrumphed. "No."

"Do you think I would choose this glorious sunny morning to change that?"

The other voice went silent, but Squirrel could hear a series of wheezes and mumbles from inside the tent. Finally the loud voice said, "You know what, Xerice? Sometimes I think your heart is almost as blistered as your hide. I'm leaving now, but I'll be back before the day is over!"

"Would you believe that I'm happy to hear it?" said the so-called Xerice, her voice shaking with chuckles. As she laughed, the tent flared open and a desert goat with a red beard stomped out, digging his hooves into the sand. Looking at Squirrel and Des, the goat said, "Try your luck, but know this—Xerice loses only if she wants to. And, with the way she's been recently, you're better off stuffing a straw into this darned sand and sucking for water than winning a drop from her." And with that dry advice, the goat stalked off, muttering and shaking his heavy head.

"Gee, thanks for the encouragement," said Des, yanking the curtain open. They entered the tent.

Squirrel's jaw dropped.

He was staring at a giant trunk topped with what looked like an oversize rugby ball. The ball was moving.

It took Squirrel a moment to realize that the ball was actually a face: a face with a snout, little black eyes, a pair of burnt-purple lips that kept chewing something, and teeth worse than a crumbling limestone wall. Squirrel dragged his eyes down the curved trunk: it was a long, sun-mottled neck that looked like it had been lopped off and planted straight into the sand.

Squirrel almost screamed—until he saw four long legs tucked under a sturdy, double-humped yellow boulder. A twisted ropelike tail lay beside it.

Des made sense of the sight before Squirrel. "You're a camel!" he said, clapping.

"And that makes you happy?" asked Xerice the camel, raising a thin eyebrow.

"Of course! Camels are tall! Are you very old as well?" yammered Des.

"Do I look young to you, little boy?" Xerice said, looking straight at Des.

Squirrel looked at the mesh of wrinkles around the camel's eyes and knew this lady must be the oldest being in Gandgoon. "Sorry 'bout my friend, Ms. Xerice. It's just that we're looking for a lady who is tall, old, and wise. Do you think you may be her?" asked Squirrel, holding his breath.

Xerice's black eyes pranced with wisps of light. "Do you expect a wise woman to admit that she is indeed wise?"

Squirrel thought about the question. "A real wise woman would not call herself wise. She would not boast."

Des whispered, "Squirrel, I think that was the most long-winded way of her letting us know that she may be the old, tall, wise woman we're looking for. Couldn't she just have said yes?"

If Xerice heard Des, she did not show it. She just stared at them, blinking patiently.

Squirrel decided it was time for him to try his luck. "I need your help, Ms. Xerice; I need some answers. Can you help me?"

"How can I give you answers to questions I don't know?" asked the camel.

Squirrel squared his shoulders. This camel liked to talk in circles. "May I ask you a few questions and will you answer them?" he asked, looking straight into the camel's big eyes.

Xerice chewed a blade of straw. "Son, how many nomads of knowledge do you know?"

Squirrel wanted to groan. "What is a nomad of knowledge?"

"Mate, I think she is a nomad of knowledge," Des whispered in his ear. "They're legendary folk who live a long time and know almost everything. You can ask them anything, but they'll never answer your question straight. Instead they just sort of guide you to the answer yourself."

Squirrel scratched his chin. "All right, so let me just ask her straight up and see what happens."

Turning to the camel, he said, "Ms. Xerice, I need to find a liquid and sip it. I was hoping that you could tell me what liquid it is."

"What do you hope the liquid will do?" asked Xerice slowly.

"If I drink the liquid, it will trigger a memory in my brain. The memory is the final clue in my hunt."

"And what will this clue lead to?" she asked, jerking her long neck.

"A key to a map that my mother left me."

"And why is finding the key important to you?"

"You kidding me?" burst Squirrel. "The key will fix everything. It could give me a name! I won't have to be a slave anymore. No more *Deliver this, Squirrel*. No more *Bring me that, Squirrel*. No more *Go drown in a pond, Squirrel*." The seasons of being bossed around made his chest simmer like an angry witch's cauldron. "And, if that isn't enough, I need to find the key before . . ."

"Before who?" asked Xerice.

"Before the bad guys," blurted out Squirrel, not knowing what else to say. "I need to find the key first. It'll solve all my problems."

Xerice squinted. "So, young one, you hope that the liquid will wash away all your problems?"

"Yes, it will solve my problems."

"But is there a liquid that can universally solve all your problems?" asked Xerice. Squirrel thought he saw her eyes glint and the wrinkles around her lids go taut, as though she were waiting.

"Yes, a universal solvent, if you please," said Des with a giggle.

"Des, this is not a time to joke," said Squirrel. Sometimes Des was just barking mad. Universal solvent? What did that have to do with anything? Universal solvent!

All of a sudden, Squirrel felt something click deep inside his skull. His eyes grew as large as the pool of water in front of him.

"That's it." He felt oddly calm. "I know what liquid I need to drink."

DIPPING AND SIPPING

I need to drink the universal solvent." Of course! The recipe for Peppered Urchin with Zesty Zucchini in Lavender Emulsion from his mother's recipe book flashed in his mind. The last thing mentioned in the recipe was the universal solvent.

Squirrel smiled. The universal solvent had to be it. It dissolved most things. It solved most problems. It was the most important drink. And the most simple.

"What you on, mate? What's the universal solvent?" asked Des.

"Water," said Squirrel simply.

Des went still; Squirrel could almost see the information trickle to his brain. When the dog finally soaked it up, he began to squeal. "The liquid is water! It's water!" He shook like a marionette who had just been electrocuted.

"But do you really think that just plain old water is what you seek?" asked Xerice.

"'Course not," piped Des. "It's water from this spring!"

A smile broke across Xerice's face. "I wonder which one of you is smarter."

"It's him. I would never have figured it out if Des hadn't said 'universal solvent,'" said Squirrel. "Now, Ms. Xerice, could I just steal a sip of the water from the oasis?" His legs twitched.

Xerice shook her head gravely. "The same rule applies to everyone: only someone who can beat me in a game of cards can drink water from this spring."

"Oooff . . . If that's what it takes, sure," said Squirrel, not hiding his impatience.

"So you make everyone who wants even a sip of water play you for it?" asked Des.

"Well, am I not entitled to amuse myself somehow? Is it wrong for me to enjoy a good game as often as I can find one?" Xerice asked, turning to look at Des, her eyes big and buggy.

"'Course . . . 'course you should," stammered Des. "In fact, the clue that led us to you said, *Back to back she hunts for game*. And it seems like you do that!"

"Is that what the clue said?" Xerice asked, turning to Squirrel. "Well, why didn't you just ask anyone in Gandgoon for someone with two backs? Don't you see that *back to back* clearly refers to me?" said Xerice, wiggling her double-humped back. "Now, have either of you played Making Family before?"

Both Squirrel and Des shook their heads.

Xerice smiled. "Better for me, then. Anyhow, I'll tell you how to play. Then let's see where luck takes you. Making Family is played with the same tiles used for Blackstubbs—except the rules of the game are different. Have you seen Blackstubbs' tiles before?"

Squirrel nodded. He was suddenly very glad that he and Des had spent most of the past desperate, thirsty night in Gandgoon staring at the goats' game of Blackstubbs. "The set has four copies of fifteen different tiles."

"And did you notice that the fifteen different pictures can be divided into five families?" said Xerice, laying out the tiles in front of them.

Squirrel looked at the sixty tiles. Each had a random image on it: a walnut, a millipede, a gazelle, a sand dune, a black buck, a sphinx moth, a mirage, a fox, an ant, a peanut, a cactus, an acacia tree, a pistachio, a desert teak, and an oasis.

"I think I see it," said Des as he began to sort the tiles into little stacks. "So the groups are: nuts, insects, plants, animals, and the landscape of the desert. Is that correct?"

Xerice checked the tiles and nodded. "Now, if I keep giving a tile to each of us, one of us will collect all three images of the same family, right?"

"You mean, like a moth, a millipede, and an ant?" said Squirrel, rearranging the tiles.

Xerice nodded. She flipped the tiles facedown, one by one, jumbled them up, and then scooped them into a large stack. "Not that hard, is it?"

"No. And the one who gets the family first wins?" asked Des.

"Are you ready to play?" asked Xerice.

"We've been ready to play since the spring equinox!" said Squirrel. He could not wait for the tiles to be dealt. He needed to win. He needed to find and drink his last liquid— the cool, clear oasis water.

Xerice distributed three tiles to each of them. They each carefully checked their tiles to see what they had been dealt. Then Xerice picked up another tile and flipped it over. It was a pistachio.

Squirrel looked at the pistachio, trying to decide what to

do. In his hand, he had three tiles: a millipede, a peanut, and a mirage. He considered putting down the mirage and picking up the pistachio. But he decided against it.

"Do we all pass?" asked Xerice.

Squirrel and Des nodded, and Xerice flipped over another tile. It was a walnut.

Squirrel groaned. If he had just picked up the pistachio, he could have swapped his millipede for the walnut. He could have won.

"All pass?" asked Xerice, and she flipped another tile. It was a fox.

Des grabbed it immediately and then checked his tiles. A moment later, he pushed two tiles forward: one of the fox, the other of a black buck. "I just need a gazelle. I just need one more tile."

Xerice winked at Des. "And what do you suppose I have?" She showed her tiles—which were an oasis and a sand dune.

Squirrel felt his narrow shoulders shake. If he had put down the mirage earlier, Xerice would have won already!

He looked back at Des's tiles. Luckily, the dog was just one tile away from winning. But then again, so was Xerice.

With a single, pointed purpose, he stared at Xerice as she dealt the next round of tiles.

A *gazelle*, he wished silently. A gazelle. If Des would just get a gazelle, they would beat the camel and win the water.

"Squirrel, I got it!" yelped Des. "It's a gazelle! I won! I won!" He launched his furry body on Squirrel in a happy maul.

Xerice shook her big head. "I suppose you want your reward?"

"Yes!" screamed Squirrel as she began to lift her body in slow jerks. She swung the weight of her humps back and forth till she stood straight on her four pole-vault legs. For a long moment she stood there, peering down at them from her full, glorious height. Then she sauntered over to the water, picked a leaf pitcher with her rubbery lips, and dunked it into the spring. She ambled back to where Squirrel stood.

Squirrel barely managed to plug his desire to scream, "Hurry up!" As soon as the water was within reach, Squirrel grabbed the pitcher from her mouth. He fumbled with the slippery leaf. A few splashes of the precious water spilled onto the sand. Des yelped.

Taking a deep breath, Squirrel tightened his grip on the pitcher and brought it to his lips.

"Well, here it goes," he said, taking a tiny sip of the pure, cool liquid.

The water coursed through his body, inflating every nerve,

making every muscle sigh with pleasure. The tingle of life surged through him.

Squirrel took another swig of the water, this one a little bigger. He handed Des the pitcher and waited for the pain.

It came. A jolt shot down from the base of his neck, arched across his cranium, and sped through the other side of his brain. His skull ripped with fresh slicing currents.

Squirrel clutched his ears. He breathed in. Any moment now his mother's voice would play in his ears. Any moment now he would discover the Key of Brittle. Any moment now his life would change forever.

The moment came. His eardrums quivered as soft words strummed against them and Squirrel got lost in the rhythm of his last, final clue.

Squirrel sat rigid, as though he were a fire-baked brick. He could not believe what he had just heard. He let the words chime through his mind again, slowly.

> *Well done, my son, you got here,*
> *You passed each test, without guides clear,*
> *Now you must solve one last clue*
> *For you're one step from treasure true*
> *Above your desk, in the nook*

In the skin of the big blue book
Lies the key to Brittle's Map
It's bright gold on a piece of scrap
The key lets the map be read
By turning letters on their head
And this key is yours to use
Say it, you'll gain; tell it, you'll lose
Unfurl the truth long concealed
Learn, my son, the power you wield.

Squirrel swallowed. His mind scanned the words again.

"Squirrel, *what did it say?*" asked Des, grabbing Squirrel by his narrow shoulders and shaking him so thoroughly that a few strands of Squirrel's fur flew off his body.

"I'll tell you when we get out of here," said Squirrel in a half whisper. Thanking Xerice for her help, Squirrel darted out of the tent and began to jog.

"Squirrel, what happened? What did the memory say?" panted Des as he chased Squirrel.

"We have to go home," was all Squirrel could say as he kept running.

Des reached out, caught Squirrel's tail with his paw, and pulled him to a stop. "Stop, Squirrel! Why're we going home? What about the key?" Des was looking at him as though he had gone as nuts as a bowl of acorns.

"We're going home 'cos the key is at home, Des," said Squirrel, jumping up and down.

"Squirrel, stop jumping like a jackrabbit. Now tell me what the memory said. Till then, I ain't goin' anywhere."

Squirrel corked his excitement long enough to repeat the words of the memory to Des. When Squirrel was done, Des too was grinning and hopping around like Bugs Bunny.

"I can't believe it. The key's at home! It's been in your room this . . ."

Des never finished his sentence.

Suddenly the dog's eyes grew fat with fear. With a shaking finger, Des pointed to the horizon. "Squirrel, over there."

Squirrel turned to look. The air whooshed out of his lungs and his head began to spin with panic.

Six figures in black cloaks were coming toward them. Only the one in the middle did not wear a hood.

Squirrel felt his numb feet sink into the hot sand.

There, a mere elephant's shadow away, was Azulfa, a smile on her hard face and her black eyes steely with victory.

THE TRUTH ABOUT
MS. CORVIDIUS

RUN!" yelled Des, pivoting on his toe like a clumsy ballerina. He broke into a sprint.

Squirrel did the same. But as plump beads of sweat dripped down his back, Squirrel knew that it was useless. He could never outrun a Kowa. No matter how fast he could run, he could not fly.

Sure enough, Squirrel heard the flutter of wings. A chilly shadow fell across his face. He skidded to a halt as Azulfa dropped onto the sand in front of him and flared her muscular wings to block both Des and himself. Face-to-face, the three stared at one another, each pair of eyes ripe with emotion.

Azulfa moved first.

With a swish she swung her wings out and snapped them together around Squirrel and Des, completely surrounding them. Squirrel tried to move back but was too slow. Before he knew it, he found himself and Des pushed against the strong crow, swept up in a big hug.

"It's so good to see the two of you," she cried.

Squirrel squirmed out of Azulfa's grip and yelled, "Don't touch me, you traitor! Kill me, but don't ever touch me. Drop the act. I know what you're about."

He wanted to push Azulfa away, punch her if he could, but his paws were clenched in her talons. "You've become more suspicious, Squirrel. I'm proud of you," she said.

When he did not speak, she said, "Squirrel, I hate to disappoint you, but I didn't betray you. I'm here to help."

"Stop lying," said Squirrel, his voice pulsing with anger.

"I can prove it," said Azulfa calmly. "Show your faces."

Slowly the five hooded figures removed their veils. Standing there, grinning, were five faces Squirrel did not expect to see: Cheska, Smitten, Akbar, Bobby, and Lady Blouse.

"No way!" whooped Des as he hugged his sister and slapped his three brothers-in-law on the back. "It's my family!"

Squirrel could not believe the wonderful mirage. What were his friends doing in the desert? What were they doing with Azulfa?

"Dahling, aren't you going to say hello?" asked Lady Blouse, smiling at Squirrel.

Squirrel gulped. As though in a dream, he walked up to Lady Blouse and bowed. "Lady Blouse, you look lovely."

"Why, thank you, dahling," she said with a small twirl, to show off her black catsuit that hugged every curve of her body.

"But why did Azulfa drag you here?" asked Squirrel, trying not to blush as he watched the Lady. "The desert is no place for someone like you!"

"I didn't leave poor Azulfa a choice, dahling. When I overheard her speaking to Smitten outside the Pedipurr, I felt just awful. I had to come to rescue you. Otherwise, who would make me those wonderful Pretty Piths? So I insisted that Azulfa let me come, and as you know, I'm a difficult person to resist," she purred, batting her curly lashes.

"You shouldn't have," mumbled Squirrel, so flattered by the fact that Lady Blouse had come to save him that he could not speak. Instead he went around and shook hands with Akbar, Bobby, Smitten, and Cheska.

When he reached Azulfa, he squinted. He did not know

what to make of her. "Azulfa, I don't get it. I'm sorry, but—"

"If you can stop judging me, I'll explain. Can you do that?" asked Azulfa.

Squirrel frowned but nodded slowly.

"Good," continued Azulfa. "Well, when you drugged me at Khoy's house—by the way, I'm impressed you managed to slip me the Skullcap so sneakily—so yeah, when you drugged me, I didn't know what to do. But then, I found this crumpled in the hallway." With that, she removed a small piece of blanched paper with Squirrel's and Des's hand-writing on it. It was the note Squirrel and Des had passed between them at Khoy's house. The last five words read: *The Desert of Blood Kings.*

Squirrel wanted to slap his red forehead.

"So I knew where to find you—"

"And then Azulfa flew all the way to Bimmau to fetch us," interrupted Cheska. "She knew that if you saw us, you'd believe that she's here to help you. In fact, I can't believe how quickly she flew to Bimmau. She found a boat and rowed us all here as quickly as she could. So fast that the oars of the boat are almost broken with the force. We'll have to find another on our way back."

Azulfa managed a faint smile. "We will. But, Squirrel, I do hope you believe that I'm here to help you. And also

I didn't send the Kowas after you to the Bone Tomb . . ."

"No, she didn't. In fact, we think the Kowas found out where you were because of the note Des sent us by BuzzEx. He had written that you were going to a Bone Tomb outside Mellifera, and when we got the message, it had been opened already," said Smitten.

"What? Who opened it?" asked Des, his tail drooping with dismay.

"We don't know," said Akbar, placing an arm on Des's shoulder. "But we'll find out."

"Do you believe me now?" Azulfa asked Squirrel.

"I don't know what to believe, Zulf. It seems possible, but I still don't get why you didn't stop the Kowas from entering the tomb. Or why you didn't rescue me when I almost drowned in the river . . ."

Azulfa paused, her forehead stretching like chewing gum. She looked as though she were locked in some silent battle. Finally her muscles relaxed and she said softly, "I'm sorry I didn't help you through the trials. It's just that . . . I promised that I would watch over you but never interfere unless you were in the most deadly scrape."

"And you didn't think that me in a dark, hollow crypt with two murderous Kowas was deadly?" spat Squirrel.

"Not really. Squirrel, you forget that I knew the Kowas'

orders. They were not trying to kill you but just capture you. So, if they did get you out of the cave, I was there, waiting to slice them to feathered meat."

Squirrel paused. "You just said you promised not to interfere unless I was in a deadly situation?"

Azulfa nodded.

"Who did you make this promise to?" said Squirrel, his heart spinning in ways he did not know it could.

"Your mother," whispered Azulfa.

Everyone shut up. Then, all together, they burst into babbles.

"Dahling, his mom's been gone for ten seasons!" exclaimed Lady Blouse, brushing a pretty paw against Azulfa as though the crow had just cracked a really silly joke.

"Whaddya mean, Zulf?" asked Des.

"She's got sunstroke," said Akbar.

Azulfa waited till the muttering stopped. When she spoke, her voice was just a notch louder than the sandy breeze. "I was born Azulfa Corvidius. I was abandoned as a hatchling. I was forced to become tough at a young age. I mean, really tough." Azulfa fixed her stare on the colorless sky. "Anyway, one thing led to another, and before I knew it, I was recruited by the Kowas."

"We know you're a Kowa. So what?" asked Des.

"One of my assignments was to kidnap a woman and bring her into Kowa headquarters. I was given her address and told to go collect her. I followed the instructions, broke into the house, and kidnapped her. But the lady turned out to be much . . . feistier than I had expected. Instead of sitting still, she grabbed a seaglass knife and attacked me with it. It was a horrible tussle and a moment later, the lady lay dead on the floor."

Azulfa plucked a feather out of her wing and began to wring it. "I . . . I . . . got the wrong lady. Instead of kidnapping one lady, I accidentally killed her sister. Squirrel"—Azulfa looked green, as though she were having her stomach pumped—"the lady I killed was your Aunt Etty—your mother's sister."

Squirrel heard the words. They went from his ears to his brain. Then they fell to his stomach like heavy, rotten seeds. He felt sick. He just wanted to bury his head in the sand, but he couldn't—not now. He forced himself to hear the crow. He felt his jaw lock, but he nodded for her to continue.

"When your mother figured out what had happened, she wanted revenge. She tracked me down. One day I got to my home and found her waiting for me. She had the same seaglass knife in her hand that had killed her sister." Azulfa choked. "I can still remember her so clearly. Her body was so straight. Her eyes were so clear. It was as though her pain had made her stronger. She was half my height but willing to fight me to death to honor her sister."

"That day, as I looked at your mother's brave blue eyes, something changed inside me. I realized that I had crossed a line that I could never come back from. I apologized to her from the core of my being, but my words sounded hollow—even to me. How could a sorry bring back her sister? I offered to do anything I could, but I knew it wouldn't help. I offered her the one thing I knew she wanted: my life. I laid down my dagger and asked her to kill me. It's what I deserved."

"Your mother, she took her knife and came up to me. For a flick of a moment, I saw her desperate desire to plunge it into my heart. But she dropped it. She said that killing me was meaningless. It was too easy an end for me. Instead she wanted something much more important than my life."

"What?" asked Cheska, interrupting Azulfa's story with a hiccup as she choked back a sob.

"She asked me to keep you safe, Squirrel. She said that she knew her days were numbered since the Kowas were after her. So she told me to look after you should anything happen to her. I made the promise. I owed her at least that. I vowed to protect you from the other Kowas." She choked. "If she hadn't died in the fire, I would have protected her, too."

"What . . . what else did she . . . she say?" asked Squirrel.

"She told me to let you grow naturally and to let you fumble through your own scrapes; I did that. She told me that when there was no other way out, I must help you. I tried to do that. I have upheld my promise to your mother to the best of my ability." She paused, and gulped. "Oh, and she told me to tell you to never feel ashamed of your acorn-shaped head or your narrow shoulders."

Cheska hugged Azulfa. "You repented for your sins. You looked after him. And my brother, too. Thank you . . ."

Squirrel felt tears spill down his cheeks—they were both hot and cold. He looked straight at Azulfa and said, "But . . . are you still a killer? Are you still a Kowa?"

Azulfa looked down. "I am who I am, Squirrel. I have done many bad things. Even after I met your mother, I've remained a part of the Kowas. But I only took the lighter jobs—no killings, no kidnappings."

"But why didn't you just quit?" asked Squirrel.

"Maybe for the same reason you were not able to quit the PetPost until right now. It's the only thing I know how to do. It is my identity. I'll always be ashamed of who I am, and what I've done. I cannot change that. But I thought you should know the truth about me," said Azulfa. She looked at the late afternoon sun. "Anyway, I vowed to look after you and that's why I'm back. Now we must get out of this desert immediately."

"I can't go with you," said Squirrel, stepping back. "You almost killed my mom. You killed my aunt!"

Azulfa looked straight back at Squirrel. Her eyes were different from how Squirrel had ever seen them. Instead of hard, black beads, they looked like dark, tortured oceans, swelling with apology, breaking with sympathy, and cresting with sorrow. "Squirrel, you should hate me. But I hope that you know . . ." Her voice fell. "I hope you realize that I'm here to protect you."

When Squirrel did not respond, Azulfa said again, "Now we must get out of this desert. The Kowas are probably on their way here already."

"Squirrel, even though she's done some mighty messed-up things, she seems to repent them. Remember, she has saved our hides many times. We would've been captured at Cheska and Smitten's wedding if it wasn't for her," Des said to Squirrel.

Squirrel knew Des was right; but when he looked at Azulfa, his mind was blank. "I will never forget that you have harmed my family, Zulf. But for now I will try to forgive you." Taking a deep breath, he said, "Let's leave.

But first we need to eat and drink something—we have a long way to go."

Azulfa looked as though she was going to argue, but she did not. Instead she opened a bag tied to her back and removed some mud biscuits, worm jelly, and thin tubes full of squid ink. "We eat and then we go."

Finding shade beside a sand dune, they camped, eating in silence.

Eventually Cheska said, "So, Lady Blouse, rumor had it that you were missing." She licked a glob of worm jelly off her paw.

"Yes, how hyperactive everyone is, aren't they, dahling? I mean, Squirrel had given me some Pretty Piths and I was not about to waste them! So I went to meet my husband in the Elephantine Islands. He was there on business, but who said you can't mix a little business with pleasure?" she said with a wink.

"Aww! That must've been fun. I can't wait for our honeymoon. It'll be fun to . . . travel with Smitten," said Cheska, turning the color of baby turnip as she spoke.

"You still haven't been on your honeymoon?" cried Des.

"'Course not, silly. Couldn't have gone when my one and only brother's traipsing across weird, dangerous lands, could I? I'd have been too worried to enjoy it," said Cheska, ruffling Des's ear affectionately.

"Oh no! I'm so sorry," Des said to Cheska and Smitten. "I had no idea."

"It's all my fault," said Squirrel, feeling slimier than the little leech that was inching its way toward Lady Blouse's pretty hand. "I ruined your honeymoon."

"Now stop. We're not going to have you guys talking like this. We can go on our honeymoon anytime, can't we, sweetheart?" said Smitten, and Cheska nodded prettily. Then he said, "Well, as Zulf said, we should make a move. While the rest of you pack up the food, Squirrel, Azulfa, Des, do you mind helping me with something?"

"Sure," they said, following Smitten to another corner of the dune.

As soon as they were out of earshot, Smitten asked, "Des, Squirrel, did you find everything you were looking for?"

"Yes, we did," said Squirrel.

Smitten looked around, as if to see if anyone else was within earshot. No one was. Leaning close to Squirrel and Des, he said, "I confirmed some stuff about the Map of Brittle. It isn't much, but I found out that the map was originally created to break society into two classes of creatures by either giving or taking away their names. All no-names became slaves, and they had to serve their masters till death."

"Y'mean, like . . . like it used to be in the time of the big cats and dogs?" asked Des.

"Yes. And whoever had the map decided who got to be the slave, and who got to be the master. That person became the most powerful person in the society.

"But then the masters began to treat their slaves very, very badly. They were cruel and arrogant, and soon anyone was being made into a slave—just for the fun of it. The power of the Map of Brittle was too dangerous. So the governors of Bimmau decided to hide it away. The map was made unreadable and hidden somewhere where no one could find it. The key to read the map was hidden too, but in a different place. And two councils were created: One became the Keepers of the Key. The other became the Wardens of the Map. There was no interaction between them; they didn't even know who the other was."

Smitten looked at Squirrel seriously. "Do you understand what I'm saying, Squirrel?"

"I think so. . . . You are saying that even if we get Brittle's Key, it will be hard to get the map," said Squirrel.

Smitten nodded. "I'm sorry, Squirrel. It may indeed be difficult for us to find the map. But the other news is that someone else in Bimmau is desperately looking for the map. And rumor has it that they've found it already."

Squirrel's pulse raced. Someone had already found the map! Whoever that someone was must be desperately trying to find the key as well.

"I need to find Brittle's Key. Just to keep it safe. After that, I can try to find the map."

"I agree. But *if* you are able to find both Brittle's Key and Brittle's Map, you will have unbelievable power in Bimmau." He paused and looked at Squirrel with a grave face. "Power you'll have to be very careful with. Power that nobody has had for ages. And, that some believe, no one should ever have again."

Azulfa nodded. "Your mother never said it openly, but I always suspected that though she was a PetPost slave like you, she had a secret. Based on what Smitten is just saying, I think it was possible that she was actually a Keeper of the Key. That's why your mother sent you on this quest—so that you would be forced to grow up before you found the key.

"In fact, she had planned for you only to start the quest after you were married. So that you would be old and wise enough to handle it. But somehow it started earlier . . ."

Squirrel felt a bizarre sense of calm fill him. Even though he was much younger than he should have been, he had passed his mother's tests. He was ready to protect the key. Just as his mother had hoped.

Suddenly, finding the map, discovering his name, getting his freedom did not matter. Looking up at his friends, he said, "I have to protect Brittle's Key. That is my destiny. But first I need to find it. At least I know where it is. We need to go back to Bimmau." The image of his room in his tree cottage, with the big blue book above his desk, flashed in his mind.

"Good, good. Well, we've delayed long enough. Let's move," urged Azulfa, looking at the sky.

"Why do you have to be such a killjoy?" groaned Des, who was still shoveling a fist of bone chips into his mouth.

Azulfa snorted. "I promised to protect Squirrel and I'll be damned if I break my word on the only vow I've ever made."

A PLACE TO REST

Their sprint south was interrupted twice. The first time, they ran straight into a band of jackals. Luckily, the jackals had just stuffed themselves on what looked like the remains of a large buck and were in such deep slumber that the entire valley rang with their guttural snores, letting Squirrel and his friends pass through their camp unnoticed. A while later, a flutter of dark wings forced them all to duck into a shrubbery. It turned out to be a family of sparrows in traveling cloaks migrating for the summer.

It was only when they found the river station, rented the Gavial Raft, and set off down the river did Squirrel relax. He let his eyes flit from Akbar to Bobby to Cheska to Smitten to Azulfa to Lady Blouse to Des, and he felt something warm and soothing, like piping hot milk, run through his arteries. Up until now he had not realized how very lost he had been, how very alone he had been . . .

"So what news from home? I feel like I've been away for an entire season!" said Des, picking at a sunburned patch of fur on his leg.

"There's been one juicy piece of drama at the Wagamutt. You remember Leggy Lex? She apparently ran away to join a visiting circus as an acrobat. Her parents are rabid with rage. Oh, and a family of rabbits has moved in down the road from us, but no one can make out a thing they say. They talk real funny," chatted Akbar.

"Oh, and Squirrel, everyone's been talking about the fact that since you disappeared, Bacchu has been delivering the PetPost Mail himself and he is very grumpy about it! No one else will work for him. No one can stand his tantrums. It's still hard to believe that you tolerated him for so long."

"I had to. I was . . ." Squirrel shook his head. "I still am the PetPost slave. Since I probably won't find the key, it looks like I'll be the PetPost slave for quite a while longer. I'll have to go back to Bacchu and beg him for forgiveness. If he reports me to the governors of Bimmau . . ."

"Actually, you don't *have* to. If you want to escape the PetPost, this is your best chance, Squirrel," said Bobby. "Bacchu—and all of Bimmau, for that matter—think that you fell into the mangrove and drowned at Cheska and Smitten's wedding."

Squirrel gulped. "Oops," he managed with a small smile. Since he had started his quest for freedom, Squirrel had not seriously thought of not returning to Bimmau. He *could* probably move to Darling. But, for some reason, it did not feel right at all.

"I don't think I'll run away," said Squirrel. "I'll go back. Even as the PetPost slave. I must face the consequences of my actions." Squirrel knew he had to go back. Suddenly the purpose of his quest had changed. He had to find the key and keep it safe. He had to protect his mother's secret.

"I think that is a good idea, Squirrel," said Smitten. "Even though it may be hard, we'll try to find your name and get your freedom somehow."

"Yes, we will," said Cheska. "And, Des, you won't believe it. Mom and Dad have been offered a formal invitation to the Pawshine with a handwritten note from Don Dane himself. Who thought that day would come? All at Baron Dyer's prodding, of course."

"I'm so sorry about it," said Smitten, going red. "I sometimes wish Uncle would mind his own business just a tiny bit." Then he added, "Speaking of minding other people's business, I have some news that concerns you, Des."

"Me?"

"Well, I don't know if you know this, but last season the Pedipurr's councillors changed. The new cats in charge have started the Diversity Directive. Basically, from now on they're allowing third-generation members to sponsor one animal to attend the Pedipurr School." He paused. "I thought I might sponsor you?"

"Why would I want to go to the Pedipurr School? Isn't the Wagamutt Pound good 'nuff? I don't know *anyone* at the Pedipurr!" said Des.

Cheska said, "You'll have access to so much, Des. You'll get to take part in such wonderful activities. You'll learn a lot."

"Not to mention the fact that you will be able to do anything you want when you come out of it," said Bobby, pushing his glasses up his nose.

"What do you think, Akbar?" Des asked.

Squirrel watched as the Alsatian shrugged, pulling at his old T-shirt. "Well, you know how I feel about all these high-society shindigs. Gimme a good ol' mug of mead with my boys at the Wagamutt any day over a stuffy apricot wine-drinking soiree . . . no offense," he said, looking at Smitten and Lady Blouse. "But the bone in the meat is, Des, that you'll learn much more at the Pedipurr. It's a great opportunity. Plus the Pedipurr kittens are known to be the best looking," he added with his roguish grin.

"Well, in that case," said Des, his face brightening, "I think I might just consider it."

As Squirrel heard this conversation, he felt his chest compress with an unfamiliar emotion. It was as though his lungs were being pushed against each other and his intestines were rolling into knots.

It took a moment for Squirrel to realize that he was jealous. He was jealous of Des's family—of so many people watching out for him and caring about him. He was jealous of Des being able to go to the best school. And most of all, he was jealous of Des moving on and finding new friends. And eventually forgetting about him.

"I wish I could go to the Pedipurr . . . or any school," said Squirrel. As soon as he had said it, he hoped it sounded like a joke. But he knew the longing rang out clearly in his voice.

"Dahling, don't fret. I can sponsor you!"

"You can?" Squirrel asked, looking at Lady Blouse with shock.

"I'm Lady Blouse. I'd be happy to—" But before she could

complete her sentence, Des hollered loudly. "YIP-woof-woof-EEE!" barked Des, punching Squirrel's shoulder. "Just imagine that, Squirrel! The two of us together at the Pedipurr. How fantastic! We can tell stories about our adventures to all the pretty kitties. "'Bout the Bone Tomb, 'bout escaping Wipsara, 'bout beating the camel at Making Family. We'll be the bad boys of the Pedipurr. And you know how all the cute kittens secretly love the bad boys!"

Squirrel felt a fountain of happiness frothing up in him and spilling into every fiber of his being. Without thinking, he too started hopping around the boat, making the boat seesaw with his thumps. The others smiled. Until Azulfa said, "I'm sure that you would make a good student, but Squirrel, you are a slave with no name. And no-names do not go to school."

"All the more reason we need to get you free from Bacchu Banoose," whispered Des to Squirrel. "We will try to find your name and free you, Squirrel. Then you can come to school with me. Think of the fun we could have . . ."

Squirrel felt his smile curl to the tips of his ears. For the first time, he felt the warmth of a family. For the first time, other people seemed to care about his well-being. For the first time, someone wanted him to be a part of his life—and it felt freakin' fantastic.

A long, howling whistle shook the boat. It was Akbar. "Ahoy there!"

"We're here—Otter's Cove," said Azulfa as they pulled up by the oddest-looking village imaginable. On both sides of the river, gnarled trees had been carved by the wind and the weather so that the trunks formed a rough landing. Lying on the trunks, a colony of otters and kingfishers waited to catch seaweed with nets that lazily swished about in the water.

"I think this'll make a good place to rest for the night," said Azulfa as the gavials slowed down.

"We're not really stopping here for the night?" asked Lady Blouse, her pretty eyes widening.

"I was planning on it," said Azulfa. "It's completely obscure. The leaves are so dense there'd be a very low chance of the Kowas spotting us here."

"But, dahling, it smells of fish," said Lady Blouse, crinkling her nose. "Is there no other place we can go?"

"Lady Blouse, I think that protecting ourselves may be slightly more important than an unpleasant smell," said Akbar with a smirk.

"Well, if you're all comfortable with this, I'm sure I would be too," said Lady Blouse. "It's just that I keep a summer home very close, just slightly upstream. Remember, I told you on our way here? It's called Cobblestone Yard. And you know what a proper home means: warm feather beds, access to a full pantry . . ."

"Lady Blouse, I thought we had already talked about this," said Azulfa sharply.

"We had, dahling," said Lady Blouse. "But we're all so much more tired now that I thought I'd offer my house again. I think that you, more than anyone, Azulfa, could use some rest."

"You keep a house nearby, Lady Blouse?" asked Des.

"Just a cottage. But it's charming, even if I say so myself. The river flows through it and it's the prettiest spot for picnicking. It'd be a nice spot to get some much-deserved rest. I keep the finest of GrandGrub's meats, plus there are always fresh, tasty lotus buds from the river. Not to mention we have one of the best-stocked cellars—a nice wildflower wine spritzer sounds sublime right now, doesn't it? And, Akbar, what would you say to a pint of chilled, aged mead?"

"Oooh . . . GrandGrub's meats! Do you have their Roasted Honey Beetles?" asked Des eagerly.

"That, and jars of shrimp-shell chips and berry-root jams."

"I don't care about the rest of 'em, but I'm coming with you, Lady Blouse," said Des, a hungry grin on his face.

"It *would* be nice to have a feathery bed," said Cheska.

"Not that I have a problem with these tree barks at all," she added quickly.

"How would we get there? We're better off not leaving the cover of the trees," said Bobby, looking around.

"This river leads right there. Just think, dahlings. My house is even more obscure than this fishing village. I mean, it's a private residence and the Kowas would never imagine that I'm here helping you. And don't you think we'll be safer inside a solid stone building than outside here, where those monsters can just swoop down and pluck our eyes out while we sleep?" asked Lady Blouse.

Everyone fell silent. Finally Smitten asked, "Are you sure it won't be too much of an imposition, Lady Blouse? We are a big group."

"Dahling, what's the point of keeping a cottage if I can't use it for myself and my friends?"

"Let's go," said Squirrel. "I don't think any of us can turn down a proper meal and a nice, warm bed."

"I'm in," said Akbar. "I'm always in the mood for some chilled, aged mead."

Azulfa frowned. "I still say we're better off here. But, apparently, majority wins."

TWILIGHT AT
COBBLESTONE YARD

Lady Blouse's house was as pretty as promised. Settled in the bend of the river, the large house was made of pink stones, draped with thick creepers. Crisp yellow buds and pale blue hollyhocks peppered the lawn, along with slender bulrushes, wild reeds, and wispy clusters of baby's breath. On top of the roof there was a large nest, from which the chirp of hatchlings fluted through the countryside. A family of butterflies flitted about, playing hide-and-seek. Oversize glass windows shimmered in the gathering dusk, throwing glints of warm orange light on the happy spring activity.

"Welcome, my friends. This is Cobblestone Yard," said Lady Blouse merrily.

"It's beautiful, Lady Blouse!" breathed Squirrel, letting the prettiness fill his lungs.

Everyone in the boat murmured their appreciation. Squirrel even thought he saw a faint smile soften Azulfa's face.

"This looks more like a country estate than a cottage to me," whistled Akbar. He sprang off the raft and began helping the others, while Smitten paid the gavials and thanked them.

"Come, let me show you around," said Lady Blouse with a pleased expression.

She led them by the river. Past a long bed of wild lilies. Onto a narrow path that led them into a small, dense wood. They wove through old tree trunks carpeted with moss, dodging the large, speckled mushrooms covering the forest floor—until the path turned abruptly.

There, wedged among the trees, stood an ancient square cobblestone yard, surrounded by pillared arches. The stones that paved the floor were every shade of gray and silver. In the center of the stone courtyard stood an old gnarled tree and an ancient well, complete with a stone pail, a cord, and a big, solid bronze bell.

"Oh, how quaint!" said Cheska, clapping her hands together in delight.

"A well! I have never seen something like this!" exclaimed Squirrel, running up to the rim. He curled his fingers on the stone well. The smooth weathered rock was cold to his touch. Ignoring the tightening in his chest, he peered down the narrow stone walls and watched dark shadows skim across the surface of the black water.

Squirrel heard the leisurely clack of steps against the cobblestones as someone else joined him at the well. By the ticktock of heel against stone, Squirrel knew it was Lady Blouse.

"It's like a preserved pebble of history," Squirrel said. "I've heard of wells like this, but I've never seen one."

"And now you can hear one," said Lady Blouse, tugging at the cord. The tongue of the bell swayed and clinked against its wide bronze mouth. Lady Blouse tugged harder. This time, the bell chimed out loudly. She kept tugging, letting the clear high chords ring into the dusk until Azulfa snatched the metal rope out of Lady Blouse's hand.

"Lady Blouse! What are you doing? We're in hiding! We must be quiet . . ." But a howl of the evening wind silenced her.

A dark smoky cloud drifted across the sky.

The crow went rigid, her feathers at attention. Her eyes went hard and she reached into her long cape.

"What happened, Azulfa?" Squirrel asked. But Azulfa did

not speak. Instead she tilted her face upward toward the sky. Her eyes narrowed.

Pounding shook the cobblestones. An awful flutter thundered in the blood-streaked sky. Everything went pitch-black as smoke clouded Squirrel's eyes and the stale stench of carrion punched his nostrils.

Then he saw them.

Strong black wings sliced through the smoke and circled downward, cutting off every possible route of escape. Loud, evil cackles tore through the twilight.

Squirrel felt friendly hands grab him and lock him between two sets of shoulders. His friends had formed a straight line and had safely tucked him between Smitten and Azulfa.

Squirrel saw Des tremble; his paws curled into fists. Bobby popped a pellet into a slingshot. Akbar pulled out a wooden club from his shorts. Smitten drew a long curved thorn sword from under his hood. Cheska cocked a tiny bow and arrow. Lady Blouse unsheathed the blade from the garter she wore with her black catsuit.

Facing them, five Kowas dropped down into a similar line. In a smooth motion, each of them whipped out a long pellet gun. A belt of stone ammunitions was slung across their shoulders. Squirrel recognized one of them, the one with the dented beak. He was the same crow who had rowed him to Smitten and Cheska's wedding.

Both camps stared at each other. Squirrel noticed that the Kowas were frowning at Azulfa. She looked straight back at them. Heavy breaths and the whispers of doom were the only sounds that swilled in the deadlocked air. And then, another set of footsteps clapped against the cobblestones.

All eyes turned to the intruders. From behind one of the pillared arches, two more cloaked, black figures strode into sight. They came and stood in front of the Kowas.

Both of them pulled back their hoods.

Smitten gasped. "Uncle?"

"Why hello, nephew! But, for now, you can call me Colonel," said the tall, elegant cat, a callous smile lurking on his face. Baron Dyer's glinting silver eyes moved down the line. As they passed over Azulfa, Squirrel heard her heart pound like an elephant's. Then the Baron's eyes settled on someone. "I've been waiting here all day. I thought you'd never come."

"Sorry about that, dahling! We were camping by a disgusting, smelly fishing village. It took all my charm to convince them to come here."

Squirrel's mind snapped like a wishbone. Why was Baron Dyer standing in front of the Kowas? Was that Mrs. Sox next to him? Was he the one who had hired the Kowas? And, why, why, why was Lady Blouse talking to him so affectionately?

Then he saw Lady Blouse break the line he was in. With a rather pronounced sway of her hips she sauntered toward the villains' camp. With growing horror, Squirrel watched as she got there, kissed Baron Dyer on his cheeks, and then, slowly, twirled around to face Squirrel and his friends.

"I'm sorry, dahlings, but this is the side I should be on," she purred. There was no apology in her smile, in her face, or in the way she wrapped her arm around Baron Dyer's waist.

"You betrayed us? You set us up?" barked Akbar, trying to charge at Lady Blouse and Baron Dyer with his club, but Bobby grabbed his wrist and stopped him.

"Easy, easy! This is the problem with dogs. They're just so . . . dramatic!" said Baron Dyer lazily. "Now I'm sure we can resolve this issue without anyone getting hurt . . ."

But Squirrel could not keep his mouth shut any longer. "Why?" he choked, looking straight at Lady Blouse. He felt the tip of his heart crumble a little.

"'Cos, my dear boy, you have something I need," said Baron Dyer. "That *we* need," he added, stroking Lady Blouse's arm.

"What?" asked Squirrel.

"The key to the Map of Brittle."

Squirrel grew quiet. His cheeks grew tight.

"Don't play dumb, dahling. I saw you, Azulfa, Des, and Smitten whispering in the desert. I know you have found something. You might as well just hand it over. Then all your little friends can run along home," said Lady Blouse.

"What is all this about?" Smitten asked. Squirrel knew he was playing dumb to buy time. "Why would you think Squirrel has the key to the Map of Brittle? What do you want with the key anyway?"

"Ha. Ha. Ha. Look at you trying to act all ignorant, Smitten. I know that you know all about Brittle's Key, nephew. I also know you've been trying to dig up information about it. And I know that the little dog over there has been sending you letters and telling you where he was going." Baron Dyer stuck his chest out. "I know because I intercepted the BuzzEx letter and read it. How do you think I knew where to send the Kowas? The dog led me right to you . . . but I guess it was a bit too late. No matter. We have you now."

"Uncle, please! See reason!"

"Listen to me. I've found the Map of Brittle. I know where it is. But I can't read it. And I was told by Falguny himself that the PetPost slave has the key. Why do you think I suggested you invite him to your wedding, Smitten? It was to get the key from him!"

"Uncle, you are a traitor!"

"Shush, nephew. Shush. No need for name calling, is there?" said Baron Dyer. "Now, nephew, stop trying to protect these nobodies and I won't harm you or your pretty wench. And, trust me, the Map of Brittle will not harm your life one little bit."

"But it'll harm my life."

The voice was so low that Squirrel was not sure he had heard it. But then he saw Mrs. Sox shuffle in her spot. "If you read the Map of Brittle, you will harm my life a great deal, won't you? I heard you say I'd be the first one you will enslave. And why would I help you do that, Colonel? I mean, Baron?"

"Madame, I do not appreciate your tone . . . ," began Baron Dyer, his voice acid.

"I don't care," spat Mrs. Sox, stepping out of line. "And I know you intend to kill everyone here. Squirrel, don't help him!"

Squirrel was shocked. Of all people he had never thought he would ever take advice from mean Mrs. Sox. And then his shock deepened as fat Mrs. Sox leaped forward with surprising agility and came and joined the line he was in, standing exactly where Lady Blouse had stood moments ago.

"You just made a huge mistake, Madame," whispered Baron Dyer, his eyes stabbing Mrs. Sox.

"I'm not scared of you anymore! Why should I be?" yelled Mrs. Sox, removing her own weapon—a slender whip.

"You should not have turned on me, Madame. You're quite right. I planned to make you my personal slave. But now I will kill you. Each and every one of you—that is, except you, Squirrel. You I need alive."

"You cannot hurt any of us," said Mrs. Sox, her yellow eyes glowing fiercely.

A tinkling laugh escaped Lady Blouse's lips. "Why, I think you forget, Madame, that these strapping Kowas are with us. We can shoot you all down right now."

"I think all this running around has muddled your pretty little brain, Lady Blouse," said Mrs. Sox, her lips turning into a snarl. "The Kowas do not report to you. Nor to you, Colonel . . . I mean, Baron." She paused, letting the truth of her words sink into the two villains. "I hired them, didn't I? Doesn't that mean that those Kowas report to me?"

The five Kowas nodded their chins slightly at Mrs. Sox as she added, "I command you to stand aside. This is not your fight." There was a slight shuffle as the Kowas looked at one another. Finally the Kowa with the dented beak nodded at Mrs. Sox. The crows separated themselves from either party and began to dissolve into the surrounding trees. But before Dented Beak himself disappeared, he looked straight at Azulfa and cawed loudly. Squirrel felt Azulfa tense beside him.

As the last Kowa backed away, the Colonel whispered, "This is mutiny, Madame."

"Yes, Baron, it is. Did you really think I'd let you treat me like that? Did you really think you could assault me, and call me a fat carcass every day? Did you really think I wouldn't figure out what you were up to?"

"Oh, foolish, stupid Mrs. Sox. I'll tell you exactly what I'm up to. I'm going to get the key to the map and make all the lower creatures slaves—the rodents, the insects, every small, lowly creature. That's where they belong. And, maybe, some of the higher creatures too." He snarled at Mrs. Sox. "I'll make Bimmau what it used to be. Few masters, many slaves."

At this point, Smitten clearly had had enough.

"Uncle! Please stop this madness. Why do you want to make everyone slaves? Don't you have enough? And you, Lady Blouse? Why would you do this? Let's forget this episode and just return to Bimmau . . ."

"Shut up, nephew! You know nothing. Nothing of the threat these dirty critters pose to our lives. Nothing of the loss I have suffered because of them. They should be locked away and be made to do our bidding. But how can I expect you to understand? You're married to her! A filthy, muddy dog . . . You are an insult to your bloodline . . . to my bloodline."

"What are you talking about, you Looney Tune?" yelled Akbar. "Bloodline, bah! I'll show you the only bloodline you need to worry about." And, with a howl, Akbar charged forward. With his beefy arm, the dog swung his club at Baron Dyer.

Squirrel watched with horror as Baron Dyer grabbed the club, halting it midair as easily as though it were a spindle of straw. Then he shoved it with so much force that Akbar lost his balance, flew backward, and hit the cobblestone floor with a loud crack. The snap of bones echoed through the courtyard as Akbar the Alsatian collapsed like a sack.

"Tut! Tut! I guess the time for violence has come," said Baron Dyer, swiveling his arms in a stretch. "Squirrel, I know that you have what I want, and I must get it. I'll have to take you with me. The rest of you, I'll just have to finish you off, like I did that dirty mutt. Now, who's next?"

"Don't call him a dirty mutt!" screamed Bobby, his eyes welling with tears as he stared at his brother-in-law lying still on the cobblestones. Taking aim with his slingshot, Bobby sent a sharp pellet toward Baron Dyer, who was striding forward, his full lips smiling wickedly.

Just as the pellet was about to strike the Baron's shoulder, he hopped out of the way and it whizzed by, not even grazing his perfect fur.

"You'll have to do better than that," said Baron Dyer as he stopped just in front of Bobby. Then, with his razor-sharp claws, he gripped Bobby's neck and began to strangle him.

Bobby rasped loudly. His eyes began to loll about in his head, when suddenly Baron Dyer screamed in pain. He dropped Bobby on the floor.

Behind the Baron, Smitten brandished his thorn sword. It dripped with crimson blood. Smitten had laid a long, shallow slice diagonally down Baron Dyer's back.

"Is that any way to treat your uncle?" growled Baron Dyer as a very concerned Lady Blouse ran up behind him and started swiveling her knife at all of them, especially Cheska.

"It is the way to treat an uncle like you," said Smitten, jabbing at the Baron's legs.

But the Baron was ready for him this time. In a flash he had untucked a crystal dagger, and as Smitten went for his uncle's left shoulder, Baron Dyer leaped up, spun in the air, and deftly punched his knife into the back of Smitten's shoulder blade. With a grunt, Smitten fell to the floor.

"SMITTEN!" yelled Cheska, pushing Lady Blouse toward Mrs. Sox and running to Smitten.

Squirrel felt his stomach drop. Smitten was hurt. Bobby was on the floor. Akbar was . . . He did not want to know. He felt fear grip him as he saw Baron Dyer grin and start moving toward him.

Squirrel tried to get out of the way, but he was blocked by the twisting bodies of Mrs. Sox and Lady Blouse, who were lunging at each other—lurching and leaning, tilting and spinning—in what looked like a tango-to-the-death.

Squirrel stepped back. Baron Dyer moved closer, ignoring the blood leaking down his back. Squirrel felt his muscles snap as the Baron grabbed his shoulders, his perfect white teeth glinting in the red dusk. "Now you're mine, you little rodent."

"Not yet, Colonel," said Azulfa.

In a flash, the black bird hurled herself at the Baron, her beak angled downward. Deftly she sliced at his arm with force, drawing a long gash of blood from his shoulder to his elbow. Baron Dyer winced, letting go of Squirrel for a moment. It was enough for Azulfa. She kicked Baron Dyer with her wiry legs, forcing him to lose his balance.

By the time Baron Dyer had picked himself up, Azulfa had wrapped her wings around Squirrel, using her tough, feathered body to envelop him completely.

"Zulf, your feathers are pricking me," choked Squirrel as

a clump of feathers thrust themselves in his mouth.

But Azulfa ignored him and continued to lock him within her body. He felt her muscles stretch with tension. Through her wings, Squirrel watched Baron Dyer swagger toward them, the dagger glinting in his wrist. The Baron was just about to try to wrench Squirrel out of Azulfa's grip when Des, who Lady Blouse had knocked flat on the floor, crawled over and bit into his calf.

"Get away, mutt," grunted the Baron, grinding his heel into Des's stomach and flattening the pulp out of the dog once again.

"Des!" Squirrel heard himself scream. He tried to run over to his friend, but Azulfa kept him firmly in place.

"Just stay with me," she whispered to him.

"Give him to me, you fetid bird!" said the Colonel, putting a strong arm on Azulfa and shaking her so hard that Squirrel felt dizzy.

"Not while I have breath in my body," quaked Azulfa.

Squirrel saw the Baron's eyes go pink with rage. With a savage growl he attacked Azulfa, digging his mouth into her neck as he tried to pry apart the wings and get at Squirrel. However, Azulfa had locked her wings together too firmly.

In his cocoon of feathers Squirrel got shunted left, shoved right, shaken front, and shuffled back. There were "meows" and "kaws" as the powerful crow and the strong cat tussled fiercely. Squirrel tried desperately to help, but he was stuck like a pea in its pod.

And, then, Squirrel heard a snap. The muscles in Azulfa's body slackened. A groan died in her stomach.

"Aaaah . . ."

Azulfa's wings loosened, and Squirrel knew something had gone horribly wrong. But before he could think, the Baron had peeled Azulfa's wings apart. He stood there in front of Squirrel, his face taut with victory.

"I've got you now," sneered Baron Dyer as he threw Azulfa off Squirrel like a useless shrug.

As Squirrel stared at the tall, muscular cat, he knew that it was time to fight. Squaring his shoulders, he took a deep breath, yanked a cord of courage from his gut to his throat, and announced, "I'm not going with you, Baron Dyer."

Then, with all the force he had in him, Squirrel thrust himself forward, driving his acornlike head into the Baron's solar plexus. Squirrel winced as his skull crashed into an abdomen that could have been forged from construction steel.

"That's your defense?" sniggered the Baron, grasping Squirrel's acorn-shaped head and pinning it under his arm like a basketball.

Squirrel slid helplessly on his sweaty heels. He tried jerking his head out of the Baron's grip, but before he could, he felt four claws pierce his right shoulder, tear through his fur, and cleave four deep gashes into his muscles. Squirrel swallowed a howl as four blistering streaks of pain seared his mind.

The damage was done. As Squirrel's energy dripped onto the cobblestones, he knew that his handicap was complete. He had just enough strength to either strike the Baron once more or try to free himself from the grip. Either way, the Baron would incapacitate him with a couple of swipes of his wolverine-like claws.

Trying to decide what to do, Squirrel eyeballed the battlefield. From the corner of his eye Squirrel saw Cheska. It seemed as though she had tucked both Smitten and Des behind one of the pillared arches. He could not see what state each of them was in, but his stomach lurched as he heard a sob burst from Cheska's lips.

Forcing his eyes away from the pillars, Squirrel saw Mrs. Sox and Lady Blouse still dueling, both covered in webs of runny red gashes. Akbar was crumpled on the far side of the yard, his body snapped on itself like a horseshoe. Bobby lay still with a smattering of thick, ruby-colored beads glistening on his neck. Azulfa lay right next to Squirrel, her sharp, strong face looking empty as it rested on a slab of cold stone.

Squirrel forced the prickly lump of fear down his throat. Then, gritting his teeth, he decided, *Well, if I'm going down too, I'm causing as much damage as I can.*

With a jerk of his jaw, Squirrel turned his chin toward the Baron's forearm that gripped his head. Opening his mouth as wide as he could, Squirrel dug his strong, nut-cracking teeth into Baron Dyer's arm. With sadistic satisfaction, Squirrel heard Baron Dyer yelp with pain and he felt bones crunch under his teeth. His mouth filled with the Baron's hot, bitter blood.

Resisting the urge to spit, Squirrel dug his teeth deeper into the Baron's flesh. He began to count each glorious moment he made the Baron squirm with pain—one, two, three, four, five, six . . .

The Baron had stopped writhing. Squirrel braced himself, preparing for the Baron's revenge.

A muscular cord coiled itself around his neck. Squirrel let go of the Baron's mangled arm as the snakelike rope slithered around his gullet three times and began to squeeze it. It took Squirrel a moment to realize that the cord was Baron Dyer's tail.

This is how I will die, thought Squirrel as a tizzy of stars burst on his pupils. The veins in his neck stiffened and his lungs became hollow lead cases. His brain was just being lulled into a coma when the noose slid off his neck.

As a gush of air inflated Squirrel, he realized that the Baron had taken a small step back. Forcing his mind to attention, Squirrel balled his fists, getting ready to defend himself against the Baron's next attack. He hopped from one foot to the other, imitating what he had seen boxer dogs do in fights.

That's when he realized that the Baron was wincing.

"Thought you were invincible, did you?" sniggered a voice behind the Baron. As the Baron turned around to face his new opponent, Squirrel saw a whip around the Baron's neck and a blade buried into the tall cat's lower back. Behind him, Mrs. Sox stood, drenched in sweat and blood. Lady Blouse lay panting on the floor next to her, her blade nowhere in sight.

Squirrel felt a soft hand grip his uninjured shoulder. He turned around and saw Cheska next to him. Silently she guided him over to the pillar against which Smitten and Des were propped up.

"Reckon we were done for," croaked Des.

Squirrel threw his arms around the injured dog. "Ouch. Careful, Squirrel!"

Sorry, sorry, mouthed Squirrel, untangling himself from

his friend and looking over at Smitten. Smitten gave Squirrel a small smile, and Squirrel sighed. They were alive.

"Squirrel, look," whispered Cheska, pointing over to where Mrs. Sox stood facing the injured Baron, a smug smile pasted on her face.

"So, Colonel," began Mrs. Sox, "what do you have to say to this fat carcass now? Any last words before I finish you off?" As she spoke, Mrs. Sox placed her hand on the handle of the blade she had won from Lady Blouse and used to skewer the Colonel. Slowly she drew it out of his back.

"Yes," managed the Colonel, gritting his teeth in agony. "Madame, don't count your kittens before they purr . . ."

And before Squirrel could shout out a warning, Lady Blouse—who had crawled over to the Madame's feet—bit into her chubby ankle.

A blood-chilling screech clanged through the courtyard as Mrs. Sox kicked at Lady Blouse, and toppled—butt-first— onto the hard cobblestone.

Her moment of imbalance was enough. Getting up, Lady Blouse wrapped the Colonel's arms around her shoulder. With a tender expression, she licked the Baron's wound. Then, with what seemed like all her might, Lady Blouse began to run toward the thicket of trees, with the Colonel leaning against her.

Squirrel watched as they fled across the yard, leaving a trail of blood behind them. It took him a moment to register what was happening. When he did, he whooped with delight. "They're running away!" yelled Squirrel, jumping out from behind the pillar. "They're running away! We won!"

But, just as they were about to disappear into the woods, the Colonel called out, "This is far from over, Squirrel. You walnut-brained buffoon, you have no idea what you have. You won't even recognize Brittle's Key if you see it! But you wait and watch, one day soon, one day very soon, I'm going to come back for it. I'm going to come back for you!"

With that chilling promise, Colonel Baron Dyer and Lady Blouse plunged into the eerie shelter of the trees.

"After them!" cried Mrs. Sox, pointing to the spot where Lady Blouse and the Baron had disappeared. As she yelled, the five Kowas who had melted away during the battle materialized again. With a quick nod of their chins, the black birds spread their wings and took off into the clump of trees.

Turning to Squirrel, Mrs. Sox said, "You should've tried to stop them!"

"With all due respect, Mrs. Sox, I thought that—" But before Squirrel could continue, the fat Persian cat bit into his words. "Whatever! You're just an empty bucket full of nothing but excuses, Squirrel! I should never have expected more from you. Now, because of you, that devil and his pretty little mistress are still on the loose. And neither you nor I is safe while they are."

Though Squirrel nodded as Mrs. Sox ranted, his attention shifted to the remnants of the battle. Three bodies were strewn on the stone yard. Squirrel felt a dark haze swirl around him. He watched Cheska wrap a handkerchief around Bobby's neck and put her ear right above his heart. He watched as her limp expression brightened and tears of relief coated her eyes. She smiled weakly, propped Bobby up, and gently shook him till he awoke.

Squirrel sighed. Bobby would be fine, but what about the other two? Squirrel's eyes panned over to where Akbar lay, broken like a twig. Smitten, who was weak but able to move, leaned over him. Squirrel watched Smitten rearrange Akbar's limbs and begin to frantically pump the Alsatian's chest with his palms. Squirrel looked away. He could not watch anymore.

Instead Squirrel walked over to Azulfa, his throat drying like ash as he saw the bird. He kneeled down beside her and turned her around. He placed his paw on her chest.

Azulfa's feathers were still warm. Her muscles were still strong. Her face was still sketched with determination. But she was still.

Squirrel looked into her hollow eyes and choked. Azulfa would never move again.

He wrapped his arms around her and buried his face in her wing. As her smell filled his lungs, he hugged her tighter and tighter. Tears from the pit of his stomach spilled down his face. Desperate to make her move, he shook her like a baby.

Somewhere, far away, he felt someone trying to pull him. He ignored them. He grasped her black feathers and buried his head deeper in her chest. This could not be good-bye.

He clutched the lady who had given her life for him. And as they swayed together on the cold cobblestone yard, Squirrel closed his wet eyes and made Azulfa rock him like a child for the first and last time.

26

A SEND-OFF

Squirrel insisted on carrying Azulfa home. The others let him. His shoulders crumbled under her weight. He did not care. He had to take Azulfa back to Bimmau—he owed her that at least.

"Reckon we'll be home by the time the sun rises?" asked Des, his feet slapping the dark street.

Squirrel could not speak. All he could focus on was the weight of the body on his shoulders.

They trudged on in silence until Des whispered, "What are you going to do with her?"

Squirrel looked straight ahead and swallowed the lump in his gullet. "I don't know."

"My house is that way," said Mrs. Sox as they entered Bimmau.

Squirrel nodded, not knowing what to say to this cat. What could he say after what they had all just been through? How could he thank her for fighting for him?

Not finding any words, he managed a small smile. She jerked her neck back at him, turned on her heel, and plodded off. Just before she turned off the road, she looked back at Squirrel. "Till we meet again," she said, giving him a small, awkward wave of her fat hand.

With all his energy, he lifted his arm and waved back at her. As she disappeared out of sight, he could not believe that a few sunrises ago, he was just the PetPost slave, Mrs. Sox was waiting for an invitation, Smitten and Cheska were not married, and he had never met Des. Or Azulfa . . .

Bobby's voice cut into Squirrel's thoughts. "I think we'd better get Akbar home. He needs to rest."

"He'll be all right, won't he?" Des asked as Bobby and Smitten supported a semi-awake Akbar between them.

"He'll be fine; Aubry will have him back to normal in less than half a moon cycle," said Cheska with a watery smile. "But we should take him home now. Why don't you come with us, Squirrel? You shouldn't be alone right now."

Squirrel knew she was right. But he also knew he would not go home with them. He had something very important to do first.

"Thanks, Cheska. I'll come over later," he said. As though in a vacuum, he turned toward his own home in Wickory Wood with Azulfa slung on his shoulder.

He was about to set off when he felt Azulfa's weight lighten. "Mate, did you actually think I'd leave you alone? I'm coming with you." Des wedged himself under Azulfa's wing. "Now, where're we off to?"

Despite himself Squirrel smiled. Suddenly he did not feel all that empty anymore. "To put Azulfa to bed."

Squirrel ripped the last bit of bark off and handed it to Des. With the vine Des tied the strips of wood together. When he was done, Squirrel wiped his hands on his torn PetPost uniform. Azulfa's raft was ready.

Gently they placed Azulfa on the wooden bed. They tucked a pillow of blue petals under her head, sprinkled her feathers with salt, and wrapped her cold body in Squirrel's softest quilt. Squirrel almost smiled—Azulfa had never looked so peaceful.

It was dusk by the time they got Azulfa to the ocean, and Squirrel was glad for it. The dipping sun tinted her black

body with gold and pink. The balmy breeze ruffled her feathers, making her look younger than ever. The water lapped around her, promising to wash away her troubles forever. Squirrel breathed deeply. It was time to say good-bye.

Squirrel waded into the ocean. He looked at Azulfa for the last time, knowing he would think about her every day he lived. He began to shake.

A paw touched his shoulder. It gave him strength; Squirrel pushed the raft into the sea.

As Azulfa drifted into the sunset, Des said, "She was a good lady at heart."

Squirrel whispered, "Go well, Zulf. Thank you." Slowly he turned around and stumbled out of the water.

In silence, he and Des walked back to Wickory Wood. Only when they were about to enter his cottage did Des say, "Mate, are you ready to go upstairs and find Brittle's Key?"

"Not today. I'll wait till tomorrow. Today . . . let today just be Azulfa's day." And with that, Squirrel crawled upstairs, got into his bed, and tumbled into sleep, with Des following him.

IN THE NOOK

It was still dark when Squirrel got out of bed. He went over to his desk and removed the only blue book from the nook above it. He stared at the big, blocky words on the front, not reading them. He felt the air rush through his teeth.

He looked at Des, who was snoring like a rocket engine. He felt a stab of guilt. Des would have wanted to find the key with him, but Squirrel knew that this was something he had to do on his own.

Squirrel peeled the glossy blue paper jacket off the book. He threw it on the floor.

He ran his paws across the leather cover of the book, feeling for a bump, a lump, or anything that could be a hidden key. He found nothing.

His heart ticked like a time bomb. Where was it? He checked the bottom of the book. Nothing. He flipped through each page. Nothing. He was about to rip the book apart to look for the key in the binding when a glint from the floor caught his eye. He looked down. Something glimmered on the back of the book's blue jacket.

Squirrel snatched the glossy blue flap and flipped it over. A blur of squares and scribbles swam on the page. Squirrel blinked. He was staring at a crossword puzzle with three rows of circles outlined in gold. Next to it was a sea of words.

Squirrel hiccupped loudly and began to read.

Squirrel squeezed his head like a nutcracker crushing an acorn. He was totally, utterly, squirrelly confused. The instructions were a higgledy-piggledy of letters—the first half made sense, the second half gibberish.

Yet, there were three things Squirrel did understand.

He understood he was holding the key to Brittle's Map in his paws.

He understood that the key to Brittle's Map was not a key at all.

And he understood that to complete Brittle's Key, he had to solve the crossword puzzle first.

Squirrel pulled the puzzle toward him. He squinted till he found the clue to the first word in the puzzle—9 Down. It said: *Gandgoon is a city in the Desert of _____ Kings (5 letters)*.

Squirrel picked up his feather pen slowly and dipped it in his pot of blue pollen ink. Carefully he wrote the letters B-L-O-O-D in the empty squares at the top left corner of the puzzle. He pursed his lips. That looked right.

The next clue was 10 Down. *A _____ is the smallest unit of money in Bimmau and is made of little mud patties (5 letters)*. Squirrel scribbled his answer down, this time much faster.

He looked at the puzzle. He had answered two questions and he thought they were right, but there was only one way to tell for sure. He had to fill up the word that connected them.

He found the clue—14 Across. It read: *The last two words of the dish Peppered Urchin with Zesty Zucchini in _____ (Two words; do not leave a space between the words; 16 letters)*.

Squirrel scratched his head. What was it? He felt the name of the dish flit around his brain, swirling in his head, teasing him. Peppered Urchin with Zesty Zucchini in . . . in . . . in . . .

Aaaah! With a rush Squirrel remembered. He scratched the letters down in the blank boxes. They fit in perfectly with the letters he had already filled in. Squirrel grinned. He looked at the next clue and filled it up. And then the next. And the next.

Squirrel was so busy scratching letters into the puzzle that when he felt a jab in his side, he jumped, tripped on his chair, and almost knocked his pot of ink all over Brittle's Key.

"Careful, mate," said Des, rubbing his eyes sleepily. "Whendhya-getchup? Whatcha-gotch-ere?"

Squirrel scrambled up and grabbed the dog's shoulders, grinning like a jack-o'-lantern. "Des, I found it!" He shoved the crossword under Des's nose. "I found the key!"

"Whatchyaonbout?" yawned Des. "This isn't a key. It's a piece of paper."

"Just read it," said Squirrel, sitting Des down at the desk and laying the crossword out in front of him.

"All right, all right. Don' get your tail in a twist. I'll read it," said Des sleepily, picking up the paper.

Squirrel watched as Des read. The dog's face changed—from sleepy to wide-awake to shock. When Des finally finished, his eyes were so big and happy he looked like he had been kissed by a mermaid. "Frolicking frog's legs! Brittle's Key is a . . . an actual code."

Squirrel nodded. "Exactly! And to complete the code, we have to solve the puzzle. Look, I've been trying to fill it up."

337

"You sure have. You've almost completed the puzzle," said Des, pointing to only a handful of blank squares. Squirrel checked the sheet. He had filled in almost every question.

"Des, I'm sorry I didn't wait for—"

Des put his paws up. "Mate, I don't care. We've almost found Brittle's Key. Now let's finish the puzzle."

Crouched over the table, Squirrel read the last three clues aloud and Des scribbled letters into the blank squares. As soon as he wrote the last letter, Des jammed the feather back into the inkpot and jumped up. "We're done!" he yelled, throwing his arms in the air like a cheerleader.

"With the puzzle, yes," said Squirrel. "But, Des, we still have to complete the key." And with that, Squirrel began to read and reread the instructions once more.

Squirrel felt Des's head knock against his as they peered over the instructions. Des's head felt a bit like a coconut. He wondered what it would be like to have a coconut-of-a-head instead of an acorn-of-a-head.

"Get a grip," Squirrel scolded himself. He must focus on the instructions now. He read them again, trying to figure out what to do next.

Des had better luck. "Mate, why the twitchy face? This is easy. It's not like you need to rob a tomb, or give light back to a city or something. You just have to copy some letters into this." Des was pointing to a two-rowed table that was smack in the middle of the instructions. The top row had twenty-one squares with a different letter on each. The second row was blank.

Squirrel reread the instructions. This time, he felt the words click into the grooves of his brain. His mind began to churn. "I think we are looking for the rows of circles in the crossword. Specifically, we're looking for the consonants in the rows of circles in the crossword."

"Here's the first letter," said Des, pointing to the top left circle, the first in the row. The letter *D* had been scribbled in it.

"Now I guess we write that in the table," said Squirrel, moving his attention to the table stuck in the middle of the instructions. Under the letter *B*, he wrote the letter *D* in the table. When Squirrel looked back up, Des was pointing to the next consonant down the circular row.

"Under C, write M—M for *Marshmallows* and *Mud Slurpies*," said Des, his eyes glowing like big bronze bowls.

Squirrel jotted M under C in the table and said, "Next."

Des found the next consonant in the circular row, and Squirrel wrote it down. And, like this, Squirrel and his friend filled up Brittle's Key.

Crossword Puzzle Clues

DOWN

1. A plant that grows in the desert, is covered in thorns, and has a sticky, clear gel inside its stem is called a _____. (6 letters)

2. From the memory unzipped after you drank the Wedded Wine: "But you must prove you're worthy; To use this weapon most _____." (6 letters)

3. A slate-blue stone hidden in the Bone Tomb, which when rubbed with another like it, can produce fire, is called a Flame _____. (5 letters)

4. The tea that can put anyone to sleep immediately is called _____ tea. (8 letters)

5. The ___ is the restricted, underground chamber in the Pedipurr that only Lords and Ladies can enter. (3 letters)

6. The tree cottage where we lived, and where you live, is in _____ Wood. (7 letters)

7. The main bank in Bimmau is owned by the _____ family. (7 letters)

9. Gandgoon is a city in the Desert of _____ Kings. (5 letters)

10. A _____ is the smallest unit of money in Bimmau and is made of little mud patties. (5 letters)

11. The open-air parliament in Darling Tea Hills is called the "Rule of _____." (8 letters)

12. You, your father, and your mother have all been slaves of the mail service called the _____. (7 letters)

13. The drink that triggered your memory in Mellifera is Marbled _____. (5 letters)

17. To unlock your house, you must insert the claw on your ____ paw into the keyhole. (4 letters)

18. In the *Original Raison D'Être*, the entry about Brittle's Map reads: "The clues to the key are _____ in one mind so that the key only he can find." (11 letters)

19. Wedded ____ is the drink that triggered your first memory. (4 letters)

21. The fruit used to make a Pretty Pith is a _____. (5 letters)

22. In the desert, free water can only be found at an _____. (5 letters)

24. To make Marbled Honey, the Queen Bee opens her mouth, shapes her lower ___ into an O, and blows out soft, golden vapor. (3 letters)

25. The animal who guards the spring in Gandgoon is an old, wise _____ with two humps. (5 letters)

26. From the memory unzipped after you drank the tea: "Where kingly ghosts roam on ___ sand." (3 letters)

28. From the memory unzipped after drinking the oasis water: " _____, my son, the power you wield." (5 letters)

30. In spring, when the mice pick the first batch of leaves, it is called the first _____. (5 letters)

32. What type of nut does your head look like, even though it is a bit squashed on the top? _____ (5 letters)

33. From the memory unzipped after you drank the Marbled Honey: "_____ ten leaves from richest soil." (5 letters)

34. In Mellifera, the outer wall is made of rows of tiled wax _____; these shapes make the wall very sturdy. (8 letters)

36. After the two stones were stolen from Darling Tea Hills, _____ disappeared from the mice city and made it hard for them to have heat or light at night. (4 letters)

39. At a wedding, the bride and groom each say a Wedded ___ to each other in order to get married. (3 letters)

40. Mellifera is always ruled by the _____. (Two words; no space between the words; 8 letters)

41. A _____ is a wooden square that is worth less than a guffling but more than a gromm. (6 letters)

42. In the *Original Raison D'Être*, the entry about Brittle's Map says: "The Code of the _____ states that the bonds of slavery can be broken if the words in Brittle's Map are spoken." (6 letters)

45. In the memory unzipped after you drank the Wedded Wine, you were asked to find "A _____ as a recipe." (6 letters)

47. A _____ is an institution where kittens, cubs, puppies, kids, and all other young ones are educated. The best one in Bimmau is at the Pedipurr. (6 letters)

51. The spearlike body part of a bee is called the _____. (7 letters)

52. At a wedding, both the bride and groom take a sip of _____ Wine. (6 letters)

54. The town that "speaks of gold" in the desert is called _____. (8 letters)

59. In Gandgoon, everyone likes to _____, especially during Blackstubbs season. (Rhymes with bramble; 6 letters)

61. The white cream that the Queen Bee is always drinking is called _____ Jelly. (5 letters)

63. When the Queen Bee dances, the part of her body that moves the most is her _____; and everyone else begins to move their bodies as well. (5 letters)

ACROSS

8. The county where you live, with the Pedipurr, the Wagamutt, and Priggle's Bank, is called _____. (6 letters)

11. The inscription "A Gift from Me" is in a thick, red leather book full of _____. (7 letters)

14. The last two words of the dish Peppered Urchin with Zesty Zucchini in _____. (Two words; do not leave a space between the words; 16 letters)

15. Each of the thirteen wise rulers of Darling Tea Hills is called a _____. (7 letters)

16. From the memory unzipped after you drank the tea: "Where _____ ghosts roam on red sand." (6 letters)

20. From the memory unzipped after you drank the tea: "Back to back she hunts for ____." (4 letters)

23. The black substance that makes Darling Tea Hills rich is ____. (4 letters)

26. From the memory unzipped after drinking the Marbled Honey: "Return what has long been stole; For that, my dear son, is your ____." (4 letters)

27. In order to hide from a Kowa, you must maintain pin-drop _____. (7 letters)

29. In order to smell something, you put your nose in the air and _____. (Rhymes with whiff; 5 letters)

31. The drink that you drank at Darling to unzip the memory was ___. (3 letters)

35. To follow the recipe for Peppered Urchin with Zesty Zucchini in Lavender Emulsion, you must "First check the ingredients and make sure they are ____." (4 letters)

37. The last liquid was hidden in the _____ of Blood Kings. (6 letters)

38. In the *Original Raison D'Être*, the entry about Brittle's Map reads: "So, if the map is used by those _____ of heart, slavery could reign in every part." (6 letters)

43. One puzzling recipe reads: "Drizzle the emulsion ____ the wok-fried urchin and zucchini." (4 letters)

44. The memory you unzipped after drinking the Wedded Wine told you to "find and ___ liquids three." (3 letters)

46. The circular bar at the Pedipurr is called the _____. (No space between the words; 11 letters)

48. The high-society country club for cats is called the Pedi____. (4 letters)

49. From the memory unzipped after you drank the Marbled Honey: "Find stolen stones that you ___ need." (3 letters)

50. In the *Original Raison D'Être*, the entry about Brittle's Map reads: "The ____ of the Map of Brittle is that a slave is the lowest critter; he is property to be traded and sold to the highest bidder." (4 letters)

53. In the *Original Raison D'Être*, the entry about Brittle's Map reads: "Brittle's Map is a string of words more powerful than a thousand _____." (6 letters)

55. The key that you have been looking for is the key that decodes the Map of _____. (7 letters)

56. The last drink to unzip a memory in your brain was the clear, cool, crystal _____ from the desert. (5 letters)

57. From the memory unzipped after you drank the Wedded Wine: "You're wed, my ___, now you'll see." (3 letters)

58. The "hills of heart" refers to _____ Tea Hills. (7 letters)

60. The walled city of bees is called _____. (9 letters)

62. The special drink you got from the Queen Bee is called _____ Honey. (7 letters)

64. The animal who owns the PetPost is a _____ called Bacchu Banoose. (8 letters)

65. The Lion's _____ is the chamber in the Pedipurr with all their volumes of books and encyclopedias. (7 letters)

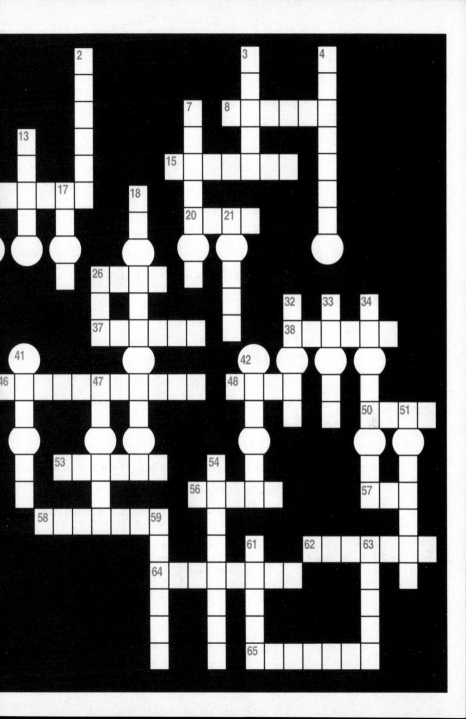

The crossword puzzle holds the key to Brittle's Map

It can make your dreams come true, but I warn you, it's also a trap.

To find the key, you must first solve the crossword based on what you've seen,

What you've heard, and where you've been.

Next, find the three circular rows when the puzzle is complete.

Notice that in these three rows no consonant does repeat.

Pluck each consonant from circular rows one, two, and three in order,

And carefully copy each in turn into the table below; son, be a diligent recorder.

So if D is the first and T is the last,

Then this table is properly cast.

And Brittle's Key is actually this very table,

For it makes Brittle's Map readable.

Note that vowels remain as they are,

As they are the most true and steady letters by far.

But every time you see any consonant in the Map of Brittle,

Replace it with the letter underneath it, in the second row of the table.

Similarly, to understand the secret words below,

Substitute the consonants in row one with those in the bottom row.

And if you manage to decode the secret words underneath,

Then you, my son, can read Brittle's Map, which is no small feat!

B	C	D	F	G	H	J	K	L	M	N	P	Q	R	S	T	V	W	X	Y

Quz dot, cg mod, hof zxe zfijwg lafz,
zxe zfal I cedziodeb qehofe
A jxoije zxaz im mo bihhijukz iz tikk fojw gou zo gouf jofe
Koow ayaid adb feab zxe zxfee fotm cabe oh mlxefem
Zxeg afe zxfee dacem mxididy zfue—
zxe hifmz goudy adb zto okb, xekb beaf
Zxe hifmz mzfil im gouf dace, gouf cozxef'm mejodb, adb gouf
hazxef'm im zxe zxifb
Zxe hifmz dace tikk yine gou zto yihzm, yihzm kiwe a qifb
Gou tikk bimjonef gouf dazufak lotef,
a lotef zxaz I bimafceb
Hof, ih gou xab aktagm qeed txo gou afe, gou toukb xane qeed
xafceb
Gou dot wdot zxe dacem oh goufmekh, gouf coc adb bab
Adb gou lfoqaqkg tadz zo zekk enefgode gou wdot zxe dace
gou aktagm xab
Hof iz jad yine gou hfeeboc adb enefgzxidy gou enef tadzeb
Mkanefg tikk do kodyef qe id gouf mzafm,
gou tikk do kodyef qe xaudzeb
Quz zxe zfal im zxaz zxeme zxfee zxfee dacem afe Qfizzke'm Weg
Adb ih gou zekk iz, iz tikk hakk idzo zxe enik xadbm zxaz qe
Zo lfozejz gou, I xib gouf ibedzizg hfoc ened gou zikk dot
Quz gou xane lfoneb gou afe feabg hof zxe jxakkedyem axeab—
mo, cg mod, zawe a qot.

"We're done!" whispered Des.

Squirrel stared at the table—the table that was Brittle's Key. Then he stared at the lines of gibberish under it. When he spoke, his voice was as soft as cotton. "Des, *we* have Brittle's Key. Only you and I have the code to read Brittle's Map. We have this incredible secret that we need to guard."

"We cannot tell anyone about the key, Squirrel. I'm not even telling Cheska. We have to pretend it does not exist. We may be the new Keepers of the Key," said Des somberly. He scratched his head and continued. "Mate, only *we* know that every letter in the map stands for another letter—and only *we* know which letter stands for which."

Des frowned and carried on. "Every letter except for A, E, I, O, and U. Look. They're nowhere in the table. It's just the consonants—every time you see a consonant in the map, you need to switch it for the consonant in the bottom row of the table. And the vowels remain what they are. Do you think that can be right?"

Squirrel felt his heart flutter like an excited firefly. "We can check. The instructions say that to understand the secret words below the table, we have to replace the consonants in row one with those in row two." He paused, flipping what he was going to say over and over again in his head. "If we replace each consonant in the second half of the instructions . . . with the letter below it in the table . . . then the words should make sense. It says in the instructions that if we can read the words below, we will be able to read the Map of Brittle."

"Woof woof!" barked Des. "Let's do it." He grabbed a blank piece of paper from Squirrel's desk and shoved it in front of Squirrel. "Let's hope it works."

Squirrel looked at the nonsensical instructions below the table. He took the first word—it was *Quz*. He looked at the table, found *Q* in the first row, and looked at the letter below it. It was *B*. Squirrel wrote *B*.

"Now write *U*, Squirrel," said Des. "Remember, the vowels are the same."

Squirrel nodded and wrote *U*.

The last letter was *Z*. Squirrel found *Z* in the table, saw that *T* was below it, and scribbled *T* down.

"Woof-my-waggity-tail. It's working," yelped Des. "Look, the first word is *B-U-T* . . . But. Come on, mate, keep going!"

Squirrel felt his own tail begin to wag like Des's. He moved on to the next word, and then the next, working slowly, carefully. He felt Des breathing next to him, puffing out gusts of excited, warm air.

351

When he was done, Squirrel dropped his feather and breathed in so deeply he thought his lungs would pop. Then he began to read the words he had just translated.

But now, my son, for the tricky part,
the trap I mentioned before
A choice that is so difficult it will rock you to your core
Look again and read the three rows made of spheres
They are three names shining true—
the first young and two old, held dear
The first strip is your name, your mother's second, and your
father's is the third
The first name will give you two gifts, gifts like a bird
You will discover your natural power,
a power that I disarmed
For if you had always been who you are, you would have been
harmed
You now know the names of yourself, your mom and dad
And you probably want to tell everyone you know the name
you always had
For it can give you freedom and everything you ever wanted
Slavery will no longer be in your stars,
you will no longer
be haunted
But the trap is that these three names are Brittle's Key

And if you tell it, it will fall into the evil hands that be
To protect you, I hid your identity from even you till now
But you have proved you are ready for the challenges ahead—
so, my son, take a bow.

Into the World of Dreams

Squirrel stared at Des. Des stared back. It felt as though a live wire was sparking somewhere in the room and they did not know what to do about it. Finally Squirrel said something he had thought he would never be able to say.

"Des, I have a name."

Des gaped at Squirrel, his eyes going as googly as spinning cricket balls. "And you know the names of your parents! I can't believe it! Brittle's Key is the consonants in your name, your mom's name, and your dad's name!"

Squirrel kept shaking his head. "I don't know what to do."

His insides felt completely full and incredibly empty at the same time. He felt himself quiver like the page in his hands. "I know the names of my parents. I know my own name."

Squirrel felt something course through his nerves. It was excitement; it was fear; it was a sense of purpose. "I found my name. Which means I don't need to be a slave anymore."

"Read the first row of the golden spheres of the puzzle," said Des gently. "That is your name, Squirrel."

Squirrel shut his eyes, trying to calm himself. When he opened his eyes, he let them wander over the thirteen letters that made up his first and last name.

He opened his mouth and said the two words. "DOMINO RYFCLAP."

As he said the words, Squirrel felt his brain rip apart, as though someone had sliced it in half. He screamed with pain. The pain shot down his body—from his brain to his ears to his neck, down his sides, to his legs. He shook as hot tears tore down his cheeks. He looked down.

What he saw made his heart stop beating as surely as if an arrow had struck it.

His sides—from his armpits to his legs—had sliced open. And, from these gashes, unfurling slowly, were tender, pink, baby wings.

"Wha-wha-what are those?" cried Des.

Squirrel looked at Des in shock. The pain had gone.

He tried to move the pink fold of muscle on his left. It twitched. He did the same with the right wing. It flapped, and streaks of blood flew off it.

"Des . . . Des . . . I think . . ." But before Squirrel could finish his sentence, he felt his eyelids shut and his head spin. The last thing he heard as he drifted into a semicoma state was Des screaming with excitement.

"Wings! Those are wings! Mate, you're a flying squirrel!

Squirrel wanted to smile, but his body could not move from shock. He knew that when he woke up, he and Des would have a lot to talk about. But, for now, he let the cool floor soothe his sides, and let his wings carry him into the world of dreams.

TO TELL OR NOT

Squirrel was having a hard time preparing his lunch. He tried to grab the jar of pickled slugs with his right paw, but his left wing swung out and knocked the stone pan off the stove. Then, when he managed to pick the pan up, his other wing flung the bowl of hazelnuts in lemon juice off the counter and sent the slippery nuts scampering across the floor like beetles.

"I quit," announced Squirrel to the empty kitchen. He marched over to the fruit bowl. With wings and arms stiff like a robot's, Squirrel managed to clasp a pomegranate. Hungrily he sank his front teeth into the fruit and began to slurp up the juicy pearl-and-pink seeds.

Just then, Squirrel heard his front door shake and Des's voice yell, "Oye, mate! Wakey wakey."

Squirrel grinned. He took the stairs two at a time and skipped across his living room. Before opening the door, he unfurled his wings all the way—just for effect.

"Yowzzaaa," said Des as the door swung open. "Squirrel, those things look awesome . . . creepy but awesome."

Squirrel began to laugh. "I know what you mean. They're still all raw and fleshy, but I bet they'll look cool in a moon cycle. And Des"—Squirrel paused and cocked a smile—"The name's Domino. Domino Ryfclap."

"'Course it is! Domino! You're Domino—the Flying Squirrel," said Des, hopping in and pointing to him as though Domino were a magnificent magician.

"I am Domino Ryfclap, the Flying Squirrel," said Domino, his heart fluttering with glee. He took a bow, twirled his wings, and then plopped onto his spongy sofa. He wiped the beads of sweat off his forehead and looked at Des.

Des sat beside him. "Mate, you've got pomegranate all over your teeth. Your face looks like a splattered fruit bowl."

"Who cares," said Domino, fanning his wings.

Des grinned. "You love them, don't ya?"

"Wouldn't you? They make me look . . . like a starfish—

but cooler. Like a red surfer starfish who can fly!" babbled Domino, trying to jump up and show off. Unfortunately, the weight of his new wings got the better of him and he fell back down like a clumsy frog. He looked at Des sheepishly. "But, I guess, they do take a little getting used to."

"You're acting more like a frog who can fly," chuckled Des, jokingly slapping Domino on the back. "But, mate, I had a question. Have you decided what to do about your name?"

"What do you mean?" asked Domino.

"I mean, are you going to tell people your name and your parents' names? Are you going to claim your freedom?"

Domino felt the needles of excitement in his muscles become needles of worry. "I don't know, Des. I mean, if I don't tell people who I am, what my name is, that I have parents, I go back to being nothing more than the PetPost slave. I want to be Domino Ryfclap." He bit his tongue. "I want that identity."

He felt a gentle paw on his shoulder. "'Course you do, mate. It's okay if you want to be Domino Ryfclap. And even if you want to tell people your mother's and father's names, I don't think there is any harm. I mean, the chance of someone figuring out that the consonants in your name, then your mother's, and then your father's, form Brittle's Key is about as likely as finding a polar bear tap dancing on the sun."

Domino smiled gratefully at Des. He did not want to hide this new life of his from anyone. He wanted to fly to the top of his tree house and shout it out to all of Bimmau. He wanted to sing it to every animal. He wanted to whisper it to every flower.

But as the excitement swelled inside Domino the Squirrel, a small tendril of doubt crept into his heart. It was a pesky doubt—small but very annoying. "But, Des, if I tell people all three names, I'm putting Brittle's Key out in the open, aren't I?"

Des looked at Domino, his eyes full of sympathy. "I'm so sorry, Squirrel—I mean, Domino—but yes. If you tell people, you're not protecting the key as well as you could."

For some reason, Des's words shot straight to Domino's heart. But, instead of wounding him, they flooded him with a new type of blood—the thick, warm blood of courage. "Des, you're right. I don't know if I am an official Keeper of the Key, but I know I must do everything I can to protect it. Like my mother. That's what I'm supposed to do. I'm supposed to make sure that it does not get into the wrong hands—like Baron Dyer's. If he gets his paws on it, then he'll make anyone he wants a slave. And being a slave is not a fate I would wish on anybody."

Domino got up and began to pace around, his body

trembling with electricity. "I will not let that happen. But"—he stopped and looked straight at Des—"I cannot go back to being who I was."

"So what will you do, Squi . . . Domino?"

"I'm going to tell everyone my name is Domino Ryfclap. But I'll keep my parents' names hidden. And I'm going to quit the PetPost. I'm going to go tell Mr. Banoose that I have found my name and according to the Code of the Jungle, I am now free. I'm not going to be the PetPost slave anymore. I'm going to create a new identity for myself." He gulped as the words left his tongue. "I have enough money in the bank to keep me fed until I figure out what to do with myself."

A slow smile lit up Des's eyes. "Now that you have a name, you could get a job. A real job. Not a slave job."

"Exactly," said Domino, looking at the book jacket with the puzzle and Brittle's Key on it. He picked it up, letting the squares, the letters, the numbers, the gibberish—all imprint themselves on his mind.

Then, without knowing he would, he tore the jacket flap. He tore it once. Twice. Three times. He looked at it. It was small enough. With a jerk, he shoved the pieces of Brittle's Key in his mouth and chewed it twice. He swallowed.

He turned to Des, who looked like he had just been

speared with a unicorn horn. Domino smiled. "I will free myself, but I'll keep Brittle's Key hidden. I will honor my mother's life. I will honor Azulfa's life. And that, my friend, is good enough for me."

30

THE PETPOST SLAVE'S LAST JOURNEY

Bacchu Banoose's eyelids began to quiver. His thick jaw swelled up. His face turned green.

"What do you mean, 'I am free'?" was all he could utter.

"Mr. Banoose, I have found my name, the name that was left to me. The Code of the Jungle—"

"I know what the Code of the Jungle says, Squirrel," snapped Bacchu.

"Sir, actually, it's Domino. Not Squirrel anymore," said Domino.

"*Domino*," mocked Bacchu, pulling a face. "*Domino*. What a stupid name. And you think that anyone else will employ you? You think you'll suddenly change your life, Squirrel? You think you've won the lottery, don't you? Let me tell you, you had it good with me. At least you had something to do."

"Sir, don't worry about me. And if you become just a little bit more, uh . . . more *accommodating*, I'm sure we can find someone to take my place at the PetPost. Not a slave, but a proper employee . . ."

"You think I need your help, you self-important pus boil?" spat Bacchu. "I don't need you. You needed me. At least I looked after you. You were the PetPost Squirrel. Now what will you be? You'll be absolutely nothing!"

"Maybe," said Domino with a small smile. "But I'll take that chance. Anyway, thank you for everything, sir."

"I'd say it back if I thought you were worth it," said Bacchu, a nasty scowl on his face. "Come to think of it, I wouldn't want those hideous wings around me anyway. You are seriously gross. Now clear out. My groomer is on his way. And I can't deal with you any longer."

"Gladly, sir," said Domino.

"And Squirrel, don't come crawling back to me. Or flapping back. Or whatever it is you do nowadays."

"I won't, Mr. Banoose. I promise," said Domino, walking

out of the room in which he had spent so much of his life.

As he left his ex-boss's house, Domino realized that he was no longer the PetPost Squirrel. He was not sure what he *should* do. He was not sure what he *could* do. But he did know what he *would* do. He would protect Brittle's Key. He would make sure no one, not the Baron, not a Kowa, not any creature, would get hold of it. He would keep the Pet-Post secret.

But it was no longer the PetPost secret, was it? It was the secret his mother had left to him. It was his, Domino Ryfclap's, secret.

As he walked away, a free creature, Domino began to hum. And skip. And flap his funny-looking wings.

He smiled for his past. He grinned for his present. And he laughed out loud at the pretty promise of his future.

Epilogue

STARTING OVER

O ye, watch it," squealed Des, diving into the closest
bramble to avoid the out-of-control whizzing fur
ball coming toward him. "Domino, you're like a
blind, red bat."

Domino crashed beside Des. "Sorry. Figured I'd try to use
these things," he said, flapping his wings. "Looks like I got
a lot of practicing to do." Domino got up and plucked the
twigs from his fur. He looked around. Behind Des stood
Smitten, clapping eagerly.

"Bravo, Squirrel!" said Smitten.

"Domino," said Squirrel, grinning. "I'm going by Domino
now."

Smitten slapped his forehead. "Oh right! Des told me you found a letter from your mother with your name in it. How great is that!"

"To think if you had found that letter earlier, you could have had a name all along. How unfortunate . . . ," said another tauntingly familiar voice.

Domino peered behind Smitten. It was Mrs. Sox.

Domino cleared his throat. "Right, but better now than later, Mrs. Sox. Anyway, Des, what's going on with you?" He wanted to desperately get away from Mrs. Sox's suspicious yellow eyes.

"Well, that's what we came here to tell you, mate. I'm starting at the Pedipurr when the first leaf falls. Isn't that great? I wasn't sure at first, but I saw some of those kittens and woof woof . . ."

But Domino had stopped listening. His heart fell to the balls of his heels and began to pulse with pain. Des would go to the Pedipurr. He would make new friends. He would learn new things. And soon Domino, the Flying Squirrel, would become some long-forgotten friend.

Domino knew his face had fallen, but he was too bummed to pull it back up. "That's great, Des," he muttered, without looking up. "I'm so excited for you."

"But, Domino, you're not listening to me!" screamed Des. "You're going to the Pedipurr too!"

Domino shook his head sadly. "Des, remember Lady Blouse just offered earlier to tease me. To string me along. I can't go. I need a sponsor. And who'll sponsor me?"

"I will."

Domino wiggled his little red ears. He was hearing things. He must get his ears checked out. Maybe it was all the flying . . .

"Well, Domino, say something!" said Des, beaming like a snowman on vacation.

"Huh?"

"Mrs. Sox has offered to sponsor you to the Pedipurr," explained Smitten. "Remember, third-generation Pedipurr members are allowed to sponsor one creature each? So Mrs. Sox has offered to sponsor you."

"Bu-bu-but . . . why?" Domino was so flabbergasted that he could think of nothing else to say.

Mrs. Sox snorted. "Oh, don't get all sentimental, Squirrel. I just figured why not. I'm allowed to sponsor someone. It may as well be you. You have a name now, so you could go to school. Plus I figured the Pedipurr could teach you to be smarter. Golliwog knows you need it after the lunacy I just saw!" She tapped her fat feet. When no one spoke, she said, "So, Squirrel, do you want the spot or not?"

Domino felt his neck nod.

He heard himself say yes.

He felt Des's paws around his shoulders.

He felt his friend jump up and down.

He heard Smitten laugh.

As his shock melted away, Domino let the happiness of this moment slurp him up. He grinned so widely his jaw hurt. This was the single best moment of his life.

He looked at Mrs. Sox. "How can I ever repay you, Madame?"

The cat looked straight at Domino, her lower lip curling into a fat, flat smile. "Don't you worry, Squirrel. We'll find a way." And with that, she turned and walked off.

In his moment of sheer bliss, Domino the Flying Squirrel, Keeper of Brittle's Key, did not notice the sly plan fermenting in Mrs. Sox's cheddar-yellow eyes. If he had, he would have wondered . . .